MW01257158

Van Horn

A Novel by

Jim Sano

Full Quiver Publishing

Pakenham ON

Published by Full Quiver Publishing
PO Box 244
Pakenham, Ontario K0A 2X0

ISBN Number: 978-1-987970-35-7

Printed and bound in the USA

Photos courtesy: Landscape Alamy, car Getty Images
Back cover photo: *Devil's Hall*, permission granted by Omar C. Garcia (Missions Pastor, Kingsland Baptist Church 20555 Kingsland Blvd. Katy, Texas 77494)

Cover design: James Hrkach and Jim Sano

NATIONAL LIBRARY OF CANADA
CATALOGUING IN PUBLICATION
ALL RIGHTS RESERVED

*I would like to dedicate this book to
my two daughters, Emily and Megan.*

*Growing up, I loved my family. I have two great brothers,
John and Jerry, and two amazing sisters, Florence and
Cassie. We remain close and I will always cherish and thank
God for each relationship. That joy of relationships inspired a
desire for a family of my own and to become a loving husband
and father.*

*From the day she was born, Emily always had a sparkle in
her eye and an infectious smile. I often wonder how I can truly
show her how happy she has made me and how much love I
have in my heart for her. She has grown into such a beautiful,
intelligent, creative, hard-working, fun, thoughtful, and loving
young woman, but she's always been all those things. I love
you, Emily, and I thank God for the gift of you every day.*

*We were blessed with Megan two years later and wanted to
nickname her "Joy" because that is what she has always
brought to our family and the world. She has been a loving
sister and daughter that captures my heart daily. Megan loves
children, animals, family, friends, conversation, and tea. She
is a beautiful young woman who is courageous, smart, giving,
thoughtful, artistic, enthusiastic, and all about others. I love
you, Megan, and I thank God for the gift of you every day.*

Chapter 1

Jack woke face down with the sting of gravel in his cheek and waves of heat rising from the scorching pavement. His head pounded as if it had been hammered by the back end of a heavy shovel. With a concerted effort, he blinked and stared sideways at the road, trying to determine his whereabouts. Before he could lift his head, the muffled silence was broken by a loud roaring sound, as if a freight train were bearing down on him. Suddenly, a hard jerk to his belt lifted his body and slammed him back on the ground a few feet away, just as a large tractor-trailer truck whizzed by, clipping the edge of his boot heel.

He twisted around and stared upward to see the silhouette of a young woman wearing a broad-brimmed cowboy hat that barely blocked the blinding sunlight.

"I didn't mean to wake y'all, but takin' a nap on the highway this time of day can be a little dangerous in these parts." She reached out her hand to lift him to his feet. "You, okay?"

He brushed the gravel from the side of his scraped face before turning to get a better look at his rescuer: a young girl, no more than twenty, with a strikingly beautiful face and hazel-colored eyes. Her brown hair, braided to one side, reflected hints of a reddish tone in the morning sunlight. Her Texan hat, complete with a teal-beaded concho band, leather cowboy boots, and fitted jeans, made it obvious that this girl was homegrown. "Thanks for showing up in the nick of time."

"I didn't have much choice. That eighteen-wheel rig was heading right for ya. The nerve of that guy driving on the road," she quipped with a smile. "What the heck were y'all doing sleeping in the road, anyway?"

"Good question," he replied, gingerly touching the back of his head. "I pulled over to help someone with car trouble. Next thing I know, I have a nice melon-sized lump on my skull and a few years less to worry about at the end of my life. My name's Jack Russo, by the way." He shook her hand.

"Siena. Siena Connors. I'm guessin' yer gonna need a ride?" she queried, pointing to her white pickup truck.

With his truck nowhere in sight and no wallet in his back pocket, Jack nodded with a half-grin, opened the passenger side, and slid into the bench seat of the old truck. She reached over to grab the handle and pull his shut. "It's a little temperamental at times. Which way are we heading?"

"El Paso," grimaced Jack, touching the bump on his head.

"You're in luck," exclaimed Siena as she slid on her sunglasses, flipped on the radio, and James Otto's "I Just Got Started Lovin' You" blared at them. She glanced over, checking him out and then sped down the road, which cut through the rough Chihuahuan Desert dotted with scrub and creosote bushes, with the bronze-red mountains in the distance.

In between lines of the song, she couldn't resist singing along as she glanced over to check out her still dizzy passenger while he stared out the dust-covered passenger window of the truck rumbling down the highway. Jack was forty-two years old and kept his six-foot frame in good physical condition. His dark brown hair showed a hint of red and gray mixed in, as did his several-day-old beard growth.

"So, what brings ya to El Paso? You're obviously not from around here."

"Just sightseeing, and what makes you so sure I'm not from around here?" replied Jack, wondering how much he should reveal about his second trip to the southern border of Texas in the past twenty years.

Siena swerved across the double line on the highway as she crowed with laughter. "Y'all look like a city-boy, more Boston than Austin if I had to guess."

"Well, this city-boy would like to get to El Paso in one piece, if you don't mind," quipped Jack.

Siena smiled broadly at his words and quipped, "By the looks of ya, I'm sorry to say your wish ain't gonna happen today. We're gonna need to take care of those cuts and bruises—and you're gonna hafta open up a bit if ya want me to be your taxi driver. You said Jack Russo, right?"

Jack nodded.

"Is that Italian or Latino? Cause you don't look like either to me!" she ventured, handing him a thread-bare blue-and-white kerchief from her back pocket to wipe the blood from his cheek.

Jack chuckled. "We've barely talked, and you already think you know where I am from and my parents' heritage? How about if we start with you? How old are you?"

"Twenty – well, close enough."

"Hmm."

"And what is that supposed to mean, Mr. 'Not From Here' Jack?"

"It explains your unearned confidence and naivete. What's your real name?"

Siena suddenly jerked the truck to the side of the road and quickly pressed an eight-inch blade up against Jack's neck. "Don't underestimate me, Russo. I've been taking care of myself my entire life, so don't tell me about 'unearned confidence'!"

Jack slowly moved the tip of the hunting knife away from his neck. "Okay, okay. So, don't answer me."

After a good stretch of the road through the rugged desert, Siena broke the silence. "Rose."

"What?"

"Rose. Rose is my real name. I didn't like it, so back when I was little, I started calling myself Siena. How did you know?"

"I didn't, but Siena sounded more like a funky hippie California name than a Texas girl to me."

"Well, I like it fine, and so do y'all unless you want to walk the next thirty miles to El Paso," countered Siena, slowing down the truck.

"No, no, no. I'm actually starting to love the name Siena. I'm even thinking seriously of changing my own to Siena," quipped Jack.

Siena raised her eyebrows and sped back up until they reached the outskirts of El Paso.

Jack peered out at the old, mostly one-story, sun-drenched stucco homes and buildings that lined the roads and ran in a criss-cross pattern. Little seemed to have changed in twenty years. This was nothing close to the winding streets of Boston with its historic brick town-houses mixed in with high-rise hotels and office buildings along the harbor waterfront.

"Hey, Russo. El Paso is a big place. Where exactly am I dropping ya off?" Siena asked, slowing for a red light.

"Ahh—" Jack struggled to find a quick answer.

She slowed down again for a crowd of people heading toward loud festive music.

"Why don't you let me off here, and I should be all set."

Siena tilted her head and squinted with curiosity. "You didn't come all this way from wherever you come from, get beat up and almost killed, just to attend some hokie festival, did ya?"

Jack jumped out of the truck and reached through the open passenger side window to shake Siena's hand. "It was good meeting you, and thanks for the ride—oh, and for saving my life, too." As Jack gazed directly into Siena's eyes, he noticed a sadness that spooked him. It felt like he had known her for more than the past hour.

Chapter 2

Jack waved until Siena's truck turned the corner, then he moved with the crowd toward the festival. Most of the people walking beside him seemed to be of Mexican and native Indian descent, many wearing colorful costumes. The music grew louder as he approached the festival area, where dancing and vendors filled the courtyard in front of an old adobe-style church building. Jack glanced up at the banner that read, *Ysleta Mission Festival.*

He stopped to watch a native Indian dance by a group in authentic dress. It brought back memories of a culture he found himself missing—the culture of his late wife's family, a history he hadn't shared with more than a few people over the past twenty years, which was how long it had been since his wife had been killed and his infant daughter kidnapped.

That was also how long he'd been trying to track down the killers who had mercilessly taken his family and life away. During that sudden act of heart-wrenching violence, he'd quickly learned not to be too open to more than a few people with whom he had entrusted his very life.

Suddenly, he jumped as he felt something press into this back.

"So, you really did come all this way to go to a hokie festive?"

Jack turned and snapped, "Didn't we just say *adios*?"

"Jumpy, huh? Didn't your mamma teach y'all any manners?"

"I'm sorry. I just wasn't expecting you."

Siena snickered. "Hey, the least ya can do is buy me a burrito. I haven't eaten all day."

Jack nodded, eyeing the "Mexican Delight" stand near them. He ordered two enormous burritos with cold drinks and carried them to a grassy spot in the shade of the only tree near the church.

5

Siena took a large bite and muttered, "So, why are you in El Paso? You can trust me with your secret."

He smiled as he took a napkin and wiped the sauce off the corner of her mouth. Her brave smile reminded him of his wife. "I'm searching for an old friend, that's all. Interestingly enough, I was told he might be at the Mount Carmel School next to this church. I wasn't expecting to find a festival here. What's this for?"

"I guess they think 327 years as the oldest parish in Texas is a big thing or something. Actually, it's kind of a cool tradition. The Pueblo Indians were pushed south after a revolt against the Spanish, and the Tigua tribe built this mission a few years later. They've remained pretty dedicated to it."

Jack glanced up at the adobe church building with the cross on the top of its rounded steeple. "Hmm. I assume the school is closed today?"

Siena laughed. "Did y'all hafta go to summer school back East?"

Embarrassment warmed his cheeks. Jack nodded and smiled. "Oh, yeah. Well, I really can't wait around for September."

Siena took another hungry bite and finished off her burrito. "Not to worry. Father Miguel runs the church and the school. He'll be around here somewhere, probably in the church showing people how beautiful it is."

"So, you're a church girl, huh?"

"Not so much these days. I went to school at Our Lady of Mount Carmel, and I sit in the church sometimes when I want to think about things. I've been doing more of that lately. Why don't we see if we can find him?" Sienna stood and peered around the festival. She approached a chubby boy playing tag. "Have y'all seen Father Miguel?"

The boy responded by pointing to the church.

Siena waved Jack toward the two old wooden doors, and

they entered the small church. Wooden pews lined each side of the center aisle, with centuries-old beams above and a colorful altar with a large hand-carved crucifix of Jesus directly behind it. As they made their way down the aisle, Jack spotted a statue of St. Anthony of Padua on the left and a priest showing some kids a strikingly colorful painting of a woman.

The priest smiled at Siena. "Ahh, it's good to see you, Rose."

Siena nodded sheepishly. "I know, Father. 'Come to Mass sometime.' I want y'all to meet someone who's looking for—well, he can tell you. This is Jack Russo."

Jack shook his hand while still staring at the painting.

"I'm Father Miguel. I see you're interested in Our Lady of Guadalupe. *¿Ella es muy hermosa, no?* I'm sorry. She is beautiful, is she not? I must tell you about her sometime, but you have a question of your own."

Jack hesitated as he eyed Siena, debating how much he wanted to say in front of her.

She rolled her eyes. "I can take a hint. If you needed to go to confession, you should have just said so." Siena walked to the front to talk to some of the kids looking around the historic mission church.

Jack turned back to the priest. "Father Miguel, you have a beautiful church. A priest I know from Boston, Father Tom Fitzpatrick, was here several months ago, and he saw a picture of a girl in the school that he thought I might know."

Father Miguel pondered Jack's question. "I remember meeting Father Tom. I liked him. Tell me, is this a girl going to our school now?"

Jack shook his head. "No. She would have gone to school here around fourteen or fifteen years ago when she was five or six."

"Wow. *No, sé.* That's a long time ago. We did have pictures of children from several years on the walls of the school this past year. That was just for a short time, but we lost them—

and almost all of our records – in a fire last month. I've only been here for five years, but Father Jose Suarez was here for twenty years preceding me. If anyone would know, he would."

By this time, Siena had edged her way back to where Jack and Father Miguel were talking. "Who would know what?"

Jack shook his head. "Father, where would Father Jose be now?"

"Are you talking about Father Suarez?" asked Siena. "He's in Juarez at the Cathedral, isn't he, Father Miguel?"

"I'll have to go there, then. I need to talk to him," explained Jack.

Father Miguel glanced toward Siena."*¿Me está tomando el pelo o está más loco que una cabra?*"

Jack turned and squinted in confusion at Siena. "What?"

Siena grabbed Jack's arm and pulled him out of the church as she waved to Father Miguel. "He said that you should take care of the scrape on your cheek."

Jack rolled his eyes. "Right, even I know that 'loco' isn't a medical term. I need to find this Father Jose."

Siena pulled him from the church grounds and down the street to a small stucco building with a worn-out sign over the front door that read *Alvita Plumbing and Air Conditioning*. She led him around the side and in through an old back door, which scraped the ground as she pulled it open.

"What's this?" When they got inside, Jack could quickly tell that this was where Siena lived. She had furnished it with discarded pieces she possibly collected and refurbished over time.

She pulled out a basket of medical supplies and damped a cloth with warm water before gently patting his wounds, despite Jack's objections. "So, what's so important that you need to talk to Father Suarez?"

Jack handed her the blue-and-white kerchief he had been using. "First, what did Father Miguel say to me?"

"He asked if you were pulling his leg or if you were crazy," replied Siena as she applied antibiotic and then a bandage to his wound.

"What's crazy about asking a priest a question? Is there something wrong with this Father Suarez?" Jack grimaced as he gently touched the bandage.

Siena took two cold drinks out of the refrigerator. "Not at all. He's really a good man, but he lives in a very dangerous place. Don't y'all pay attention to the news? Father Suarez is at the Cathedral of Our Lady of Guadalupe in Juarez, Mexico."

"Our Lady of Guadalupe does get around, doesn't she?" joked Jack. "Juarez is just over the border from here. I've gone there many times."

Siena tapped her bottle against his, pausing cautiously. "Yeah, but that was a long time ago, and things have changed—a lot."

Chapter 3

After a phone call, Siena returned to the kitchen where Jack was sitting. "I have a friend from school who I want you to meet."

"What school? Why do I need to meet your friends from school?"

"Asking a lot of questions is good, but try asking the right ones once in a while," teased Siena. "His name is Juan Sanchez, and he's coming over. We go to the University of Texas-El Paso together, and he lives in Juarez, so he can let us know, firsthand, how dangerous it's gotten there."

Jack stood up and shook his head. "I don't really care how dangerous it is. I've got to go!"

She stared at him with piercing eyes. "What's so precious that you would risk your life for? Who are y'all looking for, Russo?"

Dizziness swept over him again, so he sat down in a rickety old wicker chair and closed his eyes. He ignored her question and pretended to doze off, which worked. She went off to the next room.

An hour later, there was a rap on the back door, followed by the hinges creaking. Jack glanced up to see a young man with dark olive skin wearing a baseball-type tee shirt with "UTEP" embroidered in blue and gold colors across the front.

Siena came rushing out from the other room. "Juan, meet my mysterious hitchhiker who was almost roadkill this morning. Russo, meet the smartest, kindest guy I know."

Blushing, Jack pulled himself to a stand and extended his hand. "Good to meet you." Jack pointed to Juan's shirt. "You play ball?"

Juan nodded. "A little. You?"

Jack smiled. "Some in high school, but basketball was always my first love. Siena tells me you live in Juarez."

"I do. I grew up with my family in Guadalupe, just south of Juarez, but it's too far to travel every day to school. Baseball helps to pay the tuition bill, and I work at Jeddie's restaurant in Juarez for room and board." He helped himself to a Coke from Siena's fridge.

Jack glanced back and forth between Siena and Juan to see if there was something more than a friendship between them, but he couldn't get a read. "Did you two meet at—"

"School?" Siena and Juan said in unison.

Siena bumped Juan with her hip. "I picked up this poor ballplayer trying to hitch his way to school from here. I soon found out that he was—"

Unexpectedly riled, Jack interrupted. "You know, a young lady should be careful about picking up strange hitchhikers."

"Like today?" laughed Siena. "Juan, Russo wants to go to Juarez, and I was trying to tell him that it might not be a great idea these days. Hey, I even don't like it when you head across that border."

Juan took a swig of his soda. "Where're you trying to go?"

"Ahh—wherever the Cathedral is in Juarez. Father Miguel said it was the Guadalupe one," replied Jack.

Juan smiled. "*Catedral de Nuestra Señora de Guadalupe?* I think Siena's right. I wouldn't take a chance right now. Too dangerous."

"How bad can it be? You live there," said Jack with frustration.

"Bad. The whole Juarez Valley is turning into a war zone."

Jack paced several steps away. "When I was here last, Juarez was a great place to visit—nightclubs, restaurants, music, jobs. I never heard of any murders. What happened?"

"I guess that was when the Juarez cartel was run by a federal police commander and a businessman. Back then, they were running mostly weed, human trafficking, and other contraband. When the US cut off Colombia's distribution through Florida by water, the heavy cocaine and other drugs

11

needed another route, and Juarez into El Paso was the most coveted one. This guy, Fuentes, took over the cartel and started running a more sophisticated and bigger money operation, charging other cartels fees to use the Juarez smuggling routes," Juan explained.

"Hmm. Unintended consequences, huh?" remarked Jack.

"Yeah, it's a long story, but greed and refusal to pay fees led to internal fighting and assassinations after Fuentes' brother was killed by 'El Chapo' Guzman's Sinaloa cartel operatives when they moved in on the Juarez territory. It got very personal when the Juarez cartel responded by killing Guzman's brother in prison. The Mexican president sent in the military to try to crack down on the cartels, but that only intensified the fight for a bigger piece of a smaller pie, and in January, Guzman declared an all-out war on the Juarez cartel."

Jack pondered what he was hearing. "It seems like all the killing is between the cartels?"

Siena blurted, "Juan tells me the violence is out of control. There are two hundred murders a month. Just in May, the Police Chief was murdered the same day El Chapo's son was killed. Russo, it's insane to go there now!"

Juan agreed. "She's right. Rival gangs, like the Aztecas, have multiplied, and most of the city is completely lawless with kidnappings, extortion, and murders every night just to make a statement. It's no time to go into that area of the city."

Jack pleaded, "But, there must be a way. I have to go."

Siena pulled Jack aside and into the kitchen. "Juan just gave you a short history lesson, but this is all much more personal to him. I'm not afraid of too much of anything, but it's just too dangerous to go."

"I have to go."

Jack and Siena stood face to face staring at each other, realizing neither one was going to flinch. Finally, Siena gave in. "Fine. If you really need to go to Juarez, I'll take you."

Juan now stood behind them. *"No hay manera de que te dos locos se vayan solos."*

Jack tilted his head, and Siena explained, "He said, 'There's no way we crazies are going alone.' Well, since I'm the only one with a truck, I think we should be fixin' to go before it's too late, so we can get there and back before the sun sets."

In a matter of minutes, they slid into the front seat of Siena's truck, headed north to the Stanton Street bridge and then to the port of entry to Juarez. Only a few cars were heading into Juarez as Siena slowed down for the border check. In comparison, a long line of cars on the other side were trying to enter El Paso. The guard on their side stretched to look inside their truck, asking only for Juan's passport, while another guard peered into the empty flatbed. He quickly waved them on as Jack turned around to see the number of US Border guards with dogs checking out opened trunks, inside panels, and the undercarriages for the cars trying to enter from Juarez.

Jack scratched his beard. "Wonder why they only asked for your passport?"

Juan smirked. "Unless we're smuggling a truckload of assault rifles and grenades, they're not too worried about rich gringos coming to spend their money in Mexico. Nobody's trying to bust into Juarez with coke, human traffic, or pirated DVDs of *PeeWee's Playhouse.*"

Siena drove down side streets lined with cinderblock buildings and shops, some open and others boarded up. One looked like it had been torn open by a bomb blast and had two crosses spray-painted on the wall under the broken window with bars that no longer served any purpose. Up ahead were flashing lights of police cars where people gathered, looking up at the bridge overhead. As their truck crawled closer, Jack could see Siena closing her eyes at the sight. From the bridge, hung by the neck, was a bloodied man's body with a sign pinned to his chest. When they got closer, it was clear that the man's hands had been cut off. The sign on his chest read, *Para aquellos que no creen.*

Jack asked, "What does it say?"

Juan mumbled, "It says, 'For those who don't believe.' It's a message, a warning from one of the cartels."

Still grimacing, Siena asked, "Why cut off his hands?"

Juan responded, "It's most likely he was a thief who stole from the cartel. They must be getting bolder to do this in broad daylight."

Jack continued to stare back at the scene as one of the officers waved Siena's truck through. "Someone must have seen them?"

Juan shook his head. "No one will talk in fear for their life and their family. Sadly, the police will most likely not even investigate."

"W..what? How can they not investigate a murder like this?" Disbelief spun in Jack's mind.

Juan gave a sarcastic laugh. "Ninety percent of the murders aren't investigated, and most of the police are paid to look the other way. The Juarez cartel is particularly brutal in how they mutilate their victims and publicly discard their bodies. They use street gangs like La Linea to perform executions or Barrio Azteca to attack its enemies. As to your question about the police, most of the La Linea gang members are retired or even active corrupt police officers."

Jack shook his head. "I never heard any of this when I was here before—"

"Before we were born?" Siena turned down a side street and pulled over beside a pharmacy and a discount shoe store. The cathedral loomed across the street.

It was breathtaking with its twin towers, stonework, and fluted columns. It stood next to the original mission church built by the Franciscans that looked much like Ysleta Mission in El Paso.

A family exiting the front entrance held the wooden doors

for them to enter. Inside, the church was smaller than Jack expected. A few people gazed up at the colorful stained-glass windows while others knelt in prayer in various pews. To the side was a confessional box, where a young man, not exactly dressed for a church visit, was exiting.

They stopped at a pew where a woman sat. Juan asked, "Is Father Jose hearing confessions?" The woman nodded but didn't look up. Juan whispered into Jack's ear, "You can probably catch Father Suarez in the confessional."

Jack shrugged and waited, tapping his leg impatiently before he finally entered and knelt.

The wooden screen slid open. "Father Jose, can we speak in English?"

"If you can, I can. How can I help you today, my friend?"

"Bless me, Father, for I have sinned. It has been over a year since my last confession. I, umm—I guess I wasn't prepared for this," muttered Jack.

"Understood. Is there anything you can think of that you regret?" asked the priest.

"Oh, sure. Do you have all day?" replied Jack.

"I'm in no rush. God is merciful, even willing to give his life to forgive us."

"Well, I haven't exactly loved my enemies. I certainly can't bring myself to forgive them and haven't had good thoughts about what I wished would happen to them," whispered Jack.

"I take it you've been hurt deeply, and you struggle with revenge over forgiveness. Do I have that right?" asked Father Jose.

Jack nodded silently.

"I understand. I hear from many people these days who share your pain and this same struggle. Too many. Many of the people you see praying in the church were not here several years back, but now they suffer and pray for their families and their own souls. I have struggled, myself, with this conflict. Do you repent for your thoughts? Are you asking for forgiveness, or are you not yet there?"

"I don't know. I've never thought of forgiving them. I don't think they could ever deserve it." Jack tilted his head back in discomfort. "I thought God was fair."

"None of us deserve it, and trust me, you don't want God to be fair. We need him to be loving and merciful. He challenges us to follow his example, even when it pains us to do so, even when it feels as if we are dishonoring the people who have suffered in these horrible injustices. My son, is there anything I can do to help you today? Anything to ease your pain?"

A tear rolled down Jack's cheek as he sighed and took a deep breath. "I hope so. My wife was killed, and my baby daughter was kidnapped twenty years ago. I've been trying to find my daughter ever since," replied Jack.

"I am very sorry for your loss. How can I help?"

"A friend, Father Tom Fitzpatrick, was in El Paso several months ago, and he visited the Mission Church in El Paso, Ysleta. He also visited the school and saw a picture of a young girl on the wall. She was probably five or six years old and would have gone to the school in the early 1990s. Her name was Rosalina. I spoke to Father Miguel, and he said you were at the school during that time. I only have a photograph of her when she was a baby, but Father Tom saw something in the eyes of that girl that made him believe it could've been her."

Jack slid the small worn photo of his daughter through a slot under the confessional screen.

"Rosalina? I'm sorry. It's hard to tell from a baby photograph, and my memory is not so good these days. I don't remember the name Rosalina, but we have had many girls and boys over the years. She is very beautiful, and there *is* something in her eyes, but I can't remember. Did Father Miguel allow you to look at the records, to look through the photos?"

Jack sighed. "There was a fire, and the records were lost, so, no. If you could think of anything, it would mean everything to me."

"*Lo siento.* I'm truly sorry."

"I think I'm the one who's supposed to say that during a confession," Jack remarked sarcastically.

"Only when you are sorry—when you're ready. Bless you, in the Name of the Father, Son, and Holy Spirit."

Disappointed, Jack stepped out of the small quarters as Siena and Juan met him in the side aisle. "What did Father Suarez say?"

Before Jack could respond, Father Jose stepped out of the confessional and raised his hand. "*Señor.*"

Jack turned back and reached him in three quick strides. "There was a young girl many years ago who was adopted. The mother was a woman who was a native of Juarez, but I believe the man was an American. I don't recall their names, but it struck me that they would often go to a ranch in a small town south of here. She'd always returned with a smile on Mondays because she got to ride her horse. The town is Prâxedis. Prâxedis G. Guerrero, after a leader of the Mexican Revolution." He reached out and took both of Jack's hands in his and said, "I don't know if this is connected to your precious daughter, but I will pray for you both."

Jack pressed the priest's hands in gratitude. "*Gracias.* It's greatly appreciated." Jack took a few steps, then pivoted back. "Father, you said you struggled with a loss, with revenge versus forgiveness. I'm deeply sorry for your loss and will pray for you, too."

"*Gracias, Señor.* It was a close friend and priest who I'd known for a long time. Father Gerado loved this parish and this city. It broke his heart, as it has mine, to watch things get so terrible: kidnappings, ransoms, and killings to fund this cartel war. Scores of women have been abducted, raped, and their lifeless bodies discarded by these gangs. Then there's bribery and intimidation of the police, officials, and citizens who dare not to say anything. He spoke out at Mass many times against this violence and disregard for the dignity of human life—this assault on the children of God and God himself. They came into this very sanctuary and shot him in the head six times as he held up the Body of our Lord—in retaliation for speaking the truth. One woman ran to his aid, and they shot her in cold blood as well. I can't get the bloody images of that day out of my mind, and I can't forgive myself for not being as brave to witness the truth as Father Gerado."

Tears ran down Father Jose's cheeks. "I'm so sorry. Why don't the police find these thugs and serve justice?"

Father Jose glanced around to see who was watching before whispering to Jack, "You speak of the Guarantors. Many of the local police are part of the problem. The Juarez cartel and local gangs bribe or force the police to act as their protection, their guarantors to be able to operate their business. A good police officer who tries to do his job will be brutally murdered as a warning to others. *Plata o plomo.*"

"I don't understand." Jack furrowed his brow.

"Silver or lead. They give the police and government officials a simple choice—take the bribe or the bullet. They threaten their families, as well, so I can understand the pressure. I'm hearing that the Sinaloa cartel depends on different guarantors, the federal police and the military. There's so much money involved and a complete lack of moral conscience in these men, so there is nothing they won't do to maintain power."

Amazed at the priest's bravery in staying to serve so faithfully, Jack shook Father Jose's hand.

In turn, the priest made the Sign of the Cross on Jack's forehead, wishing him a fruitful and healing journey.

Outside the cathedral, the sunset behind the twin steeples painted the sky golden yellow, orange, and red.

Siena gazed into Jack's eyes with a look of concern. "Was he able to help?"

Jack pursed his lips. "I don't know. He said we might have a clue in a small town called Prâxedis something."

"Prâxedis G. Guerrero," said Juan. "It is southeast of here. I know the town."

"I don't know who or what we're looking for, but I need to go there. I don't feel as if I can ask you to—"

"Don't even bother, Russo," chided Siena as she rolled her eyes and headed towards the truck.

Chapter 4

Juan tried to convince Jack that going to Prâxedis G. Guerrero just before nightfall wouldn't be the smartest idea. When he motioned with his eyes toward Siena, Jack finally agreed to set out in the morning.

Siena dropped Juan off at his apartment in Juarez before heading back over the Zaragoza bridge into El Paso. The street lights and neon signs were turned on for the evening, which was preferable to the oppressive heat of the sun.

"I don't know about you, but I could use some sticky ribs and a cold beer," offered Siena.

Jack thought it was the least he could do for all the help she had been on his first day back on the border. He gave an approving nod.

Siena stopped at her place to wash and change for an evening out.

Jack stared wide-eyed at the sight of her coming into the sitting room wearing her cowboy hat, a cream-colored blouse, denim shorts, leather boots, and a smile sparkling in her eyes.

She plopped a cowboy hat on Jack's head and gushed, "Are ya ready? I think you need a bit of thawin' tonight."

Jack shook his head, catching a glimpse of himself in the mirror. "Why do I feel like protecting you is going to be a bigger deal tonight than it was in Juarez today?"

Siena laughed as she grabbed her keys.

Twenty minutes later, they pulled into the parking lot of a large building with a lighted sign over the entrance that announced *The Stampede*. "Bring your hat, cause y'all are goin' to a genuine cowboy bar tonight. Music, dancin', barbeque, and the prettiest date in Texas. What more could you ask for?"

Lively country music greeted them as they opened the door

to the nightclub. The atmosphere was upbeat with the band playing loudly and people cheering the dancers or those riding the mechanical rodeo bull that stood before the crowded bar.

As the hostess led them to a high-top table next to the dancefloor, Jack noticed that Siena attracted a lot of attention.

A waitress approached. "Evening, Siena." She eyed Jack up and down. "And who's your gentleman friend?"

Siena shook her head. "Just someone I picked up off the road. Can we get him some of those tasty barbeque ribs and a couple of Thunderbirds?" Siena glanced toward Jack. "Are ya okay with a local brew?"

After the ribs and a few beers, Siena pulled Jack onto the floor, and seeing Siena's enthusiasm as she danced, he began dancing and having fun for the first time in longer than he could remember.

When they finally stepped back to their table to take a breather, Siena shouted over the loud song, "Y'all got some moves, after all, Russo. We'll make a cowboy out of you yet!" They watched a mix of couples take the floor for a slow dance while they cooled off with another beer. "So, Russo, when are ya goin' to tell me your story? I feel like I'm getting in deep without a clue of what's what."

Jack took a long sip, pondering her question. Much of him felt as if he could trust her, but his pervading instincts were to trust no one. If his daughter were alive, he couldn't take the chance of word getting out that he was looking for her, even if it was an innocent slip. When it was obvious that he wasn't going to open up, she said, "Okay. Tell me something about yourself. Are you married?"

Jack shook his head. "No."

"Have you ever been married? Don't tell me that no one would have you. You're a good lookin' dude, and I don't think yer stupid by any stretch." She ran her finger around the lip of her glass.

Jack nodded. "A long time ago."

"Now we're getting somewhere. How long ago?"

"About twenty years."

"Wow. What happened? Sorry. Didn't it work out?" Her eyebrows arched.

"She died." Sadness returning like a body blow, Jack sighed.

"I'm sorry. I didn't mean to pry. Have ya been with anyone since? I mean, that's a long time."

Jack shook his head.

"You haven't had sex for twenty years? Sorry, that's the beer talking. Disregard that question, but—"

"Nope, and I hope you can say the same," replied Jack out of a fatherly instinct.

Siena laughed. "This is 2008. Why would you say that?"

Jack gazed into Siena's eyes. "I know. I'm old-fashioned. My wife and I waited for each other, and it was special." He paused as he drifted back, thinking of his bride. "We wanted to be faithful after we got married, but someone asked me once why I wouldn't be faithful to her before. I couldn't think of a good reason, but I finally understood why when we got married. I can't explain it, but it made it mean more. It made us closer and more intimate. I realized that she deserved that gift—and I sense that you do too." A tear rolled down her cheek as he added, "The real thing is worth it, and children deserve two parents ready to love them—for forever."

Siena wiped her cheeks with the back of her hand. "Forever sounds nice. I never had even one parent love me forever, or at all, as far as I know."

Jack reached out and touched her hand. "I'm sorry to go on like that, but you deserve real love and respect. Were you adopted? Are there no records of who your parents were?"

Siena shook her head sharply. "None. My adoptive mother was nice to me. She couldn't have children and wanted a daughter—the best money could buy, I guess. But all that money couldn't buy a cure for leukemia, so I was left with a man that drank away all her money to escape his sadness." She paused, staring into her half-empty glass. "He'd pick me up at Mount Carmel School, and we rarely made it home until late at night, stopping at one bar after another as I sat out in the car waiting for him like he promised, only to have to go into each bar to pull him out. He drank himself to death by the time I was thirteen, and I've been on my own since."

Choked up by the images, Jack squeezed her hand tightly.

Siena wiped her tears. "This is silly. Look at me. I haven't cried in years." She took a long sip of her beer. "Hey, you said 'forever' when you were talking about marriage."

"Yeah, so?"

"Well, you pronounced it, 'for-evah,' like they do in Boston." Her eyes twinkled. "Did I pick up on somethin'?" She poked at him. "Yeah, yeah, I got it right, didn't I? Tell me I'm wrong or tell me I'm right."

"Okay, you may be right."

"Ya'll been trying to hide it, haven't ya? Give me a little of the real Jack 'From Boston' Russo."

Knowing they both needed a change in the conversation, Jack grinned, and he took a long sip of this own beer. "Okay. Are you sure you're ready for this?"

"Yes, and it better be good." Siena settled comfortably on her stool.

"All right, you asked for it. My friend lives in a three-deckah in Southie. We was havin' a wicked good suppah in his pahluh on Saddedee night."

Siena laughed so hard, she almost fell off her stool. "I didn't understand a single word y'all just said. You know that, don't ya?"

Jack smirked. "Just getting stahted." He took another sip of his beer and smiled. "So, I said, 'The Sox are playin' the Yanks at Fenway Pahk,' and he said, 'No suh,' and I said, 'Yah huh, just grab the clichah ovah theah and turn on the tube.' So, my buddie says, "Bettah idear would be to get in the cah, head down Comm-av and bang a uey on Yawkee to do a packie run before we sneak inta the pahk. I wanna go.' Then I says, 'So doan I. That's a wicked pissa idear.'"

Siena's tears rolled from uncontrollable laughter. "What country, never mind, what planet are you from?"

Before Jack could respond, a young man in a broad-brimmed cowboy hat approached their table and asked Siena to dance. Jack may have been overprotective, but he could tell when a guy was a player. "The young lady is taking a break right now, and she's out of your league, anyway."

Clearly, the young man had had a few more drinks than Jack. He pointed to the mechanical rodeo bull and jutted his chin in a challenge. "Longest one on the bull gets the next dance with the pretty lady."

Jack waved his hand. "I think I'll sit this one—" He stopped short when Siena shook her head in disappointment.

With chagrin, Jack accepted the challenge.

Siena cackled. "Have you ever even been on one of these things?"

Jack eyed her, shook his head, and finished off his beer before following the confident cowboy to the rodeo bull.

Most of the saloon gathered in a circle to watch the spectacle. Jack waved him to go first. The young man's chest puffed as he sized up the crowd and then mounted the bull. He grabbed the bull rope and raised his other arm for balance as it jerked back and forth, simulating an angry bucking bull. The longer he lasted, the faster the machine gyrated, until he was finally shaken off, landing in the arms of waiting friends who hollered, "Ride'em, cowboy! That's got to be a record!"

Jack peered around at the crowd, which seemed to be impressed with his challenger's time on the bucking machine.

Siena grabbed Jack's arm. "Russo, you don't have to do this. It takes a lot of practice not to kill yourself, never mind beat that time."

The crowd cheered as Jack stared at the bull and then

stepped up to it. It took him a second to spot the stirrup for his foot to mount the bull. He grabbed hold of the rope and settled on top, getting the feel of the machine beneath his legs. He silently mumbled a quick prayer, "Please, don't let me die this way," as he grabbed the rope and then raised his left arm to signal that he was ready. He thought of everything he had been through in his life and decided he wasn't about to let this machine be the one to beat him. The sudden movement surprised him as he grabbed the rope with all his might and jerked violently back and forth, the bull trying its best to toss him from its back. The noise level of the yelling crowd grew with each passing second, thrashing him back and forth until the time ran out and the bull slowed to a stop with Jack still on board.

Jumping up and down, Siena gave him an enthusiastic hug as he dismounted to the loud cheer and approving whistles from the crowd. Even the young man who had challenged him seemed impressed, tipping his hat and shaking Jack's hand.

Siena laughed and chattered most of the way home.

Sore and exhausted, Jack had no trouble sleeping on Siena's lumpy old couch until the smell of bacon and eggs cooking on the refurbished kitchen stove called to him early the next morning.

Chapter 5

"Wake up, sleepyhead, or your eggs will get cold," called out Siena as bacon and eggs sizzled on the griddle. "I've got coffee, and I've got *coffee*. What do ya want to drink?"

Jack pulled the crocheted blanket covering from his face and squeezed his eyes tight as he stretched his body out straight, feeling the bumps and bruises acquired from the adventures of the previous day. "Smells good. I'll have *coffee* if you don't mind." He gave her a friendly smile and took a seat at the second-hand Formica kitchen table as she served him up a steaming hot breakfast plate. She plunked down her plate and two cups of hot black coffee.

"I feel like a king," he said with a grin.

"Well, you were the king of The Stampede last night, that's for sure," replied Siena with a laugh. "Y'all looked like you were hangin' on for yer life, and no one was goin' to take it from ya."

The image made Jack think back to a day he couldn't shake from his memory, the day he wished had never happened, but he never could forget. He closed his eyes to blot the sight out of his mind.

"Are you okay?"

He nodded and opened his eyes to see the sincere concern in hers. "Yeah, yeah. Just shaking the cobwebs out. Hey, these are really good," he added, pointing to his forkful of scrambled eggs.

Siena smiled and watched while he ate his breakfast and drank his coffee. After a few minutes, she broke the silence. "I like what ya said last night."

Jack squinted, scrambling to think of what he might've said. "What did I say?"

"About your marriage. I guess I've never seen a real

marriage up close—not close enough to ever want one."

Thinking all young women wanted to get married someday, he stopped to ponder what she had just shared with him. "I hope you find that right someone that makes you feel like you do want one. There's nothing more real than knowing unconditional love and friendship with someone, and then, someday, holding a precious expression of that love in your arms—together. You seem like too special a young lady not to have that someday."

Siena's eyes misted as she peered up at the cracked ceiling. "In case you were wondering, it's been almost twenty for me too."

He shook his head, and his eyes squinted at her, trying to understand what she was saying.

"I've never let anyone get close enough to me to even go there, so I guess I've got a chance for the real thing," she said, then paused before adding, "someday." She smiled and gazed into his eyes as if she had never really shared anything intimate with anyone in her life.

Siena stood up. "Well, enough of that. I have a feeling that we've got a long day ahead of us. Juan had an early morning class and should be here soon."

Jack ran his hand across his mouth. "I've been thinking about that—"

She interrupted, "Well, y'all can stop thinkin' about that. We're comin', and that's all there is to it." As she cleared the plates, there was a rap on the back door—Juan with coffee and breakfast sandwiches in hand. She shook her head as she let him in. "Good mornin', *Señor* Sanchez! Would you like some real Texan coffee?"

"Funny," quipped Juan as he broke off a piece of bacon from her plate.

"How was school? You're early," asked Siena.

"I did go, but I couldn't sit through class thinking about today," responded Juan.

Jack tilted his head toward Juan. "You guys don't have to go. As a matter of fact, I don't think you should be—"

Before he could finish his sentence, they were already packing for the trip, making him shake his head at their youthful denial of how dangerous this could be.

Juan approached Jack. "Do you have any *dinero?*"

"Money? Sure. Why?" replied Jack as he reached under his tee shirt for the hidden money belt. He opened it to show his passport and a stack of bills.

Juan shook his hand and blurted, *"Tiene más lana que un borrego!"*

Jack squinted at Siena for a translation.

She said, "These Mexicans have a lot of weird sayings. He said that you have 'more wool than a lamb'—basically, you've got a lot of money there."

"It's dangerous to carry, but we may need it to get information." Juan closed the door before they climbed into Siena's truck.

Siena checked the hunting knife on her boot and then tucked it under her jeans. She lifted the floorboard behind them, where a compartment held a rifle, pistol, and ammunition.

As they left the outskirts of the city, they drove south along the Texan side of the border. The open land had a desolate feel to it, except for an occasional 18-wheeler tractor-trailer they shared the route with.

Finally, they reached an area where he could see acres of farmland and ranches to the right, where the winding Rio Grande border divided Texas from Mexico. "You know where we're crossing, Siena, right?" asked Juan.

She tipped her hat, and a few miles down the road, she turned right toward the border crossing for Guadalupe. The road was mostly barren desert until they got closer to the river border, where there were seemingly endless farming fields and irrigation ditches. As they approached the border check station, only one car and a tractor-trailer waited in front of them.

Jack commented, "At least we should be safer in these small farm towns."

Siena and Juan gave each other a look as she turned off the engine.

"Why are we stopping? There're only a few cars in front of us."

"It'll take a bit for them to inspect that rig." Siena opened her door and stepped out of the truck.

Juan turned to Jack. "Mr. Russo, these are small towns. They are proud towns that once produced cotton that would rival Egypt's. But factories were opened in Juarez that drew workers and sent smelly sludge down river to our fields. To make things worse, we had droughts. Despite all those struggles, nothing has impacted towns like Guadalupe more than this drug war."

Jack glanced around at the open land. "Why out here? It looks like there's nothing but small towns and open farmland."

"Because there's a single highway running through the Valley of Juarez leading to the three major smuggling routes into the US. Growing up, this area was controlled by a man called *El Patron* under the Juarez cartel. There was little trouble for a long time until the Sinaloa cartel moved in. Then a lieutenant for *El Chapo* named Gabino Salas Valenciano from Durango took control. They call him *The Engineer,* and there's been nothing but murder and bloodshed since. When his brother was killed and decapitated, he ordered the burning of ranches, homes, and vehicles in the town."

Jack shook his head in disbelief. "Didn't they send soldiers down to stop it or something?"

Unexpectedly, Juan banged his fist on the dashboard. "Soldiers?! They came in and ransacked our homes, arrested and tortured families with no charges, and let the Sinaloas have their way smuggling drugs, kidnapping, killing people, and burning their homes. On the other side, the Juarez cartel has been pushed into extortion and kidnapping to fund their operations and this war. With all the murders, people are afraid to speak out, and many have been forced to leave. It's turning Guadalupe and others into ghost towns."

Before Jack could process Juan's emotional response, Siena hopped back into the driver's seat and started up the truck, slowly rolling forward until she reached the border checkpoint.

The guard peered into the truck. "Good morning, and welcome to Mexico. Are you all US citizens?"

Juan held out his passport.

"What is the purpose of your visit? You know there've been a lot of problems in the Valley lately."

Juan respectfully responded, *"Estamos visitando a la familia en Guadalupe."*

The agents walked around Siena's truck, banging their fists on the flatbed and inspecting the back cargo area before coming around to the passenger side. "What happened to your face?"

Jack put his hand to the bandage on his cheek. "Oh, that. I fell off a mechanical bull the other night."

The agent laughed and waved them on. "Have a good—and safe—visit."

As Siena drove to Guadalupe, they could see that many of the farm fields were now dry, barren plots with only weeds surviving. The sky above was a vibrant blue with few clouds to be found, but the town was desolate with abandoned cars along the way. There were rows of cement-block homes, several of which were gutted and charred from fire or explosives, abandoned without any effort to clean up the destruction.

Two boys on old bikes had stopped to watch them drive down the street, taking particular notice of Jack as he tried to give them a friendly wave. Juan said in a hushed voice, "The Sinaloa cartel often pays young kids to be lookouts. As they get a little older, they will try to recruit certain ones to be *sicarios* or hitmen." Juan pointed to the next street for Siena to take a turn and then pull up to a small, white cinderblock, single-story square of a building that was Juan's home in Guadalupe.

When they stepped down from the truck, Juan didn't go to the front door but, instead, walked to a home two doors down that showed charred burns above all the windows and on the roof. He had to push several times to get the front door open enough to step in. Jack followed him in and saw the damage of the devastating fire to what was once a family refuge and place of shared memories. A blackened family photo hung over the scorched couch, a burned Bible sat on a table, and the remains of porcelain dolls lay on the floor of one of the small bedrooms, where the blackened remnants of a crucifix were still affixed to the wall over the bed.

Shaken, his breaths coming in hard bursts, Juan trudged out the front door of his childhood home, where a woman stood at the screen door, appearing equally upset to see him.

Chapter 6

Jack and Siena stood outside the humble cinderblock home, listening to Juan arguing with the woman. "Who's the old woman?" asked Jack as he ran the bottom of his shoe across the dusty ground outside the front door.

Siena smiled. "I don't think she's even as old as you. That's his mom."

"Why is she so angry with him?"

"Because she loves him. She's saying things have gotten so bad that she doesn't want him to visit. She doesn't want him killed like his father and brother," whispered Siena. "It means the world to her to see him, but he's too precious to put his life at risk."

"Huh. I guess I can see that." Jack peered through the screen door.

"Juan's asking her about what happened to the burned-out house that belonged to their friends from back when he was a boy. She's crying about the loss of her best friend, Myriam. Their boy was only fourteen. *'Le entregaron un arma'*—they handed him a gun and told him to shoot a man in the head. Oh my gosh—when he refused, they shot *him* in the head and then the man on the ground. She says that they burned their home as punishment for their son refusing to do as they ordered. The mother and younger daughter were in the house at the time of the fire." Siena's legs buckled, and she struggled to stay on her feet. "I didn't know. I didn't know it had gotten this bad."

Jack lifted her back to her feet. "Why does she stay?"

"Juan's grandmother will not leave her home. She would rather die here, and his mom won't leave her. They said they have done nothing wrong and shouldn't have to leave. Where else would they go—Juarez?"

Before Jack could respond, Juan opened the door and waved them into the house to introduce them to his mother, Catalina, and his grandmother, whom he referred to as *Abuelita*. They apologized for making them wait and not being able to speak English. After a cold drink, Catalina asked Juan if they could visit the church for a bit. Jack nodded to Juan.

As they approached the white stucco church, Jack smiled to see its two bell towers and the name, *Our Lady of Guadalupe*. In a town that was dusty and desolate, the church seemed like a bright sign of hope and beauty. Catalina and Abuelita made their way through the door that Juan held open for them, and they walked up the aisle, knelt in the front pew, and prayed for the souls of their family and neighbors who had been lost.

Jack gazed up at the beauty of the church, most likely built by the hands of the very people who had built this community.

A man who was sweeping in the back turned and smiled when he saw Juan. "*Juan, hijo mío. Es bueno verte en la iglesia.*"

Juan smiled, hugging the man. "It's good to see you too, Padre Mira. Please meet my friends, Siena Conners from school and Señor Jack Russo."

"*Buenos días.* Good to meet you both. You are always welcome here." Father Mira waved his hand, pointing to the high-arched ceiling. "It is *bastante hermoso*—quite beautiful, is it not?"

Jack nodded. "Very pleased to meet you, Father Mira, and it is very beautiful. It seems like every church around here is named after Our Lady of Guadalupe. She certainly gets around."

Father Mira smiled. "You know the story, then?" He walked them to the colorful portrait of Mary that Jack had also seen in the two other churches.

"I guess I'm getting a little embarrassed to say that I don't know anything about it," whispered Jack.

Father Mira's eyes brightened. "Come back sometime, and I can give you the full story, but something special happened on December 9, 1531. A very long time ago, an Aztec peasant named Juan Diego experienced a vision on the hill of Tepeyac. He saw a young woman who identified herself as 'mother of the very true deity' and told him she wanted a church built on the site. Juan Diego did not know what to do, so he ran to tell the Bishop, who was very skeptical, and asked for a sign of proof.

"Juan was supposed to meet with Our Lady again on the hill, but his uncle was gravely ill, and he had to attend to him. She intercepted him on the way and said to him, 'Am I not here, I who am your mother?' She promised him that his uncle would recover and told him to pick flowers for her on the normally barren Tepeyac Hill in the cold month of December. Well, did he not find roses—roses not even native to Mexico—growing there? He took them to her, and she arranged them on his tilma, a very coarse woven cloak worn by field workers. When Juan returned home with the cloak, what do you think happened when the Bishop saw it?"

Jack shrugged. "No idea."

Father Mira smiled. "The roses fell to the floor, and on the rough fabric was this image of the Virgin Mary. The fabric and the image still exist today at the church on the hill."

"Not to be a negative Nancy, but how do we know it's real?" Jack asked.

Father Mira gazed up at the bright portrait. "A reasonable question. Over the centuries, no one has been able to duplicate it, and tests show there are no brush strokes on the fabric. The image has lasted almost 500 years. Remember, at that time, Mexico was mostly Aztec and worshipped gods, and sacrificed tens of thousands, including children, to the gods every year. Once they saw the image on the tilma and heard of Juan's testimony and the recovery of his uncle, approximately nine million Aztecs converted to Christianity in less than a decade."

Jack shook his head. "Why would a picture have that effect?"

"Ahh. The symbolism on the image had great meaning to the Aztec natives. The gaze of a mother loving her child, the clouds from heaven, the sun for the mother of light, the prayerful mode of her hands and body, the colors of a queen, the new era represented by the black ribbon around her expectant waist, the star on the mantle indicating that she comes from heaven, and the bow indicating her virginity. There is so much communicated in this beautiful image that could not have come from the hands of man—plus, if it convinced a skeptical bishop, it had to be a miracle." Father Mira laughed.

Jack thanked him for the story as he observed the portrait, feeling as if Mary's eyes greeted his. They left the church and drove Juan's mother and grandmother to the outskirts of town, where stood a desolate-looking cemetery. Stepping from the truck, Jack could see fresh mounds from recent burials and a gravedigger working on a new plot in the scorching sun, with no shade trees for relief. Juan gave him a bottle of cool water, which made him smile as he guzzled it down. "*Cinco de la semana pasada, todos jóvenes*," he said as he wiped the sweat from his brow.

Juan turned to Jack and Siena. "He said, 'Five in this past week, all young ones.' People are afraid to even come to visit their loved ones." They scanned the bleak cemetery baking in the hot sun, and there was a heavy stillness in the air with no breeze for relief. "*Hasta el viento tiene miedo*," murmured Juan as he walked his mother to the family's plot.

Jack turned to Siena, who translated, "He said, 'Even the wind is afraid.'" They passed by several mounds with no markers. One had a wooden cross with a baseball hat tied to it with a cloth. They joined the family to quietly pay respects to Juan's deceased father, Julio, thirty-five years old, killed in 1998, and his brother Jesus, twenty-four years old, killed in

2007. On their gravemarkers hung ribbons attached to their badges as police officers. Juan's mother cried at the sight while Juan stood silently, his hands clenched by his side.

Afterward, they drove Juan's mother and grandmother back home, where he gave them a long embrace. Driving away, Juan asked if they could stop at an abandoned police station they were approaching. They got out and approached the empty building. Juan touched the wall to the right of the damaged front door and shed tears for his brother that had not flowed at the cemetery. "This is where those animals left my brother's head with nothing but a sign that read, *Per orders of El Quitapuercos.* My father was a proud police officer of this town when it was a good town, a good place to raise your family. As the narcos came in, he fought back, and they killed him when I was only eleven. My brother, Jesus—" Juan paused to collect himself before continuing. "My brother only wanted to be like him, a cop to keep the peace and fight for justice. They had killed four other police officers in this war between the cartels, but he didn't give in." Tears streamed down his cheeks again. "We found parts of his body around town, but not all. They couldn't even leave his family his body to bury with dignity."

Jack could relate to Juan's emotional anger and sense of revenge, but he couldn't share his story. He glanced down at the dusty floorboards of the front entry platform. Stuck in a gap between the boards was the edge of a small tin. Jack ran the toe of his shoe over it to brush off the dust and could barely make out the words, *CD Nb Selection Especiale Cigarillos.*

Jack and Siena left Juan to have a few minutes to himself as they approached the truck. "Siena, who is 'El Quitapuercos'?"

Siena whispered, "It means 'pig-killer.' It's the nickname of a Sinaloa commander and enforcer. Most of these towns are now lawless with no police because of the killings and threats. Jesus didn't back down, and this was a message, an example for others."

Chapter 7

The ride to Práxedis G. Guerrero was a quiet one. Jack thought about the possibilities of finding his daughter or worse. The rage that remained under the surface was palpable after their visit, and he would give anything to find the men who had killed his wife and tried to kill him.

His mind wandered back to 1987 when he was only twenty years of age and on summer break from Boston University, where he had been lucky enough to have a partial scholarship. His roommate and closest friend, Sam Engres, had wanted to do something different for their final college summer and had convinced him to drive down to El Paso to find work for their summer break.

Jack had never ventured far from the Boston area. The trip south wound its way through New York, Pennsylvania, Virginia, Tennesse, Arkansas, and then they had made the long haul across Texas that had given them a feeling of freedom and adventure. If they couldn't find a cheap enough motel, they had slept in the car and saved their money for food and beer. In El Paso, Jack had found a job in a meatpacking plant, while Sam had found several different ventures to make money. Sam had always been fun and unpredictable. There was a lot that Jack admired about him, especially his determination and ability to keep going, regardless of the obstacles. Sam had even played through an entire tournament basketball game in college with the excruciating pain of a broken foot.

They both had worked hard during the hot days, but they had been free to enjoy the cooler evening nightlife, which often led them across the Mexican border to the city of Juarez. At that time, Juarez had been vibrant, fun, and different— much livelier than Boston, with different customs and visibly rich in culture. The young women had been different, as well, and seemed exotic and alluring to two handsome American college students with no responsibilities.

One night, when they were at one of their favorite outdoor bars in Juarez, there was a festival in the street with Latin music and dancing under a gorgeous starlit summer sky. That was the night she caught his eye, and he couldn't stop gazing at her. Sam poked him in the side. "Who's stolen your heart tonight?" Jack only smiled more broadly and could feel himself blushing. "Well, whoever it is, go and ask her to dance!" Sam gave him a push.

As Jack inched in her direction, he could see that she was glancing up and down at him during her conversation with a girlfriend. His heart pounded faster as he approached and wondered if any girl could have been more beautiful. Her eyes were dark and mesmerizing, her skin soft and light brown, but it was her smile that gave him the courage to make those last few steps and ask if she wanted to dance. She glanced at her girlfriend, who was nodding, and then gazed up into his eyes. Jack forgot everything else as he held her and danced under the full moon.

Her name was Maria Engando, and she lived with her parents in Juarez while attending *Universidad Interamericana del Norte.* Jack spent more and more of his time with Maria and often double-dated, with Sam dating Maria's friend, Nina. She was hesitant to take him home to meet her parents because, as she explained, her father was very old-fashioned about dating and wanted her to find someone who was Mexican and wanted to live close to family. When she did finally take him home to meet her gracious mother, Marta, her father, Hector, gave him a stonewall reception.

Eventually, everyone became more comfortable as Jack, Sam, Nina, and Maria spent more and more time at her home, which was nicer than most of the homes Jack had seen in

Juarez. Hector worked a lot of hours, so they didn't spend a great deal of time with him outside of Sunday Mass, which was always followed by a large family dinner. Sam wasn't Catholic, but he attended anyway. There would often be men, some of whom Jack recognized from Sunday Mass, who arrived at the house to meet with Hector in his back office. Maria was never sure exactly what her father did other than the transportation business. Most of the men who worked with him called him 'The Boss.' Sam even did some part-time work for Hector to fill in between jobs he had, but he never knew much about the business.

One day, Sam pulled Jack aside. "You're really in deep here, aren't you?"

Jack nodded, eyes dazed. "I think I am."

"Like how deep?"

"You've seen Maria. You've spent time with her. Have you ever met a girl like her? I can't imagine ever finding another girl like her. I don't even want to," gushed Jack.

"Whoa, whoa, whoa, boy," pleaded Sam. "What are you thinking? You've only known her for just over two months now, and we've got to be thinking about heading back to Boston soon."

Jack turned to Sam. "Have you ever met a girl like Maria?"

Sam's eyes dropped. "No, I haven't."

"So, you know what I mean."

"I guess I do."

Jack stood back. "I think I want to spend the rest of my life with her."

When he saw Maria again and danced under the stars, this time in front of their home, he told her how he felt, and she told him she felt the same way.

But she also informed him that her father would never approve. "I know him. He won't permit it. I know that part of him likes you, but I also know him too well to not know what he'll say. I'm so afraid that he'll say, 'No.'"

Maria was right. Jack got up the gumption to approach Hector and let him know how he felt about his only daughter and that he wanted to ask for her hand in marriage. Marta glanced at Hector but didn't say a word as her husband's eyes turned stone-cold. "She's only nineteen, and you haven't known her long enough to make a commitment like that."

Jack's nervous energy showed. "I will stay here and court her properly. I will prove myself to you. I love Maria, and I want to give her the life she deserves."

Hector peered directly into Jack's eyes. "The life she deserves is with a Mexican husband, not with an impetuous and spoiled Americano. *La respuesta es no. ¡Y eso es definitivo!*"

Maria cried but didn't say a word as her father escorted her out of the room and slammed the door on Jack.

Marta let him out, apologizing for the answer, thanking him for his care and respect of her daughter. He left in a daze, with no sense of peace.

Sam tried to console him the whole way home.

The small farming community of Práxedis G. Guerrero was not very far down the road from Guadalupe and even closer to the border that saw $300 billion of drugs cross it each year to feed the growing appetite of its northern neighbors. The ferocious turf war between the cartels had devastated it and turned it into one of the most dangerous towns in an already violent region. There were soldiers posted on the road as Siena cruised by and entered an eerily quiet town.

As they passed more small cinderblock homes that were boarded up or burned down, Jack asked, "Is it even worse here than in Guadalupe?"

"It's always worse when you know the people personally, but it's about the same. Mayors of both towns have been assassinated, and the police killed or chased out of town. Innocent people, not involved in the drug trade at all, have been subject to extortion, kidnapping, and murder. Most have escaped, and little remains of the life that once existed here. There is a saying, '*Pobre México, tan lejos de Dios, tan cerca de los Estados Unidos.*'" Jack shook his head, and Juan said, "Poor Mexico, so far from God, so close to the United States."

They passed a dilapidated market in the center of town populated by a few fruit and vegetable stands consisting of baskets placed on folding tables. Juan told Siena to pull over to see if there might be someone who could help them. The store windows had bars on them, and the old wooden door screeched as it opened. An old man's head snapped up as they entered. The shopkeeper had wary eyes that were surrounded by dark wrinkled skin and bags underneath. His eyebrows were dark and bushy, while his thinning hair and broad mustache were mostly gray. "*¿En qué puedo ayudarlos?*"

"Sir, do you speak English?" asked Jack, noticing the shopkeeper's right hand still under the counter, possibly with his finger on the trigger of a gun.

The man nodded. "What can I help you folks with?"

Jack stood still with his hands in full view and forced a cordial smile. "My niece used to visit this town, probably fifteen years ago now, to a ranch to ride horses. I can't remember the name of the ranch, but I want to visit it."

The shopkeeper squinted as he inspected Jack.

Juan interrupted. "I'm from Guadalupe, and he's a good guy. He's safe."

The shopkeeper let out a long breath as he raised his empty hand and leaned on the counter with both palms. "*Un rancho,* eh?" He rubbed some of the sweat from his brow with the palm of his hand. "There is a ranch on the outskirts of town off Ramirez Road, right next to the Rio. They always kept horses to ride, but I don't think it's the one you want."

Jack asked, "Why is that?"

"Because of who owns it," replied the man as he took out a cloth to wipe his forehead again. "I don't want to say any more."

"But—" pleaded Jack.

Juan grabbed his arm. "Thank you, sir." Juan touched the brim of his hat. "Is it okay if we buy some fruit from your stand outside?"

After the man nodded, Juan retrieved three plump purple plums from the basket, paid the man, and nodded to have a good day.

Outside, Jack approached Juan and asked in a hushed tone. "What did I miss?"

Juan scanned the empty streets for anyone watching. "The Sinaloa cartel hasn't been in these parts for very long, so I'm assuming the owner of the ranch is connected to the Juarez cartel—and by the expression on his face, it is most likely someone high up and dangerous. The only one I can think of in this town would be the man they call *El Patron*. I have a sick feeling that the men who killed my brother work for him."

Chapter 8

Juan clenched his jaw.

Jack broke the silence. "Juan, I don't want you or Siena involved, but I need to find out what I can."

"*Lo sé.* I know, but you can't find out anything if you're *muerto.* I need to think for a second," snapped Juan.

Siena pressed on Juan's shoulder. "Take your time. Do you know anyone in town?"

Juan snapped his fingers. He drove them down a few streets past the abandoned police station, which was riddled with machine-gun bullet holes, and stopped at an intersection where a boarded-up home had three arrows spray-painted in front. The top one, a fat solid arrow, pointed down, and the other two were open arrows pointing to the solid one. "What does that mean?" asked Siena.

"It's a message saying, 'two people were killed here.' The neighbors would know why." Juan turned the corner and then into the driveway of a small house, overgrown with weeds. He pulled into the backyard, where there was a small carport overhang. "This is Jess Alvarez's home. She goes to our church in Guadalupe and often takes my mom and grandmother. She's a good woman and has asked me to visit many times. I hope she's home."

Before anyone could get out of the car, a woman opened the back door with a broad smile on her face. "Juan Sanchez! I can't believe you came to visit." She gave him a big hug and kiss on the cheek. "Your mother and *abuelita* were good when I saw them on Sunday. Who are your friends?"

"Jess, this is Siena, a good friend from school, and Jack, who is visiting the area after many years."

Jess gave each a welcoming smile and handshake. "And your good friend from school is very attractive too. You are all very welcome to my home. Come in and let me get you something to eat and drink."

The home was simple and clean. A crucifix hung on the wall over a table with pictures of Jess's late husband and possibly her parents.

Jess brought out a tray of cold lemonade and small sandwiches to the sitting room. "Juan, after all my invitations, you finally come to visit me. Your mom says you are doing well at school, no?"

"I'm trying, Jess," Juan replied as he took a seat and reached for some lemonade. "School is going well. I do worry about *Mamá* and *Abuelita* with all these senseless killings and kidnappings going on. I worry about you too. How've you been coping?"

"I don't know if I'm coping, but I am praying a lot more these days. I never thought I'd ever see our beautiful valley called 'The Valley of Death,'" she said sadly. "There seems to be no end to it. Now, with the market collapse, there are no jobs except for smuggling and drugs. The appetite in the United States for drugs seems to only get bigger and hungrier, and the money makes people do almost anything for power. It's so sad." Jess turned to Jack. "Please take no offense, but I often wonder why a country with so much abundance has such a need for all these drugs?"

Jack couldn't have felt more ashamed than he did at that moment, but he could only shake his head.

"Maybe," the woman said, "too many distractions and choices get in the way of focusing on the important things—the only things that really matter."

Siena tilted her head. "What really matters, Mrs. Alvarez?"

Jess smiled. "To me, it's God, family, and friends. Relationships. Even when we have lost someone, I think we still have a relationship with them and will see them again."

Siena said, "What if you never met your family, never knew your parents—do you think you can still have a relationship with them?"

"They are part of you, just like God is part of you. You honor them in the life you lead and how you love others. Do that with all your heart, and you will see all of them someday— and I think you will find that it was well worth it." She reached out and clasped Siena's hands.

"Jess, do you know the ranch down off Ramirez Road?" inquired Juan.

"You must mean '*Rancho Familia.*' They were always generous to the community and used to allow the neighborhood children to come to the ranch sometimes to learn how to ride—but no one has been allowed down that road for several years now. They lived in Juarez and would come out to get out of the city. We've always suspected that they had a connection to the cartel—if not one of the leaders. We just lived with the reality of it, but it's all gone dangerously *loco* now with this insidious war."

Jack paced the small room as he tried to think of how to get onto the ranch. "Is there only the one access road to the ranch?"

"Yes, unless you cross the river from the States, which is pretty dry and shallow now, but I suspect they may have guards along the border. I don't know," replied Jess. "I don't think they'll let you drive in unless—"

Jack turned with anticipation. "Unless what?"

"I have a good friend who attends to the horses on the ranch. She may have an idea, but I don't know if she would want to take a risk like that," said Jess. "Her name is Calle. Let me see if she's free."

Calle dropped by a short time later, hugging Jess when she entered the house. She had short gray hair and a slender but sturdy frame. She became extremely fearful and hesitant when they asked about getting to the ranch. Calle's anxiety and panic became palpable as she pursed her lips and squeezed her eyes shut.

Jack sat next to her. "Calle, I want to thank you for coming over. I realize I'm a stranger to you, but I understand your concern and–"

Calle interrupted. "I don't think you do. This is not a matter of discomfort or concern; this is something much more dangerous. I have no choice when it comes to tending to these horses. If I didn't have a family, then I might have a choice, but it still wouldn't be a good one. I am under strict orders, or more like a threat, to only come with my assistant. We can't even talk about who or what we see there. I've never met the owner, and I don't know his name. I just go, do my work, and leave."

Jack replied, "I'm no stranger to threats and deadly violence. My wife was killed, and my daughter kidnapped, and I've been trying to find my little girl for over twenty years. The only lead I have, and I know it's a longshot, is that she may have ridden horses at a ranch in Prâxedis G. Guerrero."

It may have been the look of complete sincerity or desperation in his eyes that made her pause before asking, "Have you ever handled a horse before?"

Siena giggled at the question.

Calle shook her head. "This might be the stupidest thing I've ever done, but we can get you some gear so that you look like a stablehand, and we can talk about what to do when you get there."

They stopped at Calle's house and picked up a broadbrimmed hat, a heavy pair of gloves to clip onto his belt, and some boots that had belonged to her husband. On the way, she explained that he would be responsible for most of the dirty work. "Act like you know what you're doing; muck the stalls, clean tack, groom, water, and feed the horses, and do anything else I tell you to."

"Sure. I do appreciate this. One question though, what's 'clean tack'?"

Calle rolled her eyes and headed down the long stretch of

road until she reached a security guard with a long mustache and wearing dark sunglasses. "*¿Cuidando a los ponis?*" Calle nodded and commented on the hot weather.

The guard tilted his head to get a better look at Jack, whose face was partially obscured by the brim of his hat. After an anxious hesitation that seemed to last much longer than a few seconds, he waved them on and used a walkie-talkie to notify the main house they were coming.

The ranch-house was large and impressive, as was the barn that housed the horse stalls.

Calle waved to the man on the front porch of the ranch-house as she parked near the stalls and got out, gesturing for Jack to bring in their gear and supplies and get to work.

Jack tried to scan the premises without attracting attention. He noticed another large barn structure in the back closer to the Rio Grande, some jumping fences on a riding trail, and attractive gardens with palm trees behind the ranch house that may have surrounded an outdoor patio area. As he helped Calle clean the stalls, water and feed the horses, and even learn what horse tack was, he began to doubt his decision to come here in the first place. He didn't know if this was the right ranch or if the girl that Father Jose remembered was even his daughter. What were the odds? Who was he going to ask? What was he going to ask? How was he going to get any information without putting Calle or his life in danger?

After they finished their work, they drove back out, none the wiser for the experience. As Calle pulled in front of Jess's house, Jack thanked her and stepped out of the truck only to hear a rumbling sound in the back cab. The back door opened, and Siena rolled out onto the dusty pavement. Jack shook his head in disbelief and helped her up. "What were you doing back there?"

"Y'all weren't doin' too much reconnaissance in that barn."

Calle stepped out to see what was going on. "Siena?"

"I've been there before," said Siena.

"Been where? What are you talking about?" asked Jack.

"I've been to that ranch before, riding horses. I must have been pretty young, but I recognized the spot, the house, the stable, everything."

Chapter 9

Jack shook his head. "Are you sure it was *that* ranch?"

"Yes, I'm sure. It was hard to peek out from the back of her truck cab, but as soon as I saw it, I knew I'd been there. There was a girl I went with, maybe in kindergarten or the first grade. I can't remember her name. I never had a sister, and people would say we looked alike, but she didn't come back to school the next year. It was a difficult time with my parents, well, adopted parents, so it's a bit hazy," replied Siena.

Jack turned to Calle. "I have to go back there."

"Well, we can't just go back. They won't allow it." Calle paused, staring down at the ground for several moments. "Wait, there is something that might work. They are looking to sell one of their horses. When I go back tomorrow, I could bring you—maybe both of you as interested buyers. What's more natural than a father who wants to buy a horse for his lovely daughter?" Calle winked and grinned. "Think about it. I can be back tomorrow morning." As she started the truck to take off, she said, "I must be crazy."

Jess insisted that Jack, Siena, and Juan stay for dinner and spend the night at her place. She cooked up a meal of beef chili and homemade bread and kept the conversation positive, despite the hardships in their lives and all around them. After dinner, there would still be hours of sunlight, and although few ventured out at dark, Jack and Juan decided to go for a beer one block over while Siena kept Jess company.

Lou's Cantina was a small but clean and well-maintained restaurant and bar. They sat at the old wooden counter, where a small TV played the soccer game.

They watched as they sipped their cool Coronas. The bartender, Suds, was friendly but not very talkative, which wasn't a problem as they sat next to a portly local named Javier, who was more than happy to keep them company.

Javier knew enough to keep his voice down as he complained about the destruction of the town he grew up in. His son had been shot and killed for no explained reason, and his wife had disappeared several years ago. This bar was the only family he had left when his nights became too lonely to bear. Jack asked about the farming demise and then about any ranches in the area. Javier replied, "Cotton farming has fallen from being a source of pride and the ability to make an honest living to empty fields and desolation. The only real ranch in town is the *Familia*, but few people get to see it."

Jack played dumb. "Why is that?"

Without turning his head, Javier glanced around and made sure that Suds was preoccupied with cleaning the glasses. "It is owned by *El Patron*. He is very rich from smuggling oregano and *pollo*."

Jack glanced at Juan. "I must be getting old."

Juan whispered. "Oregano is pot—marijuana. They also smuggle people across the border. Human smugglers are called coyotes, and they transport their *pollo*—chickens—for a fee."

Javier nodded as he put his hand over his mouth. "*El Patron* saw himself as a 'good' bad guy because the pot was harmless compared to coke or opium, and smuggling desperate people into a better life was a good thing. In the old days, Colombia moved its hard drugs across the Gulf to Florida, but when that got shut down, the Guadalajara Cartel controlled the routes through Mexico. Things got worse when that broke up into separate cartels who got greedier and more violent. I think they let *El Patron* operate his business if he gave them access to his valued route that he has kept a secret for all these years."

Jack squinted. "Secret route?"

"Yeah. I keep my eyes and ears open, and I think I know why he has been so successful."

"And?" asked Jack.

Javier hesitated. "Well, here's my take. *El Patron* is operating out of Juarez, but does he really come down to a little dusty cotton farm town for entertainment? He buys acres of land right on the Rio and builds a ranch." He dropped his voice to the lowest of hushed tones. "Over the years, he has had heavy equipment coming in and out, and he's got that big barn right next to the border."

Jack kept his eyes on his drink as he whispered back. "So, he wants to build a ranch and get away from the city with his family."

"Well, here's the thing. Not all of that equipment or materials have been for building stables and barns, and every worker that has been brought in has been from Juarez, blindfolded, and works only at night. Since then, we've seen trucks and cars with US plates coming to the ranch and never leaving the ranch." Javier tapped his empty bottle, and Jack quickly nodded to Suds to bring another round.

Jack scratched his head. "Are you thinking he built a tunnel? And he brings people and pot under the river in the cars and trucks with US Plates?"

"I don't think it; I know it. Don't ask me how, but I do," mumbled Javier, who guzzled down his beer, holding up the bottle for another refill.

Jack and Juan made it back to Jess's place at dusk. Few people were out as a military truck drove through the middle of town. Jack and Siena practiced their parts for the next day's venture back to Ranchos Familia before they settled in for the night. At about three a.m., they all woke to screams.

Jerking upright on the couch in the living room, Juan woke up screaming, "Nooooooo!"

Siena ran in from the bedroom, her hair disheveled, and met Jack at Juan's side. "A nightmare about his brother, probably."

Jack's stomach twisted as he remembered his wife's brutal murder.

Siena pressed his arm. "You okay?"

Jack stared ahead and sighed. "Uhm, yeah. There were too many nights that I felt as if darkness was my only companion, but it was never a good one."

In the morning, Calle returned to Jess's house, appearing a bit nervous about her plan to take them back. She told them that if they found out she had deceived them, her life wouldn't be worth a *centavo*. Juan was to be Calle's stablehand assistant. Calle slowed down again for the guard, a different man than the previous day. She handed him a hot cup of coffee she had picked up at the bakery. "This is Sam Hendricks, and he's interested in buying Cortez for his daughter, Ryan."

The guard took a sip and eyed Jack, then checked the truck to see if there were any hidden guns before calling the ranch house and finally waving them on when he got the okay.

Jack's heart pounded as they approached the ranch house area. There seemed to be more activity and people at the ranch than the previous day. He noticed activity around the large barn and men on the ranch-house porch talking. A man walked toward them. His dark hair, dark skin, and scruffy beard gave him a menacing appearance as he eyed Jack up and down. "You're interested in a horse, *Señor?*"

"I am. A friend of mine knows Calle here and trusts her judgment on horses. I would like to buy the horse for my daughter, Ryan, if she feels comfortable with him. My name is Sam Hendricks, by the way," added Jack as he extended his hand to the man who didn't take it or offer his name in return.

The man waved his hand toward the stall barn. "Calle, show her Cortez. Let her ride him, and I will talk to *Señor* Hendricks about the price." He glared at Jack. "We only accept cash."

Jack nodded without flinching.

When the horse was saddled and Siena leaned over to pat the horse, Jack almost felt as if he were taking his own daughter to fulfill a dream. Her enthusiasm as she picked up the pace and even made a few jumps brought a rare smile to his face, genuine enough to apparently convince the man that he was indeed her father. "If your daughter finds Cortez acceptable, it will cost 10,000 US dollars for him. Do you have that kind of cash?"

"Calle tells me that Cortez is approaching eighteen. No disrespect, but ten thousand seems a bit steep." Jack knew that failure to bargain for the horse would raise more suspicion than arguing the price would. The man waved his hand and shook his head. "That is a firm price, *Señor*. The boss believes it's fair, and he doesn't want to negotiate. Either you want him, or you don't. Your daughter seems happy."

"She does at that. I will pay your price," replied Jack as he watched Siena bring Cortez in and dismount, giving Jack an enthusiastic hug and kiss on the cheek. "He's perfect!"

A man coming from the ranch-house interrupted their conversation as he yelled, "*Emilio, ¿qué está pasando?*"

"He is interested in buying Cortez," replied Emilio.

Jack watched the two men as they spoke. The man who yelled seemed to be more in charge as he puffed on his small cigar. He was tall and lean, with high cheekbones and a hawk-like nose under his dark sunglasses and black hat. When the man took off his glasses, Jack shuddered as he met his cold-steel squinty eyes. It wasn't a face one would forget, but Jack couldn't place him.

Siena tapped Jack's arm with the back of her hand and whispered, "What is it, Russo?"

Whispering under his breath, Jack responded, "I don't know. Something disturbing about that guy."

"This whole place gives me the spooks," said Siena. "What's the plan here?"

"That's a good question. All these years of searching, and I'm acting more on emotion than a plan." He paled as he considered the situation. "I'm also putting people at risk."

Calle and Juan were busy working in the stalls as the men continued their animated discussion. Jack sensed that something was going on and that the man with the squinty eyes wasn't happy with them being there.

When Calle and Juan were done with their stable chores, they joined Jack and Siena. Juan whispered, "What are we supposed to do now?"

Jack replied in a hushed tone. "I don't know. I was hoping there'd be someone we could talk to. Siena, do you remember anything more?"

"I'm surer than ever that I've been here and remember riding that course. I don't think that big barn in the back was there, but I'm not a hundred percent sure. I don't know. I remember riding with my friend and having lunch on the porch there with her grandmother. There were men around, but I don't recall any of them, except for one—" Siena stopped short as the two men approached them.

Emilio said, "We're going to have to finish our business another day. Cortez will be here, and you can take care of the money—cash. Calle, are you all set with the horses?"

The tall man took off his glasses again as he looked closer at Juan, almost as if he knew who he was and uncomfortably so. *"¿Cuál es su nombre?"* he questioned Juan.

"Juan," he replied cautiously.

"¿Apellido?"

"Sanchez. Juan Sanchez," responded Juan with an increasingly defiant tone.

"¿Eres de Prâxedis?"

"No, I'm from Guadalupe. I'm visiting a friend of the family and am helping out Calle. I know her from Our Lady's Church."

"Guadalupe, eh?" He narrowed his eyes as he glared directly into Juan's.

Juan returned the look without flinching, but Jack sensed that Juan was shaking underneath just as much as he was.

"Let's send them on their way," said Emilio.

"*Solo las mujeres*," ordered the man with the squinty eyes as he turned back to the ranch house.

Emilio put his hand out to divide Siena and Calle from Jack and Juan. "They can leave."

Siena pushed against his arm. "What? What's goin' on?"

Emilio chided, "I would not test him, or your chance may be lost."

Chapter 10

Jack pleaded, "Can I ask what's going on? Why are we being detained?"

Emilio narrowed his eyes. "*Señor* Hendricks, I'm sure you know the Valley has become a very dangerous place. How would we even know that you are Sam Hendricks or if this is Juan Sanchez? I'd asked for identification, but I wouldn't trust it anyway."

Jack froze. He scrambled to think of what may lay ahead of them. These men would think nothing of killing them, taking no chances. Kidnappings and murders were not investigated in the Valley these days and certainly not prosecuted, giving the cartels free rein to operate in their best interests and no one else's.

Juan asked, "*¿Qué planeas hacer con nosotros?*"

Emilio smiled. "I don't know. Maldito probably wants to wait for *El Patron* to see if he's comfortable letting you go." He proceeded to take out a gun from the inside of his vest. "In the meantime, I'm going to have to ask you to wait in the barn." He waved the gun toward the large barn in the back, the one Javier had told them about the night before. The barn was a wooden structure on the outside with large doors, but inside revealed that it was supported by metal framing, large enough to hold several tractor-trailers and stalls on the sides, which could hold several families each.

Jack and Juan were put inside one of the stalls. There were benches on each of the walls, wide enough to sleep on, and a small sink and chemical toilet for necessities. Emilio locked the heavy door to the stall area that was clearly built for human beings. Angrily, Juan paced the stall. "This is where they must keep the families being smuggled into the United States."

"You think Javier was right when he said there's a tunnel

under the river starting here?"

Juan shrugged. "I don't see where one would be. It's just a large open space. He was talking about trucks and cars traveling through the tunnel and into the farmlands on the other side of the river. I think he was spinning a story to get some free beers. One thing I do know is that the man with the evil eyes isn't going to waste a lot of time deciding what to do with us."

Jack scanned the wall for an exit from their prison cell. "Do you know anything about him?"

Juan continued to pace the stall. "He called him Maldito. The only person I know with that name is Maldito Sentenza. They call him 'Angel Eyes' because of the shape and look in his eyes, more like a dark angel."

"Anything else?"

"He's an enforcer for *El Patron*, a killer who has no regard for human life," barked Juan.

Four hours later, they heard a key open the lock on the stall door. Jack and Juan stood up and were led into the holding room, where Emilio and Maldito waited. Maldito slowly approached Jack, his steely eyes boring into Jack. Jack thought there was nothing angelic about the man in the black hat. He looked more like the angel of death.

"What brings you to Prâxedis?" asked Maldito in a terse tone.

"I was visiting a friend of my mom's from church to see how she was doing," offered Juan as a story he could back up.

Maldito stared at him with a piercing yet haunting gaze. "You have a familiar face, somehow, but I was more interested in why this man would bring his pretty young daughter to the Jaurez Valley? What is your story, *Señor* Hendricks, or so you call yourself?"

Jack scrambled to concoct a believable story that couldn't be instantly dismissed. He came to the ranch to find some answers, to find a trail that would lead him to his only child.

So far, he had nothing. He pointed to Juan and replied, "I don't know this boy, so you can let him go—"

Maldito's eyes remained serious as he half-smiled. "You spend an evening drinking together, and suddenly you don't know him? I'm not someone whose patience you want to test. *No tienes pelos en la lengua*—tell it like it is, Señor Hendricks."

"You're right. I did have a few drinks with Juan, but I didn't know him before the other day. He's a good kid and isn't a danger to you. The girl I was with is not my daughter. My name is Jack Russo, and I am searching for my daughter. I was told that she came to this ranch when she was little, about fifteen years ago, to ride horses. I wanted to know if anyone might know where she might be or who she was with."

Maldito squinted at Jack, hesitating, with only his heavy breathing breaking the silence. Jack prayed that inside that the panic he felt was not revealed on his face, but he didn't feel as if he was successful.

Maldito took a long puff of his cigarillo and let out a cloud of aromatic smoke.

Jack rubbed his nose. The scent was faintly familiar.

"A lot of young girls came to ride here back then. We don't keep track of them. Something doesn't seem right about you. I don't know what it is, but there's something," cautioned the man with the evil eyes.

Suddenly, Maldito grabbed Juan and pushed his head downward, pulling out a gun from a holster under his jacket and pressing it up against his head. Jack moved to protect Juan, but Emilio grabbed his arms from behind. *"¡Dime la neta!"* bellowed Maldito.

"Te lo juro! ¡Es neta!" pleaded Juan. "I swear to you! It's true!"

After what seemed like an eternity, Maldito pushed Juan away as he turned on his heels and walked out of the stall. The door slammed shut on the two prisoners.

"Why did you tell him that," whispered Juan after they could hear the closing of the barn door. "I have a feeling we are on death row here, and you are changing our story. I don't think it's helping. You might have a death wish, but I can't die until I avenge my brother's murder!"

Jack put his hand on Juan's shoulder. "Juan, I'm sincerely sorry for your grief. It's something we share. I promise you that I won't let you die."

"You act as if death doesn't frighten you," retorted Juan, as he peered straight ahead.

"I've already died in more ways than one, so it doesn't frighten me like it once did," replied Jack as he scanned the stall again for ways to get out. The walls were too high, with no way to climb them, and the ground was too hard to dig without a shovel. He fished a penknife out of his jeans and inspected the barn boards, pressing the sharp edge into the wood where it joined a support. For hours, he ran the blade back and forth and started to loosen the board. When his arm got tired, Juan took over until the cut went all the way through. If the next stall were unlocked, then they would have a chance to escape. They repeated the process on the bottom of the board until they were halfway through and could snap the board free. The opening was wide enough for them to slide through, but before they could do so, they heard the sound of the large barn doors opening.

Through the narrow opening between the boards on the stall door, they could see two large tractor-trailer trucks, several smaller trucks and vans, and cars behind them at the entrance. The trailer doors opened, and out poured scores of men, women, and children who were ushered into the stalls to sit or lie down. Jack jumped back as the door to their stall suddenly opened. It was Emilio checking to see that they were still there before he closed and locked the door again. Before the stall next to them was opened for the migrants, Jack and Juan removed the slat, slipped through to the other side, and carefully put the slat back in place. They stood next to the door, so they wouldn't be detected when it opened. Jack hoped that they could simply meld into the large group without being noticed due to the darkness of the barn stalls.

Chapter 11

Jack estimated that roughly twenty people looking to be smuggled into the US had entered their stall, with at least thirty stalls in the barn, which meant up to six hundred people were being transported across the border. A man standing at the entrance barked orders to the migrants, who were most likely from various countries in Central and South America, before closing the door. From what Jack could see, many of the other stalls housed all men, but the families in their stall huddled together to get some sleep before the next leg of their long and trying journey.

Jack and Juan waited until everyone had fallen asleep before they removed the board and slipped back into their original stall to decide what their plan was going to be. "What was the man at the door saying?" whispered Jack.

"He was telling them to get some rest, and he would let them know when it was time to go," replied Juan. "He's one of the coyotes Javier was telling us about. For a fee, he gets these chickens from Colombia, Honduras, wherever, across the border to escape poverty and violence. The cartels control the border, so the coyotes need to pay a fee to them to use their smuggling routes. They pay at Mexico's southern border and then at the US border, getting them into the US with fake Visas and papers. If the coyote doesn't pay the cartel, he gets killed. This is very expensive for the families and big money for the coyotes and the cartels."

Jack shook his head. "If they're poor, how can they afford the fees?"

"Some are paid by relatives in the United States, for some, it's a life's savings, and others pay by helping to bring drugs across for the cartels. Some coyotes are con artists and extortionists and will kidnap a relative, demanding even higher fees to release them. I'm guessing *El Patron* only uses reputable smugglers."

Jack whispered back, "How do you know all this?"

"I have many friends who have had to flee to the US to get away from the violence and lack of work. Some attend college with me. Many didn't have a good experience with their guides. Crossing the desert or the Rio Grande on a raft or climbing high fences is dangerous with the patrols out, so being smuggled in is seen as safer and more successful."

Jack said, "I think we need to see if we can meld in with these chickens if we want to have any chance of getting out of here alive."

Juan agreed.

They quietly slipped back into the next stall as surreptitiously as possible and replaced the slat they had cut out. At around three a.m., the door of the stall opened up, and their guide brought in some bags of food and water for the trip and moved them into the open area, where they lined up to board one of the trucks. The barn remained fairly dark to avoid attracting any attention from reconnaissance planes or border patrol agents. With blankets over their heads and a package in hand, Jack and Juan shuffled onto the large tractor-trailer truck holding crates that most likely held marijuana, cocaine, or other contraband being smuggled that night. As Jack walked up the ramp, he could hear the sound of large hydraulic lifts. The ground in front of the vehicles began to elevate.

With the migrants, they crowded into the trailer and waited for departure while the tractor diesel engines revved. Suddenly, the trailer jerked, began to roll forward, and then down a steep incline until the trailer was again horizontal and moving forward. Jack imagined the underground tunnel that must have been a tenth of a mile in length. The trailer stopped, and then the sound of hydraulic lifts could be heard again as the trailer ascended upward and onto solid ground.

They must have driven up onto a dirt road in the fields of a farm on the US side of the river. The truck drove slowly, presumably with no lights, until they hit the highway and sped up to normal speed for over an hour before they stopped.

Jack wondered how many people and families had made this trip, rocking back and forth in the back of a dark trailer truck into a strange land. Finally, he heard the sound of a large garage door opening and the trailer once again moved forward.

They sat in the dark for several minutes before the back of the trailer rolled open to what appeared to be a dimly lit metal storage building. The man who had spoken to them at the ranch waved them out and into another set of holding rooms, this one with cots and tables, until they could be moved to their final destinations, rather than dumping five to six hundred people onto the streets at the same time. Jack was surprised at how organized and professional the entire operation was. He also knew it wouldn't take much time for Maldito to figure out how they had escaped and where to find them.

Morning twilight was still more than an hour away, so most of the immigrants tried to grab some sleep while the storage facility hummed with activity, unloading crates and bundles from the trucks. The door to their holding area was not locked, and Jack and Juan stepped out to watch the operation. Jack reached down to grab a bulky burlap bag and swung it over his shoulder to block his face since a *gringo* would stand out like a sore thumb.

Trying to appear as if they knew what they were doing, Jack and Juan cautiously made their way across the unloading area toward the doorway where people were entering and exiting. The closer they got, the more men crossed their path, but it was dimly lit, and people were moving too quickly to notice. Jack glanced up at a lighted office above, where a man stood holding a rifle on a small landing outside the office door.

Just as they reached the doorway, a loud voice from behind said, "*Oye. ¿A dónde vas con eso?*"

Jack didn't overreact, nor did he turn his head as he slowly placed the bundle on a table near the doorway and held up his hand. Knowing there'd be no positive outcome to turning around, he grabbed Juan's arm and bolted out the doorway. Two men chased them out into the pitch-black lot where several trucks were parked. They circled behind one of the trucks and ran along the tall chain-link fence that surrounded the lot. His heart was pounding as more men exited the building in pursuit. They ran along the fence looking for openings, feeling very much caged in.

Desperate, Jack grabbed Juan by the shirt to stop him as he breathed heavily and sweat streamed down his face. Voices were closing in as one man yelled, "*¡Mira allá!*" Jack remembered his promise to Juan and pointed upward, climbing a fence that must have been fifteen feet in height. Juan didn't hesitate to join him. They frantically grabbed the metal fence and pushed off with their toes and grabbed an opening.

Two feet from the top, they heard one of the men below yelling, "*¡Allí arriba!*"

By the time the other guards joined that one, both Jack and Juan had reached the top, painfully maneuvered themselves around the barbed wired, and jumped to a hard landing below.

Scrambling to their feet, they ran in a panic toward the highway.

Behind them, they heard the engines of vehicles starting up to chase after them. Adrenaline pumped as they frantically raced to the empty highway. There they spotted headlights moving out of the lot. Jack didn't know which way headed to town, but he knew they couldn't outrun the men driving after them.

As they ran along the edge of the highway, they spotted a

lone vehicle heading their way while the pursuing vehicles were quickly catching up, possibly with guns at the ready.

The only chance they had was to trust the pickup truck approaching them from the other direction.

As Jack and Juan waved their arms in desperation, the truck slowed down, and a voice called out, "Jump in the back!" They grabbed the tailgate, pushed off the bumper, and landed inside the bed without the truck ever coming to a complete stop. As it sped back up, their bodies were tossed to the back of the truck bed. The cartel men in pursuit were gaining as the pickup raced down the road at something near 100 mph. Suddenly, a set of blue flashing lights appeared on the side of the road, pulling out to chase down the pickup truck. Jack looked back beyond the police lights and could see the men who had been in pursuit pulling back and turning around. He breathed a sigh of relief when they slowed down, and the police car pulled behind. The cop in the cruiser was taking his time to call in the plate, and Jack and Juan continued to breathe heavily.

A voice came from the driver's side window. "Y'all sightseeing?"

Jack lifted his head. "Siena?"

"Were y'all expecting a limo pickup?" quipped Siena with a facetious tone and a giggle.

Jack sat up with Juan in the flatbed. "How did she know where we were going?"

Juan shrugged. "When we were at the ranch, I sent her a text saying we were heading across the border in some trucks through a tunnel in the big barn. She must've, um, hightailed it down the only road on this side and looked for a convoy of trucks."

Jack leaned back against the metal side panel and smiled as the police officer approached Siena's old pickup, flashlight shining in their eyes. "Good mornin', ma'am. I can see y'all have had your mornin' coffee already. Do y'all know how fast you were going?"

Siena peered up into the young officer's eyes and smiled. "Was I goin' too fast, officer? Some boys were chasing after me, and I didn't feel comfortable being alone on the highway with some bad actors; ya know what I mean?"

The officer let out a long sigh. "I can totally understand that," he drawled out, "but you ain't exactly all alone, are you?"

Siena looked surprised as the officer pointed to the truck bed. Siena opened her door and walked around to the back with the officer. "Oh, my gosh."

Jack hopped off the back with Juan. "We are sorry, ma'am. My friend and I were tired out from our travels from El Paso, and we took a nap in the back of your truck. We didn't expect you to be taking off so early in the morning. She's right, officer. She was traveling at a pretty normal speed until those trucks started bearing down on her a few miles back. They got so close; I can understand why she picked up speed."

The officer glanced back at Siena, but her eyes only widened as she continued to stare at him with huge doe eyes. He tapped his pad of tickets against the back of his hand, glancing at each of them and stopping at Juan.

Juan didn't wait for a question. "I go to UTEP."

The officer nodded, pointed at Siena, and warned, "If I see y'all goin' a hair over the limit, I won't be so generous next time."

As he drove off, Siena gave Jack and Juan a hug. "I was worried sick about you two."

"I can't believe you found us," Jack said. "Is Calle okay? I'm feeling awful about getting people involved in this. These aren't your garden variety kidnappers. They'd just as soon kill you as look at you."

They all slid into the old truck's front seat and drove into a magnificent sunrise of gold, yellow, and reddish-orange over the distant mountains. Hours later, Siena pulled up to an unassuming café called Lizy's. "Y'all hungry?"

Juan chuckled. "You're always hungry, girl."

As Jack held the door to the café, Siena grinned. "Now, don't you think a girl deserves a free breakfast for saving y'all's hides?"

Chapter 12

The waitress gave them a friendly smile, pointing to an open booth by the front window, and held up a coffee mug with an inquiring look. Siena replied with a nod and three fingers raised, then slid into the booth with Jack sliding in across from her and Juan beside her.

"So, how was the underworld?" she whispered.

The waitress put down three piping hot mugs of coffee. "My name's Maggie. Would you like a few minutes to decide?"

Jack nodded.

Siena waited until Maggie stepped away. "Juan texted something about a tunnel under the river."

"Oh, yeah. I never thought texting would save my life. I wanted to thank you for that, by the way." Jack gazed into Siena's eyes to let her know how very much he appreciated her being there for him, for being who she was.

Maggie came back to get their orders and recommended the Mexican omelet or the egg and cheese burrito. When she returned a mere few minutes later, Juan smiled, pointing to the plate. "Now, this is authentic Mexican cuisine. None of that Tex-Mex imitation fast food. You're going to like this."

Neither Jack nor Siena disagreed as they chowed down.

Siena lifted her eyes, taking a sip from her refilled coffee mug. "Russo, yer are goin' to hafta open up a bit. You gotta trust us enough to let us in."

Jack's eyes narrowed as he sat quietly, circling his forefinger around the brim of his mug. He started to speak but hesitated, pondering what he should do. He had relived the event every night for the past twenty years, but the resistance to go there during the day was an overwhelmingly hard force to overcome. He let out a long breath and took himself back in time. "I came down to El Paso in the summer of 1987 with my closest friend. An adventure. Something different for our last college summer. We worked hard during the day, and in the evening we went to Juarez for the nightlife. It felt so alive, exhilarating, but nothing compared to the girl named Maria, who I met one amazing night. Saying we fell in love doesn't seem to capture how I felt about her, how she felt about me. I couldn't imagine living my life without her, and we wanted to marry, but her father was adamant that he was not going to allow it—ever."

Jack's eyes drifted to the coffee swirling in his mug. "Well, I couldn't leave her. I knew we were right, and I'd take care of her. We knew we were meant for each other."

Siena tilted her head as she listened.

"After her father forbade us to see each other, we met secretly and decided our only chance was to run away together, to elope. On the last day that my buddy Sam and I were to be in El Paso, we met Maria in Juarez and drove back to Boston. It was freeing, the best I had ever felt in my life— or so I thought. Getting married, sharing a small apartment, and having a baby girl together made us feel like the richest people in the world. I loved being married to Maria and sharing my life with her, starting a family. Despite having so little to live on, I felt that I had everything."

"That's so beautiful, Russo. I would never have guessed you had it in you," said Siena with a broad smile on her face. "Sounds almost too good to be true."

Jack's head dropped, and a tear fell into his coffee. His throat tightened. "I felt the same way, but Maria was so special, she added to everything in my life. One nice thing was that I didn't have to lose Sam because of Maria. He was my best man at the wedding and grew even closer as a friend to both of us. We had as good a time together in Boston as we'd had those nights in Juarez.

"Having a daughter only made life more special until…" His throat choked up. He tried to clear it several times and he squeezed his eyes tight in a poor attempt to stop the flow of tears.

Siena silently handed him a napkin.

"I, ah—" He sucked in a deep breath as the nightmare replayed itself in his mind. "On the day we had her baptized, we had a party at our apartment in Boston, and—"

He nodded as he closed his eyes again to see the scene. "Several hours after everyone had left and we were putting our daughter in her crib for the night, there was a loud bang on the door and then another. The door broke open, and there were four men, masked, all in black with shotguns in their hands. I panicked and waved Maria into our room as I pleaded with them that there must be some mistake. One of the men, h...he—he said, 'The mistake was yours.' I don't even remember the shotgun blast, but I was told that it blew a hole through me and knocked me out the window of our second-story apartment, onto the street below."

"Oh my gosh," exclaimed Siena. "No!"

"They didn't stop there. They burned the apartment building down to the ground with Maria inside and kidnapped our baby. She was gone without a trace." Jack stared directly into Siena's eyes, his heart pounding, his throat clenched in pain. "They burned her to death, my sweet Maria—for what?!"

Juan said in a hushed voice. "I'm so sorry, *Señor* Russo. I can't imagine the pain that still lives with you. How did you survive?"

"I don't know. I had a hole through my abdomen and a broken back when they took me to Mass General Hospital. It took them days to stabilize me and years for me to recover physically, but I never recovered emotionally. That nightmare never leaves me, but I was determined to recover for the sole purpose of finding my daughter and avenging my wife's death. The fire was so fierce that they found only her charred bones and a locket I gave her when we were in Juarez. She wore that every day we were together. Her death keeps running over and over in my head and wakes me night after night."

Juan nodded. "You said you've been hunting down these killers for twenty years. Didn't you suspect her father?"

"I did. While I was recovering, Lieutenant McMahon from Boston traveled down to Juarez to confront Maria's father. McMahon felt Maria's father's grief was so real, so intense, that he had a hard time believing he had anything to do with it. It took me a long time to get to the same place, but I can't imagine him ordering Maria's death. He loved her too much. I knew that when I spent time with them and when he ordered me to stop seeing her."

Siena put her arm around Jack. "I'm truly sorry for your loss. I can't imagine your baby girl being out there all this time, and you've been robbed of her too."

Jack nodded. "Except she's not a baby anymore. I've been to every state in this country, to Canada and Mexico, to the FBI, and every police department I can find. The trail is nonexistent."

Juan said, "I admire your commitment. I don't know how you keep going. I could be wrong, but I'm guessing they were after your girl all along. If they were after you, then they would have come back to finish you off."

"They did," muttered Jack.

"What?" queried Juan, but Jack didn't respond.

Chapter 13

Maggie came back with a pot of coffee. "How was breakfast?" Jack and Juan each lifted one side of their empty plates.

She grinned. "We may not even need to clean those. I'm glad you enjoyed it. Any more coffee?"

Jack shook his head. "Just the check, please. Could you tell me what town we're in?"

Maggie smirked. "You're in Van Horn—that's Texas, just in case you weren't sure of the state either. Where're you comin' from?"

"Prâxedis G. Guerrero," replied Siena.

"Ahh, down in Chihuahua, huh. Things have gotten pretty nasty down there in the Valley. It's a darn shame. My entire family left Juarez when the military came in. It's only gotten worse on both sides of the border—smuggling drugs and people one way and guns the other. Greed and poverty are a tough combination," replied Maggie.

"It must be a little better up here, off the border a bit?" queried Jack.

She replied, "We thought so, but those Texas border towns have been flooded. You said Prâxedis, right?"

Juan nodded. "There's a rumor that cartel smuggler *El Patron* was operating out of there, but when the war started with that other cartel a few years back, he bought a large ranch in Van Horn. I think he has some businesses here in trucking or something. I get a lot of truckers through here, but they don't talk about it. I'm a Mexican American now, and I want my family to grow up here—safe."

"*El Patron.* I've heard that name before," said Jack with an innocent tone.

"Well, if you've ever been to Juarez, you would know of him. Everyone does. He's very powerful."

"Does his ranch have horses?" questioned Jack curiously.

"Oh, yeah. I hear he has horses, stables, barns, and a beautiful ranch house—a *hacienda*. I believe his family spends more time here now that things in Juarez have gotten so dangerous." Maggie stacked the plates and put down the check. "I hope you all have a good stay. Sorry, I got a bit on a negative roll with all the goings on around here."

Jack stood up. "You've been nothing but a pleasure this morning. Thanks for helping us get our day going."

Maggie nodded, and her eyes widened when she saw the large tip Jack was leaving.

They gathered outside the café in silence before Siena spoke up softly, almost as if she didn't want to break the peaceful moment. "What are y'all thinking?"

Jack replied, "I don't know. I'm trying to get a sense of whether or not we're here for a reason. It seems as if everywhere we go *El Patron's* name comes up. His men are certainly after us. Juan, sorry to bring this up, but do you think your brother's death could have been committed by this *El Patron* group?"

Juan paused. "I haven't been able to figure that out, but my gut tells me it could be the Sinaloa Cartel that's responsible. The Juarez Cartel certainly used intimidation and sadistic tactics to rule by fear, but it was the Sinaloa Cartel trying to control the highway along the Valley that caused the violence to erupt, and they are suspected of most of the police killings in Guadalupe. I don't know. I've never heard of *El Patron* ordering any police hits in Juarez."

Jack put his hand on Juan's shoulder. "Juan, I can't know the personal grief you feel for your brother and your father's grief as well. I can only tell you that I know how unnerving that grief can be when those responsible haven't been held accountable and don't even seem to want forgiveness. I hate those men because of what they did to my family, and revenge seems like the only possible source of relief—even though I think we both know it won't stop the pain or heal the hole in our hearts. You're young, and I only hope that you can find peace so that you can live the life your family would want you to live."

Juan dropped his gaze. "You were my age when you lost your family, and here you are, twice my age, and still in as much pain, if not more. I don't think I will ever let my brother go."

Jack glanced at Siena, who seemed to be lost in her own thoughts. Maybe she wished she'd even had a chance of a family to lose. Her loss was different. She never knew if they loved her or even cared enough to know her. While their loved ones were gone forever, her parents may still be alive. There would be no solace in that for her because she would never know.

Jack cleared his throat. "Look, I know we have had this conversation before, but it's time."

Siena lifted her head. "Time for what?"

"Time for you two to head back to El Paso and your lives. Time to get out before something really painful and irrevocable happens. I can't stop, but I need you both to do as I ask." Jack took on an authoritarian tone, said, "If you care at all, I need you to be safe and away from here. I don't think I can do what I might need to do with you here."

"Russo—" started Siena.

Jack raised his hand to stop her. "Do this for me...please. I need to figure out if there's a connection here—a lead of any sort."

Siena pleaded, "We can help you. We can watch your back." She pursed her lips and lifted her eyes to hold back the tears. "I don't want to lose you, Russo."

Jack gave her a long hug and whispered in her ear, "I know. I feel the same way. Don't worry about getting rid of me so easily." Jack reached out to shake Juan's hand, but they found themselves hugging each other instead. "Juan, I, um—"

Juan interrupted, "Me too. Be careful. Be really careful." He dug into his pocket and handed Jack an object. "Here. It's one of those pay-as-you-go phones. I got it for my mom, but she won't use it, so I took it back for you. Please call us, and we can be here in a few hours. You can text too," Juan said with a forced smile.

Jack put the phone in his pocket. "I appreciate all you've done, much more than you know. I just may need to get dirty to get close enough to find out anything."

Juan laughed. "Sure, you look like a *narco*. You'll blend right in, no *problemo*."

Siena glanced back as she got into her truck. Her expression seemed half-angry and half-worried.

Jack hoped his expression showed that he was deadly serious. Juan waved as they drove away, leaving Jack standing alone in the dusty road in front of Lizy's without a clue of what he was going to do next.

Chapter 14

Although he was used to not getting a full night's sleep, being up all night and out-running the men at the storage facility had left Jack feeling beat. He tried to hitch a ride into town, but the first few trucks passed him without even slowing down. He smiled to himself as he lifted his pant leg, feigning to be a woman raising the hem of her dress to show some leg at the next old pickup truck approaching. He hadn't expected it to stop and turned beet red as he lowered his head to look in the window.

"Need a ride, Miss?" sputtered the old man sporting a wink in the driver's seat.

"Very funny. I just need a ride into town if you're heading that way," replied Jack.

"Young man, I'm 95, so I don't really need to be anywhere right now. I'd be happy to take you into town. It's a small town, and it's not far."

Jack tipped his hat and opened the door of the antique forest green truck that must have been at least fifty years old. "Much obliged."

"Did you leave something," inquired the old man. "Is that your bag on the ground there?"

Jack glanced down. It was Siena's small backpack. He picked it up and could feel what was inside. "Oh, yeah. Thank you, sir."

"Anytime. My name is Homer Beeker. I told you I was 95, didn't I?" The old man smiled, put the truck in gear, and pulled away from the curb. "It's my birthday today, so I thought I'd mention that. Born in the next town in 1913, but I've lived in Van Horn ever since. I think there were only thirty people in town back then. I guess I'm going on. Did you tell me your name?"

"It's Jack. Jack Russo. I guess you've seen a lot over the years? Done a lot."

"Now that you've asked, I've done farming, mining, tried to join the Texas Rangers for a while, oil drilling, ranching, and a bit of park rangering for a while when I retired. You know Guadalupe National Park over there. Did you know Guadalupe Peak is the tallest point in Texas? Over 8,000 feet up. There's the Devil's Hall Trail that people like to check out." Homer turned right at a two-story farmhouse.

"How about the town? Lots of changes?"

"Some. It's still a pretty small town. It's eighty percent Mexican these days, but that's not a problem for me. They're friendly, hardworking family people, for the most part. It's the other ones that leave a bad taste," grumbled Homer.

"You mean—"

"Criminals. The drug gangs and all they bring. Most of the violence is a few towns down across the border. But we had a murder here two weeks ago, a police officer: family man, churchgoer, and Mexican descent too. Shot down in cold blood on the highway pulling over a truck. They had a big funeral service for him at that Catholic church in town. What's it called? Our Lady of Fatima. That's it. A lot of police officers and families went to pay their respects. All of this started just a few years ago when the ranch was bought," grumbled Homer.

"*El Patron?*"

"Something like that. Well, I don't know where you want to be dropped off in town, but this is the center. There's a place to stay over there if you need something for the night. Daisy has been around a while, and she takes good care of her boarders."

Jack shook Homer's hand and thanked him for the ride.

"Oh, I'm usually around, so if you need a ride again, just wave me down."

Jack stepped down from the truck and closed the door as Homer added, "Or flash a little leg, and I'll be right there."

Jack could hear Homer laughing and coughing as he pulled away. He had no idea how long he would be in town, but he figured it would be at least one night, so he approached the door with a hand-carved sign for *Daisy's B&B*. Inside, he found an intimate lobby with a desk. He ran the bell as he glanced at the photos and paintings of Van Horn and its history on the walls.

An older woman, large but able-bodied, came in with a smile. "How can I help you, my friend?"

"Good afternoon. Are you Daisy?"

"Until they put me in the ground and carve some other name on my gravestone, I'm Daisy, all right. Would you be looking for a room, or can I help you with something else?" She wrinkled her nose at his dirty clothes.

"Thanks. I do need a room, and a hot shower would feel good."

"I have a nice single overlooking the town if that works for you. The bathrooms are shared." Daisy pointed to his small backpack. "Do you have more luggage?"

Jack shook his head. "I was robbed outside of El Paso. My truck, clothes, and wallet are all gone, but they did leave me with a nasty bump. I guess they thought it was a fair trade. I do have cash, though."

Daisy looked him up and down. "Six feet, one-eighty-five or so?"

Jack smirked. "Or so. Why do you ask?"

"I have people leave all kinds of things, including clothes. There may be some that fit you until you can get restocked at Friedman's. He's an odd duck, but he's got everything you might need for clothes, gear, guns—whatever it is, he's probably got it." Daisy handed him the key for room 13 and a fresh set of towels.

The room was small but comfortable and clean. He could see

down the main street in both directions from his windows.

He immediately opened up Siena's small backpack, which, as he had suspected, held the handgun from her truck. He smiled as he grabbed a towel and took a long, hot shower. The hot water on his back felt good as he considered the leads this small town might hold.

Clean and dressed in a new set of clothes that Daisy had left on the bed made him feel like a new man. He looked a little more like he fit in this South Texan town he had never heard of before. He tested out the bed. It was as comfortable as it looked, and he dozed off. It was several hours before the familiar nightmare kicked in, and he jumped as the shotgun blast knocked him backward, and his eyes opened in horror, trying to get the image of Maria being burned to death out of his mind. Sweat poured down his forehead, and rage filled his veins. He wondered if Juan experienced the same uncontrollable desire for revenge.

He needed to get outside, so he headed downstairs. In the lobby, Daisy sat at a desk doing paperwork. "You look a bit more Texan now, Mr. Russo," she said, glancing up.

Jack smiled. "Thank you, Daisy. They actually fit."

Daisy nodded.

"Oh, and thanks for the toothbrush."

"So, what are your plans for the day?"

"I don't really know. Just getting my bearings. Daisy, when I was at Lizy's this morning, I heard there've been some border issues hitting Van Horn now. Illegals. Drugs. You even lost an officer recently."

"Officer Pete Rizza. He was a good man, a family man. It's been a long time since we've had any real trouble here, but now it's here. I wouldn't know who to blame. A lot of people in the US have lost their way. They want to avoid their own pain, deal with fear, or they're just plain bored, so they resort to drugs. Without the demand for them, Mexico would still have its poverty but not the drug cartels—not the brutal

Jim Sano

murders and the greed—not the destruction of all those families," replied Daisy, running the palm of her hand across the desk.

Jack said, "There's always more than one side to every story, so I think there's a lot of truth in what you're saying. Do you think there's an operation here in town now?"

Daisy paused. "There are lots of rumors going around this small place: businesses opening up with mysterious owners, ranches being built that no one knows much about."

"Someone mentioned a ranch being built a few years back. Do you think they're involved in some way?"

"Ah, the *El Patron* rumors. I know they have had some beautiful horses being transported there. The owner is very private and has a family there that I think he wants to protect. I don't know what he does, but it does raise some interesting questions," replied Daisy. "I've talked to Sheriff Ramos about the ranch and goings-on there, and he's not sure either. I trust he'll figure out if they're connected to his deputy's death or some of the things going on lately."

"That'd be good," replied Jack, peering out the window. "Do you trust him?"

Daisy leaned back. "What do you mean? Do I think the sheriff is on the take or something?"

"A lot of the police south of the border have been bribed or coerced into going along. I was wondering what you thought of Sheriff Ramos."

Daisy shook her head, apparently disturbed by the question. "Pete Rizza is dead and his family fatherless because Ramos wouldn't turn a blind eye. I think Sheriff Ramos is a man of honor and doesn't bend with the wind."

Jack held up his hand. "Sorry to ask you that. These are tough times. No disrespect intended."

Daisy offered him a half-smile as Jack walked out onto the wooden platform and scanned the sun-drenched downtown that was no more than a square mile in size, mainly dotted

80

with one-story, stucco-covered homes and businesses.

He stepped out onto the street and then jumped as he heard the sound of an old horn beeping behind him. He turned to see Homer smiling behind the windshield of his old truck. "Did Daisy fix you up with a place to stay?"

Jack walked over to the open driver's-side window. "Yes, she did. Thanks for the recommendation. I like your truck, Homer."

"I do too, but the missus doesn't like me driving around as much these days, so I make sure I can get out when she takes a nap. Get in, and I can show you the town—it shouldn't take too long."

Jack stepped around and opened the passenger's-side door, only to see a pug dog flopped on the bench seat.

Homer patted the dog's head. "Rambler, move over for our guest." The pug lifted his head lazily and edged himself over as Jack slid into the seat. "Someone found him abandoned in the mountains and brought him back to town. He went from one house to another until he settled in on us. I can't say he's been living up to his name the past few years."

Jack stroked the dog's brow, and Rambler edged himself closer to Jack's thigh as Homer slowly pulled from the side of the road and drove up and down the streets of Van Horn, pointing out anything of interest. "If you need a haircut, Carlos does a nice job. That's the courthouse, and up here is the school. It's small, but still, they've had real competitive baseball and basketball teams. There's Jake's Garage if you had a car that needs fixin'. Bargain him on his rate, though. A lot of people hang out here at the Haney's Hardware and Feed if you're ever looking for company or information."

Jack smiled to himself, thinking about how much Homer enjoyed both driving and talking.

"If you're hungry for dinner, Chuy's Restaurant over there has good Mexican food, if you like that, and Mom's Kitchen has a good burger and such."

They drove up and down and then across each of the streets with its modest homes, none of which were boarded up or burned to the ground as in Guadalupe or Prâxedis. A few more turns, and Homer slowed down in front of Our Lady of Fatima Church. "The missus and I are Baptist, but a lot of folks go to the Catholic church here. Seem like good folks, and Father Diaz does a lot of things for people down on their luck, even if they don't go to his church. Can't beat that."

From the other direction came a jeep with police insignia on the hood. He pulled in front of Homer's truck, slowly stepped out, and walked to Homer's driver's-side window. "Homer. Hot one today, isn't it?"

"Sure is, Sheriff. I was just showing Mr. Russo around town," replied Homer.

The sheriff wore a white cowboy hat, blue jeans with a sidearm on this hip, and a badge on this work shirt. He lowered his head to get a good look at Jack, eying him up and down before he reached across to shake his hand. "Sheriff Ramos. What brings you to Van Horn?"

Jack extended his hand and shook his. "Jack Russo. I had my truck stolen in El Paso and hitched a ride from Homer. I thought I'd stay a few days to get a feel for the area."

Sheriff Ramos glanced at Homer and back to Jack. "You may have just seen everything in town if Homer has given you his grand tour package. Let me know if you need anything. I'm at the courthouse or around town." He tipped his hat. "Say hello to the missus, Homer." Then he got back into his jeep and took off.

Homer drove to the outskirts of town, passing by a large warehouse building that made Jack wonder if it was the place he had narrowly escaped from the night before. Outside of town, there was a lot of open space, and they passed a gate with the name *Ranchos Famalia Dos* above it. There was a black SUV with darkened windows parked by the gate. Jack imagined armed guards sitting inside.

"Is this the ranch you mentioned this morning that belongs to *El Patron?*" Jack stretched his neck to peer down the long road on the other side of the gate. He could see some buildings in the distance and what looked like men spaced out along the fence.

"Yep. No trouble there, just rumors and stories. Sheriff Ramos hasn't been shy about checking them out and letting them know we have a law-abiding town."

"The big storage warehouse we passed back there. Is that new too?" asked Jack.

"That's been there for about five or six years. Lots of trucks come in and out. Sorry to end the tour, but I'm guessin' the missus' nap is over by now, and I should be gettin' on home. Feeling a little more tired than usual, myself." Homer dropped Jack back off in front of Daisy's B&B and drove off.

Jack stood and thought about why he was in Van Horn. The only connection he had was the warehouse facility and possibly the ranch. Did someone there know anything about his daughter's whereabouts after all these years? Down the street was the county courthouse and in front stood Sheriff Ramos talking with a man who appeared to be around Jack's age. He shook off the passing thought that he knew the man and walked in the other direction toward the barbershop. Two older men sat on the bench outside, having an animated conversation until Jack approached. They nodded as Jack tipped his hat before entering the shop where the barber was finishing up one customer while another waited, reading the local paper.

The barber smiled at Jack as he sat down next to the man commenting on the paper. "Carlos, the Astros won another game last night. Maybe they can finally get back to the playoffs?"

"*Si*, all they need to do is hit, pitch, and field better," said Carlos as he brushed the cut hair off his customer's shoulders. "I like that left fielder who's hitting all the home runs. What's his name again?"

"His name is Carlos, Carlos! You ask that every time I'm in here." The man chuckled as he pointed Jack to the standings in the paper. "I hope you are an Astros fan, *Señor*."

"Well, you've got a pretty good club with Oswalt pitching and Lee, Tejada, and Berkman's bats, but I grew up with the Red Sox in Boston," replied Jack.

The man rolled his eyes. "Carlos, *otro!*"

Carlos waved Jack to the now vacant barber's chair. "What would you like, *Señor?*"

"Wasn't he waiting first?"

Carlos shook his head. "He's just here to stir the pot. Miguel, take off your hat."

The man was completely bald and laughed. "My wife thinks I'm bald because I spend so much time with Carlos."

"You got that right. You spend a lot of time and no money to take up one of my seats all day," blurted Carlos.

"I could use a cut and a shave," said Jack as Carlos put the plastic apron cover over him. "What was that you said after I told him I was a Red Sox fan?"

Carlos brushed Jack's hair back as he responded, "Oh, *otro* means 'another one.' There's another Boston fan in town." Carlos gave Jack a clean shave with a straight-edge blade and a decent-looking haircut.

"I guess I am a long way from Fenway Park."

As Carlos brushed him off, the tall man Jack had seen with the sheriff entered the barbershop.

"Speak of the devil!" exclaimed Miguel.

Jack peered over and blinked his eyes at the man, who looked as white as a ghost. The man attempted to take a step forward and then dropped to the ground, unconscious. Jack jumped up to see if he was okay. When he turned the man's head, he couldn't believe his eyes. It was his old and dearest friend, Sam.

After being lugged to a chair and given a cool cloth to his forehead, Sam regained consciousness and shook his head in disbelief. "Jimmy! How can it be?"

Chapter 15

By the time Jack and Carlos had Sam back on his feet, he was feeling better. Jack said, "Let's get you into the fresh air." He left Carlos with enough for the cut, shave, and a generous tip and walked Sam outside. "Are you okay?"

Sam was still shaking his head. "Yeah. I can't tell you what a shock this is—a very good one, mind you, but, Jimmy, how is this possible? Are you real?"

Jack scanned the street in front of the barbershop before responding. "Do you have a car?"

Sam nodded and pointed to a black SUV. "Let's talk somewhere else."

They drove outside of town, down a dirt road to a pullover area facing the Guadalupe Mountains. Sam pulled over and turned off the engine. "I still can't believe this. You died!"

"I did," muttered Jack.

"Jimmy, you died! How can you be here—alive?" Sam turned in his seat and poked Jack's shoulder, almost as if to see if he was real. "I have mourned you for over twenty years. How can you just say, 'I did'? What is going on? Tell me how this is possible."

Jack pressed Sam's shoulder. "Sam, I can't tell you how sorry I am for not contacting you for all these years, not letting you know the truth."

Sam covered his eyes and shook his head, sucking in ragged breaths. Tears streamed between his fingers. "I've missed you. I gave the eulogy at your funeral!"

"I know," Jack choked out his words. "I know."

Sam lifted his face and stared at Jack with red-rimmed eyes. "You were there—I mean, you were there alive?"

"No. I was dealing with a very long and painful recovery process, physically, emotionally, and even spiritually. I saw your eulogy on tape. It was very moving and heartfelt. I could tell how much pain you were in. It mirrored my own pain to be exiled from my best friend. I can't say it enough, but I'm so sorry."

Sam narrowed his eyes at Jack. "Someone taped your funeral? I'm even more confused."

"When I was shot and—" Jack hesitated as that familiar lump grew in this throat, "and they killed Maria and kidnapped our baby, the detectives believed that this was a professional hit. If I survived, the assassins would only come back to finish the job. I needed to make sure everyone believed beyond any doubt that I was dead. A pronouncement of death, a closed-casket funeral, and a change in identity had to be the plan. It was months before I could even engage with what was going on, and I desperately wanted to track down the killers and find our daughter. I could only do that if I were 'dead.'"

Sam got out and leaned against the side of the SUV.

Jack came around to Sam. "I'm sorry, man. You were the only real friend I had left, and I missed you more than you can know. How can I make up for twenty years of deceiving you?"

A smile slowly edged at the corner of Sam's mouth. "Jimmy, you owe me a lot of beers. That's all I can say."

Jack put his arm on Sam's shoulder and pulled him into a hug. "Now, you tell me something—what the heck are you doing in this dusty town in the middle of nowhere? What's a Boston boy doing in Texas?"

Sam stared at the mountain range. "I don't know where to start. I was devastated and lost after what happened. You, Maria, and Rosalina were my life, my family. I had no other family. I was Rosalina's godfather, and I was picturing finding the right girl and being family together forever. I just felt lost. I wanted to go to Maria's funeral and tell her parents how happy she'd been that year. They were still in shock and so angry, saying that she'd still have been alive if you hadn't taken her to Boston."

Jack's stomach clenched. "I knew her father hated me for doing that, maybe even enough to have me killed, but I could never believe he'd be responsible for taking his daughter's life. He loved her too much, and her mother would never get over it."

"You've got that right. They were devastated, and there was nothing I could do to ease that pain for them—or for me. I think they knew I missed Maria as well. I tried to think of where I was going to go, and I felt no desire to be in Boston. It seemed too painful, so I decided to stay in El Paso. Maria's father, Hector, had liked the work I had done for him and started giving me some projects. Nothing big. Little by little, I started doing more work and coming up with ideas for expanding their transportation business. I'm not sure how legit all the stuff Hector was involved in really was, but I was getting them into more businesses that were above board. I think Hector liked that and could be more open and proud with Marta."

Jack shook his head. "So, you've been working for Maria's father all these years?"

"Yeah. It wasn't the plan, but I was pretty good at business and have helped to build something here. It helped me to stay busy and find some purpose in my life."

"So, why are you in Van Horn?" queried Jack.

"Things in Juarez were getting too crazy with all the killings from the drug wars. It's nothing like when we were there. I'm still headquartered across the border in El Paso, but we were expanding routes, and Van Horn has its small-town charm. There's an airport up the road, a hospital, the mountains, and it's less than two hours from El Paso," replied Sam. "I've been thinking about moving out here, somewhere."

Jack laughed. "I never pictured you to be a small-town cowboy, but here you are. Did you ever get married or close?"

Sam shook his head. "Maybe close, but no marriage. I guess

I've been too buried with the business, and time has moved a lot faster than I thought it would. Enough about me. How are you doing?"

Jack let out a deep breath. "Okay, I guess. I won't rest until I find Rosalina. I still have nightmares about that day. We were so happy, and everything seemed so right at the baptism. I'd never have guessed that day would be the worst day of my life. The memories won't let go of me, and I can't let her go."

"I'd feel the same way. Maria was incredibly special, and you were so happy together." Sam paused, wrinkling his brow. "So, why are you in Van Horn? Do you think there's something here that can help you to find Rosalina?"

Jack kicked the dirt. "I don't know. I had a long-shot lead that brought me to El Paso and then to Juarez, but the trail seems dead. Someone thought that a young girl, about Rosalina's age, may have gone to a ranch in Prâxedis G. Guerrero to ride horses, but—I don't know. I just don't know."

Sam patted Jack on the shoulder. "Jimmy, if there's one thing I know about you, it's that you don't give up—and you obviously haven't in all these years. Hey, I do have some work to attend to, but are you up for dinner tonight? We have a lot to catch up on."

That night, Sam took Jack to the Van Horn Cattle Company for some steaks and beer. They reminisced about their college days, happier times, and reviewed the last twenty years. At moments, Jack felt like a twenty-year-old again and was able to laugh, but, for much of the time, seeing Sam brought home painful memories. Sam knew Maria. He knew the two of them together, was his best man and Rosalina's godfather. He was Jack's best friend, and it made him feel more alive—and with rekindled joy, came tangible memories and pain.

"Jack, I'm sorry that you're still in so much pain. I know you can't let either of them go, and I can't blame you. What's your plan here? What can I do to help?"

Jack glanced around the steakhouse and dropped his voice low. "The only thing I have to go on is a priest's belief that he saw something in the eyes of a photo of a five-year-old that reminded him of a baby picture of a girl he'd never met. All the school records and that photo were burned in a fire, but another priest thinks a girl in that class may have gone to a ranch in the Juarez Valley to ride horses. If that's not far-fetched enough, another girl from that school, the same age as Rosalina, remembers going to that ranch around the same time, vaguely recalling a girl fitting her description."

Sam sipped his beer and wiped his mouth. "Wow. She described the ranch to you or knew the name?"

"No, we went to the most likely ranch in Prâxedis, and she had a visceral reaction, a reclaimed memory of being there," replied Jack.

"You met a twenty-something-year-old girl in Prâxedis and took her to the ranch?" Sam scratched his head, his eyebrows raised.

"It's a long story, but I was robbed and left on the highway outside of El Paso, and she literally saved my butt. It turns out that she attended this Mount Carmel School about the same time as Rosalina may have. She and her friend insisted on coming with me to Prâxedis to find the ranch, and we were able to manage our way onto the premises."

Sam smirked. "This is getting interesting. So, what did the owner of the ranch say when you got there? Was he the same person that owned it twenty years ago?"

"We never got to talk to him. Rumors are that it's this cartel leader called *El Patron*. His enforcers were suspicious of us and held us in a large barn with holding stalls."

"Crap. That sounds dangerous. How the heck did you get here then? Did they just let you go?" Sam leaned in.

"Not exactly. We hopped on a truck moving out with a large group of illegals being smuggled across – or should I say under–the border. We ended up being transported to a warehouse facility on the outskirts of Van Horn, and here I am, having a steak with you."

"Wait. Wait. Wait. What do you mean under the border? Do you mean one of those tunnels? But the Rio Grande is on the border, so how did they get the trucks there?"

Jack raised his eyebrows. "It's a tunnel under the river and big enough for trucks to drive through. Imagine how many drugs and people can get across in the dead of night."

"Holy crap! You're serious. I've never heard of anything like that, and I've been down here for half my life." Sam rubbed his chin. "So, what happened at the warehouse, then?"

"We slipped away, but not without a chase—and, believe it or not, that was this morning." Jack wiped his brow.

"How the heck did the three of you get away?"

"I was just two of us. The girl was let go at the ranch. Good thing, too, because she's the one who picked us up during the chase. No way I would be here now if it wasn't for her."

"Huh. So—so what does this all have to do with the ranch in Van Horn?"

Jack sat up and squared his shoulders. "Ah. I was told it may be owned and run by the same *El Patron* that owns the ranch in Prâxedis, so I have a plan."

Chapter 16

Outside the restaurant, Sam patted Jack's arm. "So, what exactly are you thinking? Why don't you just go to the police?"

"Okay, this goes nowhere. If I can prove there's a tie between the smuggling operation I saw in the warehouse and the owner of the ranches, I may be able to leverage that information to get some answers from him, even if it is *El Patron*. I need some time and networking here to somehow make that connection."

Sam started to laugh. "Are you crazy? If the owner is a cartel head, they aren't going to let you leave the premises, never mind get any answers to your questions. Look, Hector may be able to help if I don't let him know it's you who's asking. He's actually a good guy who grew up in a tough situation with some dirty players. He's done some smuggling and other things, but nothing he thought was harmful to anyone. Since we've been working together, he's been very keen on all legit businesses. That's where I come in, and I've been pretty good at it. However, he does have some connections, and I could try to feel him out a bit for some useful information about this guy. What do you think?"

Jack nodded. "Sure, anything would be helpful. I understand that he wouldn't want to see me. He's probably glad that I'm dead."

"Someday, I hope he can get to the point where he can forgive you for taking Maria to Boston. His grief was pretty intense after the murders, and he tried to find out who did it. He tried to find Rosalina, too. After years, he lost hope but not his anger. I'll see what I can do. Question for you: Do you think anyone at the warehouse would recognize you?"

Jack replied, "It was pretty dark, and we were running, so no, unless Emilio or Maldito from the ranch in Prâxedis were there."

"I'd assume they're working the Mexican side of the operation, but you never know."

"Sam, why do you ask?"

"Like I said, I've done some trucking through them and haven't found anything underhanded. Maybe I can get us on the premises if that helps? Maybe tomorrow? Where are you staying?"

"Daisy's B&B in town."

"She's got a nice place. I'm at the *El Capitan*. If you have a phone, I can call you."

After exchanging numbers, Sam dropped Jack off at Daisy's. Although he felt bone-tired, he tossed and turned in his sleep. He had endured so many dead-end trails over the past twenty years that his anticipation was now more realistic than it had been in the beginning. While he tried not to get his hopes up too high, Jack would never give up his search for Rosalina. He drifted off to sleep, comforted by that thought.

The next morning, Daisy fixed a huge breakfast of scrambled eggs, bacon, grits, fresh fruit, and coffee.

A few hikers sitting next to Jack mentioned that the mountain trails were practically deserted.

One of the girls exclaimed, "You should check it out. The trail is raw and rugged but incredibly beautiful." She turned to her boyfriend. "It's the best hike we've been on, don't you think, Lee?"

Lee, with a brillo-type hair braided back and a sparse attempt of a beard, nodded. "Unbelievable! But take some water with you. It gets pretty hot up there."

"I might just do that." Jack nodded as he finished the last of his breakfast.

Showered and dressed, he stepped onto the street and smiled as Homer Beeker came around the corner with his old truck and gave him a beep. "You're looking dapper, Mr. Russo. Where are we headed today?"

Jack laughed, then thought he should take advantage not

only of the transportation but also Homer's local knowledge if he was going to pull off his newest plan. "Homer, I'm not sure I can afford your rates." He climbed in and asked if he could see the ranch from a different angle, if possible.

Homer chuckled. "There's an old dirt road running behind it that might work."

Fortunately, Jack was able to see how many buildings and people were at the ranch. They watched for quite some time while Homer chewed Jack's ear off chatting about local gossip. Jack held out hope that he might catch a glimpse of a young lady.

"What are we looking for, exactly?" asked Homer.

"I am hoping to see someone I lost many years ago..."

Homer nodded and must have decided not to pry any further as he continued to give Jack a history of Van Horn and the area he had lived his entire life.

Finally, Jack called it quits, and Homer dropped him off at the B&B, and headed back home to the 'missus.'

Just as Jack mounted the front porch steps, Sam drove up and waved for him to get into his SUV.

Jack stepped to the curb. "Sam, what is it?"

"Good news. I spoke to the assistant manager at that warehouse you talked about. He's fine if we stop by to see their operation, hoping we can do some business." Sam grinned.

As they approached the entrance of the warehouse yard, Jack tried to picture the exact route he and Juan had run in the dark of the night to escape their pursuers over that tall barrier. With his shave, haircut, and change of clothes, he knew he'd look different to anyone who may have caught a glimpse of him in the dimly lit warehouse, but he still felt nervous that someone might recognize him as they walked across the parked tractor-trailers in the yard. They entered the same doorway he was sure he had run out of that night.

A man approached them as they looked up at the sheer size

of the warehouse building. "Gentlemen, welcome to our humble business. We are honored to have you."

"Jimmy, this is Andre Bravo. He was generous enough to show us their operation to see if we might be able to do some business together with our transportation routes," said Sam.

Jack nodded, studying the highly organized operation. "This is impressive. You should be proud of this facility and how well-managed the team seems to be."

"We are, Mr.—" Andre paused.

"Russo. Thanks for asking. How many tons of goods come through here in a week?"

Andre half-smiled. "Let's just say a lot. Let me show you the entire process from inbound deliveries to outbound shipping and transactional processing, accounting, and quality control. Andre showed them the large power doors to the warehouse while letting in another trailer load of goods. He took them to a back area, where a dozen or more men were assembling packages for shipment.

A man yelled out from an office along the sidewall. "*¡Andre! ¿Puedes venir aquí?*"

"Gentlemen, I need to see to some business in my office. Would you follow me?" snapped Andrew and he pounded away.

They entered his office, where a single light hung over the desk, leaving the corners of the room darkened. Andre picked up the phone. "*Andre, ¿qué es?*"

As they stood patiently waiting for Andre to finish his call, Jack had a foreboding feeling running through his veins. The feeling continued to grow when the sound of a scratch and the sudden light of a match came from a dark corner of the room. A man, clothed entirely in black from his boots to his hat, stood partially visible as he lit his small thin cigar, puffed a cloud of smoke, and began to emerge from the darkness—a silhouette of a man, long and thin, exuding a sinister aura. Jack's attention was quickly drawn to the wastebasket when a tin container was flicked into it by the dark stranger. He tried not to react; something didn't feel right.

As Andre continued his conversation, the man in black stepped out from the shadows, and Jack recognized the devil-like coal-black squinted eyes of Maldito. Outwardly, Jack remained composed and nodded to the man who took a few steps toward Sam, staring into his eyes with a wary examination. Sam didn't say a word. He remained relaxed, not a sign of nervousness as the man silently assessed him, then shifted his attention to Jack, his eyes narrowing even more.

Sam said, "He's okay. He's with me."

Maldito turned and landed a jab into Sam's ribcage, doubling him over in pain.

Jack reached out and pulled back on Maldito's shoulder, who quickly turned and stuck Jack on the cheek with the back of his hand. The large ring on one of Maldito's fingers cut into Jack's skin and sent him to the floor with a heavy thud.

Sam quickly pulled the exposed gun from Maldito's holster and held it firmly with two hands, waving everyone to the ground, while he pulled Jack up and toward the door. "Everyone stays down, or this thing goes off."

Sam turned off the light and closed the door to the office, quickly heading out through the back area, through the receiving area, and out the side door, where he tossed the gun into a bush. They scrambled for his SUV, sped out of the parking lot, and down the highway until they reached downtown. "I don't know what happened there. That guy looked like he recognized us or something. Was it from the other night, Jimmy?"

"He's definitely the guy from the ranch in Prâxedis. I don't know the reason, but he seemed to have a problem with me from the get-go," stammered Jack.

Sam rubbed the side of his face. "I'm trying to think of the best thing to do here. I don't know if we can trust the police in these parts or not. Um, why don't you get your stuff ready while I pick up mine at the hotel? I have a gun in my bag just in case we need it. I'll be back in ten minutes, okay?" Sam turned Jack's head to look at his cheek. "We should take care of that."

Sam drove off while Jack went back to his room at the B&B to gather his things. He pulled Siena's small backpack from the drawer and recognized the weight of a handgun inside it. He checked to see if it was loaded before placing it back inside the backpack and headed to the shared bathroom down the hall. A young woman with wet hair and a towel wrapped around her stepped out of the bathroom and scampered down the hall. He shook his head and entered the steamy room to check out the gash on his cheek. He used a wet towel to dab it, which stung. The bruising around it stood out more visibly than he thought it would.

Downstairs, Jack rang the bell, but Daisy didn't answer. He looked up at the notice board behind the desk and read, *Visiting/Be Back This After.* Jack pulled out some cash from his pouch and slid it into an envelope from the desk, writing on the outside, *Daisy, thank you for your kind hospitality. Something unexpected came up, and I had to leave. I hope this covers the expenses. Jack.*

By the time Jack had exited the front door of the B&B, Sam was back outside waiting in his SUV.

Jack came around the front of the car. "Where are we headed?"

"I don't know yet, but it's probably a good idea to make ourselves scarce." Sam reached over to open the door for Jack.

As they reached the outskirts of town, Jack could see the flashing lights behind them in the rearview mirror. Normally, Jack would feel panic when police headlights flashed behind, but the two times he had been to the warehouse, those lights brought a sense of relief—until a voice blared from the megaphone, *Please, step out of the vehicle and put your hands on the hood of the car.*

Jack glanced over at Sam, who shrugged and said, "I don't know. I don't think it'd be smart if the people from the warehouse reported us—they attacked us!" They slowly stepped out and walked to the front of the SUV and placed their hands on the hood, waiting for the officer to approach them. A flood of possibilities ran through Jack's head, including the possibility of a paid hit by a crooked cop. When Jack looked up, he could see Sheriff Ramos walking toward them.

Chapter 17

"Please spread your legs," ordered the officer.

"Sheriff Ramos, we met the other day. Can you tell us what we are being pulled over for?" asked Jack.

"We'll get to that. For now, just remain still and keep your hands on the hood," warned Ramos as he patted Jack down and then Sam. He pulled a gun from Sam's shoulder holster and carefully placed it in a plastic bag. "I hope you're licensed to carry that." When he was done with his body search, he said, "You can turn around now. Keep your hands where I can see them."

They slowly turned, leaning against the front bumper of Sam's car with their hands in the air. Sam demanded, "Can you tell us, now, why in the world are we being frisked?"

Ramos took a step closer and tilted his head to get a better look at the wound on Jack's cheek. "That's a nasty cut there. Looks like you just got it today?"

Jack winced. "I did, and I'd like to report it."

"Hmm. That's interesting. Well, for now, I'm going to have to cuff you two and bring you in for some questions," responded Ramos.

"Bring *us* in? We were the ones attacked, and you're bringing us in?" snapped Sam.

"He's right, Sheriff," added Jack.

"Hmm. I see. Well, we can sort this out at the courthouse," countered Ramos as he put cuffs on each of them and led them to the back seat of the police jeep. Ramos returned to Sam's SUV and opened the door to pull out Jack's backpack. Jack could see him unzip it and look at the contents. He brought the backpack and Sam's bag with him as he locked up the SUV and put his bags in the back with the guys before driving to the Van Horn Courthouse.

At the courthouse, Ramos uncuffed them and directed them into a jail cell.

"I have no idea what just happened," groaned Sam as he paced the small cell from one cinderblock wall to the other. "If this has anything to do with that warehouse crew, they've got another thing coming."

Equally dazed by the turn of events, Jack whispered, "Is it possible the sheriff is on their payroll?"

"I don't know, but I'll get my lawyer on this once we can call!"

It wasn't long before Ramos came back and took Sam out of the cell for almost an hour. He returned, opened the cell to let Sam back in, and waved Jack to come with him. Sam stared wide-eyed, a man frozen in shock. Ramos led Jack to a small interrogation room where he sat on the other side of the table from the sheriff. Ramos wore neither his hat nor his gun as he sat to question Jack. His skin was rough and dark, but his hair much darker, with strands of gray mixed in. Homer had told Jack that Ramos was a good guy, so Jack tried not to let anxiety overwhelm him and forced a calm composure. He couldn't read Ramos, either, as the sheriff glared into Jack's eyes for several moments.

"Mr. Russo? Is that what you said your name was?" Ramos flipped open his notebook.

"Jack Russo," Jack nodded slowly.

"Your friend there said your name was Jimmy O'Connell. Any reason he'd be confused about your name?"

Jack pursed his lips and exhaled a long breath. "Sam knew me over twenty years ago in Boston when my name was James G. O'Connell. I unexpectedly ran into him down here and haven't had a chance to tell him about changing my name."

"Any special reason? Did you get married or something?"

Jack shook his head.

"So, you're from Boston. Boston, Massachusetts?"

He nodded.

"And, what brings you to little old Van Horn, Texas? I would assume the weather is kind of nice in New England now. What's that place with the nice beaches I hear about all the time—Cape something?"

"Cape Cod." Jack tried not to fidget in his seat.

"Is it as nice as they say?"

Jack nodded.

Ramos scratched his scalp. "So, why are you in Texas, Mr. Russo, or should I say, O'Connell? Which name would you like to use today?"

"Russo's fine. I came down to search for someone I lost a long time ago," said Jack with a tone that became obviously more serious.

"Good enough. No law against that." Ramos crossed his arms against his chest. "Tell me about your morning. What did you do? Don't worry about being too detailed. I like details."

Scratching his scalp, Jack responded, "I'm renting a room at Daisy's B&B and had breakfast there and then a shower. After that, I stepped out of the B&B, and Homer—Homer Beeker—picked me up, and we drove around a bit." Jack, tried to figure out where this line of questioning was going. What did Ramos think he had done to warrant putting him in a cell?

"Okay. Where exactly did you go for a drive this morning? Can you tell me that?"

Jack straightened. "Um, we drove to the outskirts of town, down a dirt road behind that big ranch. I believe it's called *Ranchos Familia Dos*. Sheriff, can you tell me what you're looking for?"

"Okay. Ninety-five-year-old Homer Beeker was found in his car on that dirt road behind Ranchos Familia," replied Ramos as he leaned forward against the table between them, "with a bullet in his head."

"What?! Who would shoot a man like Homer?" Jack questioned, horrified.

"Personally, I'm sick about it. I had to go out and tell his wife, but I didn't get into any of the details. So, tell me why I shouldn't be considering you as a suspect?"

"Me?!" Jack shouted. "You think I did this? I would never kill anyone, never mind a sweet old man like Homer. Why would I? I didn't do this!"

Ramos glared at Jack, "You're going to have to do better than that. This is what I have right now: You were seen driving with Homer several times and heading out of town this morning. He was killed on that deserted dirt road you said you drove to with him. That gash on your face has the partial imprint of a letter. Homer Beeker wore a large ring with the raised letters *HB* on it." His words were spoken with a cold, hard edge that left Jack in no doubt about what Ramos was thinking.

Jack exclaimed, "He never hit me. I got this from a man involved with that warehouse facility—"

Ramos interrupted. "He had the ring on this finger, and it had blood on it. For your sake, I hope it's not yours, but we'll be checking. Even without that, my real problem is with what we found in your backpack."

Jack continued to shake his head. "Backpack? Oh, you mean the gun? That isn't mine, and I haven't fired it. Check it."

"There was money in the backpack—some hundred dollar bills. His wife didn't like it, but Homer liked to carry a few with him to flash as if he were rich."

Jack pleaded, "I don't know where those came from. It must have been from Siena. She's the one who left me the backpack."

Ramos tilted his head. "I don't know anyone named Siena. Did she leave a money clip with HB inscribed on it, as well?"

Jack dropped his head in disbelief.

"Finally, the gun in your backpack has been fired very

recently, and we lifted prints from it. I'm sure if you're as innocent as you say, you won't mind us taking your prints— to rule out a match, of course."

Jack sat frozen. How was this happening? His mind scrambled to organize his thoughts. "Sam. Sam knows I didn't do this."

Ramos' head bobbed in agreement. "Sam's a good friend. He told me the same thing—and in the strongest of terms. But, he's your friend. He told me about the incident at the warehouse. We can check his story out, but he can't account for your whereabouts in the morning, only after that. You two were scrambling to get out of town pretty fast. How did you say it in your note to Daisy? 'Something unexpected came up.' Was that right? Well, the tread of Sam's tires had the dirt from that road. I suspect he picked you up. You were seen together at the Cattle Company last night. Someone there said you two looked like you were 'planning something,' and the next day, you're stopped hightailing out of town, packing guns." Ramos paused as if to let it sink in. "See what I'm dealing with?"

Chapter 18

Sheriff Ramos had separated Sam and Jack to avoid the two of them comparing stories, so Jack sat alone in his cell. The only defense lawyer in town was a grandson of Homer, so Jack was still without counsel and felt as if the world was caving in on him. He had always felt as if he could depend upon himself, no matter what the circumstance, but this was different. Locked up in this cell, he was helpless on a whole new level.

That afternoon, a man was brought into the adjoining cell to sleep off his drunken state. When the guy was awake enough to notice that he had a neighbor to talk to, there was no stopping him.

The man narrowed his eyes as he checked Jack out. "Are you that guy?"

"What guy?" replied Jack.

"The guy they're sending to death row. That guy," said the man, pressing his head between the bars to get a closer look.

"I don't plan on being *that* guy," mumbled Jack.

"No one does. Did you know that over half of the executions in the country are in Texas? They don't fool around."

The door opened, and the sheriff came in. "Now, Marvin, don't go scaring people. Are you sober enough to head home?"

Marvin nodded. "I know. No stops on the way."

As Ramos unlocked Marvin's cell, he glanced over at Jack. "How're you doing, Mr. Russo or O'Connell? Which do you prefer, again?"

Jack replied, "Russo is fine. O'Connell died twenty years ago."

Ramos tilted his head, confused, as he escorted Marvin out of the holding area.

Jack thought again about his predicament. Who could he turn to here in southern Texas? He didn't want to involve Siena or Juan, especially with the recent turn of events.

In Boston, there were only two people he could trust when his family was attacked. Police Lieutenant Kevin McMahon and Father John Doherty from St. Francis Church in the South End where Rosalina had been baptized the day she was kidnapped. They had devised the plan to announce his death and have the funeral to protect him from another attack. Both had been close friends of Jack's before the attack, and they did an incredible job of keeping things quiet while Jack recovered and assumed his new identity. Father Doherty had talked with Jack almost daily to counsel him and attempt to heal his pain, anger, and desire for revenge. When Father Doherty died, the younger Father Tom Fitzpatrick became the pastor of St. Francis and had remained there throughout the past ten years. Jack had continued to work on his grief and pain with Father Tom. Even though Jack found it too difficult to forgive God for the horrific tragedy his family had endured, he remained close to Father Tom to this day.

Early evening, Ramos brought in a tray with his dinner. He met Jack's wide-eyed stare with a chuckle. "My wife made it. It's a Mexican stew and some homemade bread."

"Thanks, Sheriff," replied Jack as Ramos shut the steel door. "I heard about Officer Rizza. I think Homer said his name was Pete, and he had a family. I'm sorry for your loss."

Ramos's back was already turned when he nodded and headed to the door. He stopped and hesitated. "You want some company?"

Jack was surprised by the offer. "Sure." Ramos came back with his own piping hot dinner and pulled a chair up on the other side of the bars. "Don't you get to eat with your family?"

Ramos blew on the hot stew. "I try to make it a habit, but I can't leave you here alone either. Thanks for the condolences, by the way. Pete was a good man, the best. These drug cartel gangs have no conscience. There seems to be no end to it."

Curious, Jack asked, "How long have you been a policeman?"

"Just coming up on thirty years. It's tough on the family when things get hairy."

"I can only imagine." Jack considered what it would have been like to have had a family all these years. "Could I request a visitor?"

Ramos tilted his head forward. "Who're you thinking of?"

"He doesn't know me, but Homer had told me about the priest at the Catholic church in town."

"Padre Diaz from Our Lady of Fatima? If it's about a confession, God can forgive you, but you'll still have to pay the price down here," chided Ramos as he stood to take Jack's empty tray. "I'll see what I can do."

After a difficult night of sleep, visited by his familiar nightmare, Jack woke up to the sound of a cock crowing, not something he was familiar with in Boston. He looked up at the same dirty ceiling that numerous drunks and robbers had probably stared at, which made him wonder how many actual killers had occupied this same bed.

After breakfast, Ramos stood in the doorway. "You have a visitor, Mr. Russo."

Behind Ramos stood a man wearing black pants and a black shirt with a white collar. He stood maybe five-five in height and had a kind face. "This is Father Raphael Diaz from Our Lady, who was kind enough to come over."

Father Diaz clutched a book in one hand and a priest stole in the other, in case Jack was looking to make a confession. "It's always good to meet a new face. I would ask how you are this morning, but I imagine being in there isn't pleasant. Sheriff Ramos said you wanted me to visit you." Father Diaz turned to Ramos. "Is it okay if I sit with Mr. Russo?"

"Oh, sure. I'll get a chair out here for you, Padre." Ramos

hurried out the door.

Father Diaz's gaze was fixed on Jack's. "No, please. May I sit inside with Mr. Russo?"

Ramos exhaled. "I don't know about that. You know why he's here, don't you?"

Father Diaz nodded. "Please—if it's okay with Mr. Russo."

Jack nodded. Ramos unlocked the cell and stepped aside to let the priest enter. The priest put his sacramental stole around his neck.

Jack said, "I don't want to make a confession, Father."

The priest removed the stole and laid it on the bed along with the book. "How might I help you, then?" He nodded to Ramos to leave them alone to talk.

Ramos hesitated, concern in his eyes.

Father Diaz waved him out and turned to Jack. "Mr. Russo—"

"Father, please call me Jack. I don't know exactly why I asked for you, but I have no one to turn to." Strong emotions filled Jack as he described the entire of his family and his purpose for coming back down to Texas. He told him about his time in Van Horn, how kind Homer Beeker was to him, and that he didn't have anything to do with his death.

Father Diaz leaned in, his forehead furrowed in concentration.

After he was done, Jack leaned back, one concern dominating his thoughts. *Does he believe me?*

Chapter 19

Fear, helplessness and boredom fought for the upper hand in Jack's mind.

Later that day, muffled voices rose from the room outside where the sheriff sat. It was only when the voices became louder that he could make out the conversation.

"I can't go by how I feel or how you feel for that matter. I've got to go on the evidence and the facts I have!" Ramos intoned, apparently something he'd said many times.

"I don't believe he did this, Nick," replied the other voice. "I think he's telling us the truth."

"There's too much damning evidence, and he has no explanation. His friend is getting out on bail, and I think he would say anything to cover for him," countered Ramos.

"I called—" Jack could not hear the full sentence. "Nick, they confirmed his story and his character. They said that he's an honest man."

Jack felt sure the other voice was Father Diaz's. Who did he call? Why was he trying to make a case for someone he just met and didn't seem to believe when Jack talked to him just that morning?

"But he wasn't charged with murder when they knew him, and that can change a man's desperation to avoid the penalty at any cost," chided Ramos.

They must have moved closer to the open door of the cell area because the voices became clearer. "Nick, the Boston police lieutenant and Father Fitzpatrick both convinced me that Mr. Russo could not and would not have done this. They think he must have been framed."

"Framed?!" Ramos exclaimed. "That would be a lot of framing in a very short window of time. How likely is that?"

"No matter how unlikely, no one is looking to see if he might have been framed, right?"

"I don't know. This is crazy talk. Let me do my job, Padre, and you do yours. Can we do that?"

The door closed between his office and the cell area.

A little over an hour passed with nothing to look at but the walls and his shoes. Then the door opened again. Ramos brought in a chair, which he placed outside of Jack's cell, and in came a short man in a suit carrying a leather briefcase. "He's right here, Mr. Chaz."

The man gave an awkward half-smile as he straightened the wire-rimmed glasses sitting on the bridge of his nose. "Thank you, Sheriff."

Ramos left, and the man sat with his case on his lap. "Mr. Russo, I'm Enrique Chaz. I am representing Mr. Sam Engres, and he requested that I come to offer you legal counsel, services which he said he would pay for."

Jack moved to the edge of the cell and gripped the metal bars. "Is Sam okay?"

Mr. Chaz nodded. "I will be securing his bail release by tomorrow. They don't believe he was directly involved, but they are attempting to charge him with some sort of coverup. He is very concerned about your well-being and the charges against you. I don't believe they'll allow bail for you, but I can push for it if you permit me to act as your legal counsel."

Thoughts quickly raced through Jack's mind. *I hate rushed decisions on things like this. I need to get a hold of McMahon— but how's he going to help me down here? Crap.* "Look, Mr. Chaz, I appreciate the offer. I need to think about what to do here. Tell me how you think you can help."

Mr. Chaz frowned. "Well, I can make a plea for your bail and start gathering information to assess your case. Mr. Engres believes you are innocent, but we will need more than that to convince a judge and jury."

Jack snapped, "You think this is going to trial?"

Mr. Chaz tightened his lips and raised his brow in response.

As he stood, he added, "I will do everything I can to get you released, or we may be able to bargain for a lesser charge than the one they are planning on entering."

Hopelessness filled Jack in the silence of his cell.

Voices from the outer office caught Jack's attention. A moment later, Father Diaz stood in the doorway.

Jack half-chuckled. "Did you miss me already, or did you talk to my lawyer, and you've come to give me last rites?"

Father Diaz sat in the chair outside of Jack's cell. "I'm glad you've kept your sense of humor. I don't know if I'd be able to do so under your circumstances. I wanted to talk to you about a few things if you're not doing anything."

Jack smirked. "Maybe we both have a sense of humor. I'll check my calendar, but I think I'm free at the moment. What did you want to talk about, Father Diaz?"

Father Diaz leaned forward. "You can call me Father Ray if you like. I want to apologize for not getting your permission, but I was profoundly struck by your story and the tragedy of your family. My younger brother was a parish priest outside of Juarez and was killed last year for speaking out. Sadly, another priest in the city was shot more recently, so I can empathize with your loss on a personal level. I hope you are reunited with your daughter soon."

Jack pulled closer. "And I'm sorry to hear about your brother. That must make you pretty angry. Did they catch the people responsible?"

"No. They haven't seriously even looked for them. Many murders go uninvestigated these days in the Valley of Juarez. Sure, I was angry, but I know my brother is in heaven now, and I pray for the killers to find Christ in their hearts and repent."

Jack smirked. "You pray for his killers? I understand that concept in my head, but I can't imagine ever feeling that in my gut, in my heart."

Father Diaz opened up his bible to a page marker and read, "I have been crucified with Christ; it is no longer I who live, but Christ who lives in me; and the life I now live in the flesh I live by faith in the Son of God, who loved me and gave himself for me."

"And what does that mean?"

"Jesus was a friend like no other, willing to give his life for us so that we could live fully in him. We let go and try our best to live like him and follow his example. Well, he asked us to love our enemy. We don't have to like them or forget what they did or ignore justice being served, but we can pray for those who have been lost to find their way and that we can forgive them."

"*Forgive* them!" Jack reared back. He had heard all the words before, but here was someone who should feel as angry and vengeful as him, and he wasn't exhibiting either one of those.

"Mr. Russo—Jack, I believe you when you say you are innocent. My gut feelings were split when we talked this morning, but my stronger instinct was telling me you were truthful. I'm sorry for not getting your permission, but I called Father Tom in Boston, whom you talked about, and then the police lieutenant, McMahon. Both were appropriately cautious of my questions until I told them the predicament you were in. They both adamantly defended your integrity and character. Both swore you wouldn't have committed this crime, but they did seem worried about you."

"They're worried? I'm worried!"

"They weren't talking about this charge. They were worried about your obsession with vengeance. You've spent all these years trying to track down these men who committed evil against your family. They said you've had no life of your own for the twenty years since it happened."

Jack turned his back and shook his head. "Life? What's life without Maria? What's the purpose of it without my family—

without Rosalina? How can I find her when I'm locked up in here?"

Father Diaz reached in through the bars and touched his shoulder. "I can understand that. Just to let you know, I felt the anger and desire to hurt someone, just like you, but it was eating me up and wasn't doing my brother, or me, or my parishioners any good. I have to leave you now. Our daily Mass is at six p.m., but know that I am praying for you, my friend."

After Father Diaz left, Jack could hear muffled voices in the office but couldn't make out what was being said. About fifteen minutes later, Ramos came and sat outside Jack's cell. Neither spoke for several moments until Ramos said, "Homer was a pretty likable and generous guy."

Jack nodded in agreement. "Yes, he was. He was also a big part of the history of this town. I was getting to like him quite a bit."

"And you had plenty of your own money on you long before you met Homer?" inquired Ramos.

"That's right," replied Jack.

"So, who do you think would have set you up?" pressed Ramos.

Jack paced and shook his head. "I don't know. The only one I can think of is this Maldito guy from the warehouse. We met him on a ranch in Mexico, where he held us against our will. We escaped with a bunch of illegals being smuggled across, well under, the border to that warehouse. When Sam and I went to visit the warehouse, there he was—and I got this from him," replied Jack pointing to the bandaged wound on his cheek.

"I want to believe you as Father Diaz does. I keep running into dead ends for explanations. I went to that warehouse earlier today. It looks like a legitimate and well-run operation. They never heard of this Maldito character and said your visit with Sam was business-related with no incidents like the one you described."

Jack exclaimed, "What? Sam can back me up on this."

Ramos said, "I need more than a man's attempt to save his friend from the chair. You've got to help yourself out on this." Ramos walked out of the cell area and came back with a hot homemade dinner for Jack. "Sorry, you'll have to dine alone tonight. I've got to go home for a bit." He left.

A few minutes later, Jack heard the front door to the sheriff's office slam shut. What Jack noticed was that Ramos had closed but not locked his cell door. Jack thought Ramos was too methodical to forget something like that. What did he mean when he said, "You've got to help yourself out on this"?

Chapter 20

Jack sat frozen. *What's the right thing to do here? Was Ramos giving me a sign, an opportunity to slip out? He kept saying that he had to go on the evidence, which all pointed to me being guilty. If he didn't leave that door open on purpose, running would only make me look more guilty. But I'm not going to find Rosalina by rotting in jail or worse.*

He pressed his hand against the hard steel door and slowly pushed it open. The building was unusually quiet as he crept, one footstep, a pause, and then another step. He hesitated, not knowing if this was the right thing to do or where he would even go.

He paused in the empty office at Ramos' desk. A photo of his wife and another of two boys were positioned by the phone. On the wall was a news clipping titled *Officer Slain. Family Left Homeless*, with a photo of the young Officer Pete Rizza.

As Jack began to turn away, he noticed a piece of notepaper in the middle of the desk with two words handwritten on it, *Good Luck.*

He stood and stared at those two words thinking, *If there's ever a time I'd need it, it's right now—no gun, no money, no place to go, and a grieving town full of people that probably want me hanged.* He slid out the front door, scanning left and right to see if the street was clear, wondering if most people would be home having dinner or getting ready to watch *American Idol* or reruns of *Lonesome Dove*. The only safe place to gather his thoughts was the church less than a half-mile from the courthouse, even less if he cut through empty lots.

When he reached the small adobe church, there were a few people still congregating out front after evening Mass, so he slipped down a path behind the churchyard.

He entered a grassy area with a large rock formation

enclosing one side. A statue of a woman in long white garments, a golden crown, and rosary beads in her hands stood in a carved-out section of the rock. He felt her gaze as if she were looking upon him, and he had her full attention. As he gazed at the statue, he wondered what his daughter looked like today, almost twenty years old now. Would she look upon him with love and admiration, or would he be a stranger that let her down by not finding her earlier?

Anger flooded him when he thought about being cheated of their lost time together. His anger grew almost out of control at the thought of Maria being burned alive in that inferno. How much did she suffer, knowing what had just happened to her family? She was the last person on earth who deserved such an injustice, and he alone could set it straight for her. He could not let her down again.

He had to get back to the warehouse or onto that ranch and see if any connection even existed. He wasn't afraid of dying. He'd already suffered worse than death, but dying now would mean his daughter would never be found, and Maria's killers would never be held accountable.

Exhaustion overcame him, and he stretched out on a stone slab, closing his eyes, trying to ignore the conflict between the peaceful spot and the unrest in his soul. He tried to focus on a scheme for gaining access to the warehouse but kept drifting off until he fell asleep, curled up on the cool stone surface while the evening sunlight began to fade, and one of his all too real dreams took over.

Jack felt the panic in his chest as he scaled the chain-link fence to escape his armed pursuers. He chastised himself for putting another person in danger as he tried to help Juan clear the fence, landing with a painful thump before running at full speed into the pitch-black darkness of the night. The salt from the sweat streaming down from his forehead and into his eyes stung as he tried to wipe it off to see what was in front of him— he halted in front of an adobe building. A muffled scream came from Juan's pain-stricken face. In front of them was the horror of his brother's decapitated head on a stake staring back at them.

Jack recoiled at the sight, the blood, and Juan's devastating reaction. He tried to turn away, but there was only the dark of night. Suddenly, he was inside a room and couldn't breathe as he stared at an old wooden door, fearing what was on the other side. He tried to yell to Maria before the door burst open and four men in black, with black masks and shotguns, entered. They were yelling something, but he could only hear the high-pitched sound of a muffled ringing in his ear. One of the men puffed on a small brown cigar and then flicked it to the ground just as there was a bright flash of light, a delayed sound of a cannon blast, and the sensation of being hit by a truck. The heat of the flames all around him was too much to bear as he screamed, and his arms flailed in a useless attempt to find Maria and Rosalina.

He jerked violently awake, feeling a hand on the side of his face that was now dripping with salty sweat. In the dark, he couldn't see who touched him, but he instinctively reached down to feel the hole torn in his chest but found only his dampened shirt.

"Jack, you're okay. You're okay."

Jack shook his head and quickly sat up.

"You were having a nightmare."

Jack's eyes adjusted to the dark, and he saw Father Diaz. He exhaled a long breath. "I'm sorry. I didn't mean to trespass or disturb you. What time is it?"

"Come in. The nights can be a little cold for sleeping outside." Father Diaz helped Jack to his feet and onto the path to the rectory. In the small kitchen, he waved to a chair at the table. "I have some tea that calms me down when I have nightmares of my brother's murder, and I wasn't even there. Would you like to try some?"

"Thanks." Jack glanced at the clock on the wall. It was just after midnight.

Father Diaz placed two cups of hot tea down on the small kitchen table and sat across from Jack. "If you don't mind my asking, are you on a temporary furlough?"

Jack grinned and shook his head. "Not officially. I appreciate your trust in me. Now, I may need your confidence for a little while to sort things out."

Father Diaz's eyes squinted as he sipped the hot tea.

"Father, can I ask you something that's been on my mind? You talked about forgiving your enemies. Have you really forgiven the men who killed your brother in cold blood?"

Father Diaz lowered his head as if searching for a response. "I'm working on it. I do pray for them to turn back to God. I refuse to hate them and let them win, to let the devil win. Jesus gave us a new commandment—I guess that means it wasn't a suggestion. *Love others, as I have loved you.* I'm guessing he meant everyone when he also said, *Love your enemies and pray for those who persecute you.* He didn't give us easy things to do, but there's always a very good reason for whatever he asks."

"What good reason can there be in asking for the impossible?"

Father Diaz smiled. "Alone, many things are impossible, but in Christ, nothing is impossible. He gives me the strength, the example, and the grace to try."

Jack shook his head. "I don't know. Sounds like a lot of unrealistic thinking and expectations."

"I thought the same way when he was only a concept, words on a page and in my mind. The difference came when I started realizing that Jesus is a real person, offering to be my friend in a real way."

"Hmm. I don't know. I feel let down by your friend."

"I felt the same way but realized he'd never let me down. We have free will so that we can choose a real relationship with him, but that free will means we can choose to do bad things too—and that is what those men who took my brother from me did, not Jesus."

Jack stared into his half cup of tea.

"I'm sorry—you didn't come here for a sermon. I have a spare room you can stay in. It's small but better than a stone slab, and it comes with breakfast."

Chapter 21

Jack had grown up a Catholic but didn't think much about his faith in college, even if he tried to defend it when it was being trashed by one of his schoolmates. It wasn't until he began getting closer to Maria that he was exposed to actual questions about his faith and what he truly believed. Maria wasn't intense about it, but her faith was part of who she was, where she drew her strength. As strongly as she felt about Jack, she wouldn't agree to marry him if he wasn't open to sharing their faith with any children they would have. He was surprised by how much that meant to her as a young woman when none of the friends he knew went to church or talked about God. Classmates generally wanted to live and do the things they wanted to do, unencumbered by responsibility or selfless giving to others. To them, faith and religion seemed like a roadblock, while, for Maria, it seemed like the source of her freedom. He didn't think about it much, but he subconsciously admired her for it. *Little good it did her in the end.*

The bed was more comfortable than the stone slab, but Jack felt restless. He didn't want to think anymore. He finally drifted off to sleep, but with it came the images of his apartment above ablaze while he lay on the pavement with a broken spine and blood pouring from his chest. A man taking a long puff of smoke kept demanding his attention as he suddenly saw himself inside the office at the warehouse. The man in the black hat sitting in the dark corner flipped a metal case into the wire wastepaper basket.

Awake, Jack sat up and slid his legs off the bed and onto the floor. *Where have I seen that tin before? What did it say? CD something,* he thought. *Cigarillos. Wait a minute, that guy wasn't smoking a cigarette—CD Nb Selection Especiale Cigarillos, that's it! Where have I seen that?* Jack stood up and paced the floor of the small spare room, trying to think of where he had seen that name on a small tin case before, but it wouldn't come to him. He tapped his thigh in frustration, knowing the information was there, but he couldn't retrieve it.

Jack returned to bed, but after a sleepless night, he wandered from the bedroom to a bathroom off of the narrow hallway. He stared into the old mirror, noting how tired his eyes looked before he lifted the bandage from his cheek. The cut from the ring on Maldito's hand that Ramos had cleaned and dressed was healing well. Jack let the water in the sink run until it warmed before cupping his hands in it and splashing it on his face. Looking back up the mirror, watching the beads of water run down his cheeks, he thought, *What am I doing here?*

Father Diaz gave a friendly smile as Jack entered the kitchen, where he was cooking up an omelet on the stove. "*¿Descansaste bien, Señor Russo?* I hope you were able to sleep on that old cot."

"Let's say it was softer than the stone slab in your garden." Jack accepted a fresh cup of coffee from Father Diaz.

"Well, you're just in time for that breakfast I promised, if you don't mind an old bachelor's cooking."

As they ate in the kitchen together, Father Diaz pointed to the yard. "It's a grotto, by the way. The area you were in last night is called a grotto, or at least our attempt at one to give people a peaceful place to be with Mary or to just to be."

"I'll have to check it out," Jack replied. "I need a place to think about what I should do."

Father Diaz pointed to the empty chair and the black shirt that hung over it. "You may want to wear something that will avoid unnecessary attention."

Jack smiled at 'unnecessary attention' and looked at the clothes. "Is that what I think it is?"

Father Diaz nodded. "It's just an idea. If you're sitting in the grotto or the church to think or even to pray, I can let people know you are a friend stopping to visit."

Jack sipped his coffee. "Why are you doing this?"

"I think you need help."

Jack asked, "What kind of help are you talking about?"

"Well, something tells me you are a good man who's up against not-so-good forces trying to stop you on your journey. You're also a grieving man, and the anger is as strong today as it was when you lost your *esposa* and your daughter."

"Maybe so, but I think she deserves justice, not to be given up on."

"*Señor* Jack, you express deep, sincere love. That is good. I'm jealous of it," said Father Diaz with a smile. "But remember that desire for vengeance is like an infection that will spread throughout your soul."

Put off by the comment, Jack leaned back in his chair. "Are you going to tell me to forgive and forget? Act as if nothing happened to my wife and daughter—and not be angry about it?!" He clenched his fists.

Father Diaz sat back. "Jack, you are a guest in my home. I don't want you to feel anything except my respect and welcome. I'm sorry for touching on a sensitive area. I can understand."

It was a full minute before Jack could respond, taking several deep breaths as he stared down into the dregs of his empty coffee mug. His eyes welled up with hurt and anger. "Those men deserve to pay for what they did! I have a right to be damn angry! I don't understand this 'love your enemies' stuff. It doesn't make any sense to me."

Father Diaz held up the pot of coffee to see if Jack wanted a refill. "Jack, the last thing I wanted to hear were the words forgiveness or love when my brother was murdered—assassinated by what I called 'animals.'"

"You should have been angry, shouldn't you?"

Father Diaz nodded. "Anger is a human emotion and a

legitimate one in response to the pain of injustice. It is a passion to set things right."

"So, then why are you worried about me? Why is Father Tom so worried about my desire to set things right?"

Father Diaz's voice lowered to a hushed tone. "It has to do with those two words I didn't want to hear when my brother was assassinated—love and forgiveness."

Jack scratched the side of his head as he squinted in confusion. "Love and forgiveness? You just said that anger was a legitimate response? I'm confused."

"It *is* confusing. I had to learn to trust God again to begin to understand it. I still fall back and struggle some days, but I think He's right—as usual." Father Diaz shrugged. "God only gives us commandments and guidance that end up being for our own good. We often prefer human plans, but they never really work."

Jack abruptly stood up. "Yeah, well, I'm not really up for a Sunday School lesson today, Father. Thanks for breakfast. I think I'm going to excuse myself if you don't mind."

Father Diaz stood and put his hand on Jack's shoulder. "No problem. Please treat this as your home. I would just be careful about being recognized, but you know that already."

Jack went into his room to decompress. When he heard Father Diaz leave, he stepped out into the kitchen to grab the clothes left on the chair and held them out in front of himself, conflicted about putting them on. Before he could talk himself out of it, he slipped on the black shirt and pants and then played with the stiff white collar to figure out how to slip it into the shirt collar. Shaking his head, he got a kick out of seeing himself in the mirror, dressed like a priest. The pants were a bit short, and his boots were dark but not black, making for an interesting look. At a glance, he certainly didn't recognize himself and felt a little freer about walking the premises.

Chapter 22

Jack thought about sitting in the grotto area but was curious about seeing the interior of the church and turned himself in the direction of the side door. Inside, the church was small, with simple wooden pews on both sides of a single-center aisle, original wooden beams bracing the ceiling, and arched windows down both sides with Stations of the Cross between. A large crucifix hung above the tabernacle, which held the Eucharistic Host, the Body of Christ, in the form of simple bread.

Jack sat down in one of the pews and allowed the quiet sacredness to seep into his being. *What should I do next?* He needed help because nothing he was doing on his own was working. With surprising urgency, he slid to his knees on the kneeler in front of him. Instead of praying, he just listened for an answer, some kind of sign or direction. Before he could discern any answer, he heard the sound of the front door opening and closing behind him. Hoping it was someone who simply peeked in and then closed the door, Jack didn't turn to see who it was, but then he heard the sound of someone struggling to shuffle down the aisle, emitting a smoker's cough.

"Father." Cough. "I'm glad you're here," said the old woman as she sat down in the pew behind him.

Who is she talking to? Jack continued to look forward.

She reached over and touched his shoulder, and Jack finally turned to look at her.

"Oh, you're not Father Diaz," said the woman, clearing the phlegm from deep in her throat. "I wanted to make a confession."

Jack had forgotten his priest's attire as he responded, "I don't think the Father is around right now. Maybe later?"

She laughed through her congestion. "You'd be fine."

"I'd be fine?"

"Well, you're a priest, aren't ya?"

Jack glanced down at his black attire. "Oh, yeah. Right. Well, I'm in training and haven't gotten to the forgiving sins part," he said with a nervous smile.

"Oh. Huh. Well, my name's Arletta. I come by once a week to give Father my confession, but we really just talk sometimes."

Jack turned in the pew to see her better. Her house dress, gray hair, and the lines on her face showed signs of a woman who'd lived through a less-than-easy life. "Well, I can certainly talk with you."

She laughed again. "I hope so, or you're in the wrong line of business. You're a good-looking priest, but no kid. What made you sign up? No one would have you?"

"Well, my wife died."

"I'm sorry to hear that. My husband died almost fifteen years ago, and I still miss him. He was some kinda man, and I know for sure he's in heaven right now. That's the reason I've come to confession every week since he passed—I want to make sure I can see him again, and I can't do that if I don't get to heaven."

"Hmm. You really believe that, don't you?"

Arletta coughed. "Henry was the best man I've ever known. I was never as good a person inside as he was, but I've got an incentive to make up for it. It's a challenge, but that's what I've been trying to do."

Jack turned to the crucifix over the altar. "I guess all we can do is try our best. I believe you'll see Henry again," he said with a smile. "Arletta, did you know Homer Beeker?"

"Oh my gosh. What a tragedy that was. I've known Homer for fifty years. He was the sweetest man in this town. Why would anyone do such a thing? I hate to say this in the house of the Lord, but I'm hopin' they catch that son-of-a-bitch," she said with a nod.

"Under the circumstances, I'll forgive you for that—and I hope they catch him too. Homer was a good man."

Arletta thanked Jack, picked up her cane, and made her way to the back of the church, leaving it quiet again—but only for a few moments before he heard another set of footsteps heading his way. Jack laughed to himself as he glanced up. *Maybe something doesn't want me talking to you today?*

He could feel the presence of someone in the aisle next to his pew and then a familiar voice. "Don't let me disturb your prayers or quiet time."

"Father Ray. No problem. I've already given a few confessions to parishioners today," replied Jack as he motioned for him to sit next to him.

"How do you like the forgiveness business?" he laughed.

Jack gazed up at Jesus on the crucifix. "Certainly, there are some sins that aren't forgivable—don't you think?"

Father Diaz kept his eyes on the crucifix. "Hmm. Jesus was God yet humbled himself as a man. He did nothing but love us, teach us wisdom, teach us about God, show us how to live—and we abandoned him, betrayed him, spat on him, beat him to a pulp, and then nailed him to a cross. On that cross, what did he do?"

"I think I know what you are going to say, but what if someone wasn't sorry at all for what they did?" asked Jack.

"That's a great question. Do you know that line in the Our Father, *forgive us our trespasses as we forgive those who trespass against us?*"

Jack squirmed in his seat. "I guess I've never stopped to think about it. So, you're saying it doesn't matter if they're sorry? That makes no sense."

"Not at all. God has even more passion for setting things right than we who were wronged to ensure there is justice. Forgiveness doesn't cancel the requirement for justice or pretend the wrong didn't happen. Forgiveness acknowledges that there was an injustice, and God doesn't forgive those who do not repent."

"Oh, okay then," said Jack in relief.

"But, he desires that all men to be saved, to come to know the truth. That is the key to love and forgiveness. He asks us to be open to forgiveness, to be willing to forgive. I said that anger was a legitimate response to injustice, but the single-minded desire for vengeance is a deadly sin," replied Father Diaz.

Jack shook his head. "So, someone can burn your wife to death, and if they just say, 'Oh, I'm sorry,' we have to forgive them?"

Father Diaz turned to Jack. "Remember I said this was about love and forgiveness? I didn't really understand it fully until my brother's death. It challenged me to look at where my heart was and if I was willing to accept Christ's example, his challenge to us. Look, the person that was in the wrong has to sincerely repent for their sins, and forgiveness doesn't remove the requirement for justice. It's just that we have to trust God with the justice part."

Jack asked, "What exactly does that mean?"

"Jack, my brother's brutal death devastated me. I was in a deep state of depression and then anger. I was almost angrier at God than the men who did this to him. It was the anger and desire for revenge that drove me, but I could see that I was becoming what I hated. I wanted to hurt them. I hated those men and thought that delivering justice would relieve my pain and make things right for Roberto."

Jack replied in a quiet tone, "Roberto, that was your brother's name?"

Father Diaz nodded. "I had to really think about what I was becoming. I hated the violence of the world around me, yet I wanted to become a part of it—seeking vengeance, wanting the worst to happen to those men. I wanted them to pay."

Jack could relate strongly to Father Diaz's feelings. Anger and hurt resided in his own heart full-time. "Sorry, but why shouldn't they pay—bigtime?"

"I understand. I do, but I had to think about what Jesus wanted from me. Love and forgiveness were central to his whole life on earth. Even if it was hard, what did he want from me, even while I was faced with this horrible experience? Last Martin Luther King Day, it finally seemed to make more sense."

"Why Martin Luther King?"

Father Diaz gazed up at the crucifix again. "I asked myself, was Martin Luther King angry at the often brutal injustices against black Americans? I think he was. Did he want to destroy them or redeem them? You see, love is an act of the will, not a feeling. Instead of clinging to anger and moral superiority, instead of resorting to violence, he chose love and peaceful protest. It didn't mean that he wasn't angry, and it didn't mean that justice shouldn't be served, but he didn't assume that delivering justice or wrath was his place. He willingly and purposefully worked to bring those who cause injustice to the truth back to community. He willed that they would see the light and come to God. I realized I wasn't doing any of that."

Jack didn't respond. He felt numb and extremely uncomfortable with Father Diaz's words. His whole life since Maria's death had been defined by a very different and singular purpose. It was the thing that allowed him to crawl out of the grave and push himself through the suffering. *Has my desire for justice and revenge turned me into a man of hate?*

Chapter 23

Jack sat alone for several hours in the quiet of the church. He didn't know how to process the world any longer without the frame of reference he had used to define and orient himself for twenty years. Although he sat in the church with God all to himself, he didn't ask for guidance or a sign. Finally, he could sense himself fighting the impulse to give in and shut down. He stood up and headed back to the rectory where Father Diaz was heating water for tea.

"Would you like a cup?" asked Father Diaz.

Jack nodded.

Father Diaz pointed across the room. "Can you get some out of the cupboard there to the right of the sink?"

A rap sounded at the kitchen door. Father Diaz cracked it open to see who it was. "Can I help you?"

The muffled voice replied, "I know this is an odd question, but I've been looking around town for someone, and I was wondering if he might have come by the church?"

"Did you look inside the church to see?"

The man said, "Just a second ago. No one was there, so I wanted to ask. I'm looking for Jimmy O— I mean, Jack Russo. Have you seen him? I'm a close friend."

The priest opened the door wider, and Jack angled his body so Sam could see his face.

"Jimmy! I like the new look. It suits you."

Father Diaz let Sam into the kitchen.

"You look like a cross between Johnny Cash and Father O'Malley." Sam reached out his hand. "Father, I'm Sam Engres. A very old friend of Jimmy's."

Jack glanced out the kitchen window. "Sam, how did you find me?"

"I was released on bail today and went back to the courthouse to talk to you about what we were going to do.

Sheriff Ramos said you were gone, escaped. I didn't know what to think, so I started checking around town. Went to Daisy's, to see if you returned for evidence; Friedman's, to see if you were getting a change of clothes—I would have never guessed a priest's collar." Sam smiled. "Then I came here. Have you come up with a plan?"

Jack glanced at Father Diaz and then back at Sam. "I don't know. I'm stumped."

"Well, I told you that I was going to try to talk to Hector. He may not want to see you yet, but I could see if he could offer any help. Are you up for a trip to Juarez to find out?"

Jack paused to think about what he would gain from leaving the town where his only lead existed, but he also knew his access to the warehouse or the ranch was greatly compromised, and he was a wanted man in town. "Okay, let's see what you can find out. Father Ray, I want to thank you for your hospitality—and caring enough to share your thoughts, as well."

Father Diaz smiled, but his eyes narrowed, showing his concern. He packed some fruit and water and handed the bag and his black cowboy hat to Jack.

Then Jack and Sam headed to Juarez in Sam's SUV. Jack was still wearing the priest's clothes, which may have been a good thing since he was still on the run, now from both sides of the law.

Soon out of town, Sam headed eastbound on Route 10 with clear skies overhead and the sun beating down on them. "What in the world did you do, Fr. O'Connell?"

"Funny," smirked Jack, running his hand along the edge of his collar. "What wasn't funny was that frame-up. I had no chance of fighting the charge, and that lawyer of yours didn't look like he had much fight in him. And I wasn't going to find Rosalina in jail or in the ground."

"I guess you've got a point there, but how the heck did you get out? Ramos doesn't impress me as a pushover or a careless kind of guy. I guess I shouldn't ever underestimate someone who's come back from the dead," responded Sam, as he sped down the highway, passing a tractor-trailer truck that honked its horn in a friendly way. In less than an hour-and-a-half, they were in El Paso driving down some of the same streets that Siena had taken him when she picked him up off the highway. At one point, they passed a white pickup truck that Jack thought was hers, but he figured it must have been someone who looked like her. Sam entered Juarez through the same port-of-entry as he had a few days earlier.

When they passed under the bridge where the man had been hanged and mutilated, Jack noticed a new arrow spray-painted pointing to the spot of the hanging. A few more turns, and Sam pulled over beside the Cathedral. "What are we doing?" asked Jack.

Sam unlocked the power doors. "I don't think surprising Hector with you out of the blue would be a good idea. With that priest getup on, I figure you could hang out here without attracting much attention while I see how Hector might be able to help. He'd be just as interested in finding his granddaughter if there's any chance she has been on that ranch."

Jack nodded, stepping out of the car. "I guess that makes sense. How long do you think it might take?"

"Probably an hour or two. I'll meet you back here if that works for you." Sam took off, leaving Jack in the sunny plaza of the Cathedral of Juarez.

Jack sat on a bench and smiled as he watched three young girls skipping rope in front of him. One of the girls asked him if he would hold something for her. It was a small plastic bag with colored hair elastics.

At one point, he saw Father Jose crossing the plaza, and he started to call out but remembered what he was wearing. Several minutes later, he noticed a young man mulling around the area, coming closer and then backing off. Finally, he came and sat next to Jack on the bench. There was a long silence before the young man murmured, "*Padre, ¿puedo preguntarte algo?*"

Jack turned to the young man. "Sorry, *no hablo español*. Do you speak English?"

"*Un poco.* I am dating a *chica*, and I like her very much," said the young man.

"That's good. What's your question?" asked Jack.

"*Si realmente te gusta mucho ella*—if you like her very much, very, very much, when is it okay to be with her?" asked the young man, now blushing.

Jack understood that the young man was asking him as a priest. "Hmm. Do you like her because of what she does for you or because you care about her?"

The young man pulled back. "Because I like her—very, very much."

"Okay, good. Then you want to do what's best for her as a man—*un hombre autentico.*"

"Sure," said the young man confidently.

"Okay. A real man thinks about what is best for his girl. He doesn't use her or treat her differently than he would want a young man treating his own daughter—honoring her dignity."

The young man nodded, listening intently.

"Now, since sex, if that is what we are talking about, makes babies, then a real man thinks about what that child needs—parents in a committed relationship ready to take care of that child for many years or two kids trying to figure things out?"

The young man shrugged his shoulders and then nodded.

"Remember, no birth control is a hundred percent effective. God has a better plan for us. He designed that special intimacy for marriage and for family. If you really like this girl—very, very much—a real man would think about that girl more than himself. Sorry if that is not the answer you wanted, but it's going to be the best one for you and her. Something to think about. Date her. Be her friend and grow together. See if it grows enough to want to be with her for life and then ask her to be yours."

The young man stared at the ground in front of them. "Huh. You really believe that?"

"I do. Someone much smarter than I made it that way, and I trust Him."

The young man stood up. "Yeah, but you never have to live in the real world, Father. It's not so easy."

Jack lifted his head and gazed into the young man's eyes. "Men of honor don't run from 'not so easy;' they rise to the challenge. They sacrifice themselves for the girl they love and for their family. They fight for them with everything they've got. I know it's not easy, but you said you wanted the best for her. I wish you good luck, my man."

The young man sat in silence a few moments, then stood, waved, and walked away.

Jack laughed to himself. *I think I'm getting this priest thing down.*

Sam pulled up to the curb, rolled down his window, and waved Jack over. "Hector was adamant that he doesn't believe *El Patron* would have his granddaughter at his ranch, but he's willing to have a few of his men check it out. We're supposed to meet them a couple of blocks over. Hop in."

Sam parked in front of an old bar on a side street. Inside, the lighting was dim, but there were people enjoying conversation and drinks. Sam glanced around the premises and saw a rough-looking character at the corner of the bar waving him over. The man had a friend with him, and both appeared intimidating. Sam asked, "Do you guys work for Hector?"

"*Señor* Engres, we were given orders to be at your disposal. You will need to make sure you keep your mouths shut, and we handle the business of checking the situation out. We are not talking about any guarantees of results for your safety. Is this still something you want to do?" asked the man with the rough dark skin and dark glasses.

"Yes, it is," blurted Jack.

"No one said anything about bringing a priest!" chided the man.

Sam raised his hand and interrupted, "He's okay. Father O'Connell can help to identify the girl. He won't get in the way and will follow your instructions. I guarantee it."

Jack couldn't see the man's eyes behind the dark glasses but felt that he was studying him in silence.

"Well, we can't go until the morning, so we might as well see what your Father O'Connell is made of," commanded the man.

"What do you mean?" asked Sam, concerned as he squinted his eyes.

"*Camarero, cuatro tragos de Tequila*," said the man as he slammed money on the counter. The bartender placed four shots of tequila in front of them. The man with the dark sunglasses held his up and drank it down in a single gulp. His companion did the same, and Sam followed suit. The man in the dark glasses downed his drink. No American salt or lemon, just hard liquor. "*¡Otra vez!*" ordered the man, and the bartender poured another shot into each of their shot glasses. The man ordered a third round, and Jack sensed nothing good would come of trying to match these men all night.

He tried to think of how to handle a man that didn't seem to be in the mood for an alternative way to pass the time. In his side pocket, he could feel the plastic sandwich bag with the girl's elastics. The children had left without asking for them back. When the man was busy ordering another round and putting more cash on the old wooden bar, Jack pulled out the baggie and tore it in half under the overhang of the bar. When the next shot was poured, he slid his hand over the top of the glass, covering the top with the clear plastic. It was barely visible with his hand around the top of the glass. Down they gulped their shot as Jack feigned doing same, except his drink stayed in the glass, stopped by the plastic. Jack shook his head as if he was trying to keep from passing out from the alcohol while the others laughed.

"*¿Siente bien, Padre?*" said the man as he laughed louder. "*¡Otra vez!*" he said to the bartender.

Jack didn't like where this was going as the next three shots came, and he was able to keep fake drinking and then dumping the shot under the bar. The men were getting drunk, but they had obviously built up a high level of tolerance while Sam seemed incoherent. Since Jack was supposed to be a priest, he took no shame in acting light-headed and then passing out on the bar to see what would happen. Sam had basically done the same, and one of the men lifted Jack's hand and then one of his eyelids to see if he was out. Jack tried to keep his eyes open enough to see some shadows of what was happening as they each lifted him and Sam, dragging them out a back door and into the alley where a black Hummer was parked.

"*El Patrón quiere que se ocupen de ellos esta noche. Muertos,*" said the man in the dark glasses in his gravelly voice.

Jack could pick up enough to know they had planned on killing them tonight. There was no way he was going to let them get Sam or himself into that vehicle. As the other man held him under his arm and dragged his heels on the ground toward the Hummer, Jack shifted his weight to his feet and kicked back into the man's groin, turned and landed a blow against the man's jaw, sending him to the pavement in the dark alley. He jumped the man with the dark glasses, grabbed him around his neck from the back, and forced him to release Sam, who dropped to the ground.

By this time, Sam had regained consciousness, shook, and steadied his footing in order to help Jack.

Jack still gripped the man around the neck as Sam landed a blow to the man's ribcage. The other man on the ground pulled out a gun and shot at Sam, sending him sprinting down the alley. Jack let go of the first man's neck and kicked the gun from the hand of the man on the ground. Knowing the man with the dark glasses probably had a gun as well, Jack scampered around the side of the Hummer and then sprinted down the alley in the opposite direction. His heart pounded against his chest as he heard a shot ricochet off the side of the building. He could see lights at the end of the alley and heard the Hummer's engine start up, then roar down the alleyway behind him. He had reached the end of the alley when a pickup truck almost ran him over.

"Get your tail in here!" yelled a voice from the truck.

Chapter 24

"We're going to have to stop meeting this way," said Jack as Siena stepped on the gas. She took a series of sharp turns in and out of side streets to make sure she lost the men who were chasing in the Hummer.

"What in the world are ya doin' in that outfit? It's not goin' to look good for a priest to be beating up on some poor cartel killers. Ya might give them and priests a bad name."

Jack looked over his shoulder to make sure there was no one behind them. "How the heck did you find me? I didn't even know where I was going."

Siena smirked. "Neither did I, Russo. I dropped Juan off after his class and did a double-take when I passed a black SUV and saw you. I tried to yell out, but you were focused, so I turned around and followed you. I watched you in the cathedral plaza for quite a while before you got back into the SUV again and then into that bar. I was getting a lot of bad vibes, so I stepped into the bar and saw y'all popping those shots, one after the other. When they started draggin' y'all out the back door, I thought I'd better get my truck to that alley, and there ya were runnin'."

Jack gazed at her a long moment. "Thank you—again."

She slowed to a stop at an intersection and leaned over to kiss him on the cheek. "For some reason, I missed you too."

Jack smiled as he put his hand on her shoulder.

"Let's see if we can stay with Juan tonight and figure out what ya want to do. Make sense, Russo?" Before Jack could respond, Siena was already on the phone with Juan. They pulled up in front of his apartment several minutes later.

Juan hugged Jack. "We were worried about you, amigo."

With her hands on her hips, Siena wanted some answers. "Are you both okay? What happened?"

Jack shook his head. "I don't know. I really don't. I met my best friend, Sam, in Van Horn after you two left. We went back to that warehouse where you and I escaped from, and that guy, Maldito, was there. Things gót a bit ugly. We had to escape and, out of the blue, I was arrested for murder. Sam and I were both in the Van Horn prison. He got bail, and I, um—"

"You what?" interrupted Siena.

"I escaped."

"You escaped from prison after being arrested for murder!" she blurted.

Jack nodded. "I didn't murder anyone, and escaping seemed like a good idea at the time. Sam found me at the church, which explains these clothes, and he wanted to see Maria's father, Hector, to find out if he could help us." Jack turned to Siena. "That's why you saw me waiting in the plaza. When Sam came back, he said Hector had offered some of his guys to check out the ranch with us. Next thing I know, they are getting us drunk and trying to take us out—and I mean trying to take us out permanently. We managed to get out of the alley, which is when my princess in shining armor showed up to save my bacon again, and here we are."

Juan dropped down into his chair. "Why did they want to kill you?"

Jack shrugged. "I don't know. Hector must have suspected or found out that I was with Sam. I'm beginning to wonder if Hector did have something to do with the attack on Maria and me and the kidnapping of his granddaughter. My mind is spinning right now. Why would he kill his daughter? Did he feel so disrespected that he would not only disown her but have her and me killed?"

Siena flapped her arms in helplessness. "How are y'all goin' to find out? This isn't sounding good at all."

Jack shook his head. "I really don't know, but I have a feeling that he didn't want me going back to that ranch, which, of course, means that's exactly where I need to go."

Siena chided, "Well, that's not goin' to happen tonight. Juan, is it okay if we crash here tonight? I know ya have summer finals tomorrow to study for, so we'll let you study."

"Yeah, like that's going to be easy now." Juan chuckled. "My roommate is out, so one of you can take his room and the other the couch."

Jack insisted on the couch, but the scare he and Sam had that evening was running through his head, making for another restless night's sleep. He had no idea where Sam had gone and hoped he was safe. He kept picturing a furious father-in-law. He just couldn't believe he could do something like this, but he also didn't know what impact the cultural disrespect they showed him might have had on him. Exhaustion soon won over his busy mind, and he drifted off to sleep, only to be visited by his familiar nightmares.

Maria laughed as Jack rocked Rosalina in his arms before putting her into her crib. He walked out into the living room and turned to the loud thuds against the front door, like an explosion, as it burst open. Four men in black masks and shotguns rushed in. He could feel the panic-induced adrenaline streaming through his veins and the pounding of this heart as he waved Maria into another room, pleading with the men. "The mistake is yours," kept running through his head and then a bright flash of light—a deafening silence, a burning in his chest, but then everything stopped. This time, unlike all the other versions of this recurring nightmare, he could see the man puffing on a small brown cigar just before he flicked it to the ground. It was a cigarillo, and he could smell the strong-flavored aroma.

Suddenly, he was in the dimly lit office in the warehouse. Cigar smoke rose from a darkened corner. He breathed in, and the aroma was the same. His head turned as the small tin hit against the metal wastebasket. CD Nb Selection Especiale Cigarillos. He could clearly see the name on the tin and the man in black who puffed on the cigarillo. Jack's body twitched as he saw himself now standing in front of a small dusty police station. A man in black puffed on a cigarillo as he pushed a small tin into the floorboard with the sole of his boot. Jack lifted his gaze and recoiled as he saw the bloody head of a young man on a stake in front of the station. The man in black was hanging a sign around the head that read, "Per orders of El Quitapuercos, 'pig killer.'"

Jack turned away from the grotesque sight and felt the blast blow a hole through his chest, propelling his body out through the crashing glass of the apartment window. Just before he hit the ground, he woke with his body snapping upward, sweat streaming down his brow, yelling, "Don't! Don't!"

Juan's and Siena's voices broke through his dream. "Jack, are you okay?"

Jack wiped the sweat from his brow with the sleeve of this tee shirt. "Sorry. Nightmare."

Siena pursed her lips and gazed at him. "Have you ever talked to anyone about these nightmares?"

Instead of responding to her question, Jack turned to Juan and grabbed his shoulder. "I may know who was responsible for your brother's death."

Chapter 25

"*¿Qué?* What are you saying?" pleaded Juan.

"I don't *know* anything for sure, but there was a small tin on the wooden platform in front of that police station you took us to in Guadalupe. It seemed familiar, but I couldn't make the connection until tonight. When we were at the warehouse, Maldito flipped an identical tin for cigarillos into the wastebasket, and he was smoking one of those small, thin cigars. In my dream–well, nightmare–one of the men in a black ski mask was smoking the same type of cigar with the same aroma. Like I said, I don't know for sure, but if he is the enforcer for the cartel in the Juarez Valley, it would make sense that he was involved. He looked at the two of us, not just me, as if we were uncomfortably familiar to him— familiar enough to hold us. Do you mind my asking if you and your brother look similar?"

Juan nodded, his eyes narrowing to slits of anger. "I'm coming with you tomorrow!"

Siena leaned forward. "Juan, don't you have your finals tomorrow?"

He turned sharply to her. "I'm going!"

Siena glanced up at Jack, eyebrows raised, and he instinctively knew that Siena had never seen Juan so enraged.

In the morning, Juan's mood had intensified. Jack couldn't say that he felt any different as he thought about how he would handle Maldito while ensuring he didn't lose the path to finding his only daughter.

Jack and Juan were intently focused in their own worlds as Siena drove down Route 10. "I'm not feeling great about this," Siena interjected into the silence.

"About what?" asked Jack.

"Y'all don't know who did it, where they are, or how to get to them even if you did. That's what."

Juan let out a deep sigh. "She's right."

Siena laughed. "Y'all should be used to that by now."

"We need a way into the ranch," Jack said. "We can't walk in or storm the place."

Siena snickered. "I'm glad yer thinkin' about havin' a plan this time."

"There are a lot of unknowns and dangerous people there," Jack said. "Sam and I had a plan the last two times, but things went awry pretty quickly. I hope he's okay."

Siena smiled. "Yer pretty fond of Sam, aren't ya?"

"He was my closest friend when I was your age, and he's put his life on the line for me twice now. I think we'd do anything for each other."

"That's nice to have in life. I don't know if I've ever had a friend like—" Siena broke off as Juan glanced over, his mouth open. "As I was sayin', except for Mr. Juan."

Jack patted Juan on the shoulder. "I'm glad she knows what a good friend you are. I guess we've all had to deal with tragedy. Sam had a rough life growing up, too. An alcoholic father who deserted them and a mother who couldn't cope. They ended up shipping him from one relative to another until he roomed with me in college and during the summers as well. We were the only family he really had."

"And he's been livin' down here all these years?" asked Siena.

Jack nodded. "I was surprised, but I think he really liked it down here. He visited a few times during the school year when Maria and I were first married. To us, he was part of our family and Rosalina's godfather. He was devastated by Maria's death and the loss of Rosalina. And for the past twenty years, he thought I was dead."

Siena pulled off the exit for Van Horn, and Jack pointed down the road to a turn that brought them behind the church.

"I think I should return to my holy attire."

They walked around the side of the rectory, and Jack could see Father Diaz talking to someone in the kitchen. He couldn't tell for sure, but Jack figured it was Sheriff Ramos. Father Diaz caught a glimpse of Jack in the window and made a stealth motion toward the side door. He must have excused himself from the conversation as he let the three of them into the hallway, signaling to them to be completely quiet as he ushered them into a small room before returning to the kitchen. From their room, they could catch most of the conversation.

"Father Ray, has Jack Russo been here at the church since he escaped from the courthouse cell?"

"He was, but left with his friend, Sam something-or-other, to get some help finding his daughter and the one who might have framed him."

"You really believe he's innocent, don't you?" asked Ramos.

"I'm not the only one who believes that to be a distinct possibility, wouldn't you agree?"

Ramos gruffed. "I don't know what to think these days. Look, I've been to the warehouse he claimed to have been assaulted at and found nothing to support his story. I'm going out to the *Ranchos Familia Dos* tomorrow morning. I'll be by around ten o'clock and expect you to be here to give me my last rites."

"Nick, do you really think you should be going out there alone?" Father Diaz sounded concerned. "Maybe I should come with you."

"I really need people who can identify some of the individuals, so if Russo makes his way back here, maybe he'll consider stowing away in the back of my jeep to help make those identifications," responded Ramos. The chair squeaked as it moved across the kitchen floor and Ramos said goodbye to Father Diaz.

Father Diaz retrieved Jack and his companions from the

small room and led them into the kitchen. "Can I get you something to eat or drink?"

Jack responded, "I'm all set. This is Siena Connors and Juan Sanchez. They've saved my life a few times over the past couple of days. Did I hear right—Ramos wants me to go to the ranch with him?"

Father Diaz scratched his head. "I think he did. I've talked to the sheriff many times about the changes over the past few years. He's had his suspicions about the owners of the warehouse and ranch, and I'm guessing he's pretty sure you aren't a killer type, but he needs to do his job."

Jack shook his head. "I don't think they're going to let him drive in with me in the front seat."

Father Diaz paused for a second. "I think you're right, and what he said is true. He has a pretty big cargo area in the back of the jeep. Maybe he really wants you to stow away inside?"

Jack shrugged, thinking that he didn't want this to be a setup to get him back behind bars either. He continued to consult with Father Diaz, while Siena and Juan went over to Friedman's to buy Jack a change of clothes.

After an early dinner and an uneasy night's sleep, Jack wandered into the church in dawn's dim light. He sat in the second pew before the altar, wondering what he was going to do if he found his daughter or Maria's killers at that ranch. He had pictured himself seeking revenge for their evil, to stop them from ever doing this to another family—or so he told himself. He had held onto his anger so tightly that he felt as if he wouldn't be able to control himself if he came face to face with the perpetrators, the men with no conscience. The chances seemed so slim, but he felt a dark presence in Van Horn. Was it his imagination or his hope to be finally done with the cancer that had grown inside him over the years?

He tensed as the side door edged open and then relaxed when Father Diaz leaned in. Jack waved him over and stood to meet him. "Do you always get up this early?"

"I could ask you the same question, but I imagine you have so much on your mind that I don't want to disturb you. Are you okay?"

Jack nodded. "Can I ask you a question that's been on my mind?"

"You can ask me anything."

"I heard you tell Officer Ramos that you believed I was innocent. I know you've heard it from others, but how do you trust someone you don't really know? "

Father Diaz smiled. "That is a very good question." He stepped to an alcove to the right of the altar area. Below the statue of Our Lady of Fatima was a nativity scene Jack hadn't noticed before.

"Are you getting ready for Christmas early this year, Father Ray?"

"I know it seems different, but we have this scene of the birth of Jesus up all year to remind people of why he came."

Stepping forward, Jack gazed down upon the baby resting in the bed of straw. He couldn't think of what to say.

"I trust in you for the same reason I trust in God."

Jack cocked his head at him. "Sorry?"

"I can see it in your eyes and hear it in your voice. You still love your wife as much as you did twenty years ago. After all these years, you still love your daughter, even if she may not know you. We have a Father in heaven who will never give up on us, who will never stop loving us."

Father Diaz's eyes welled up. These weren't just words he was saying, but something real that touched him deep inside. "Every Christmas, I point to this scene and ask the parishioners what He is doing there. He did not come to bring peace but to rescue us, to reclaim us as sons and daughters of His Father—and He was willing to sacrifice Himself to save us from evil and harm."

When Father Diaz turned to Jack, tears welled within his own eyes.

"Jesus came to fight for us. Our Father will never stop loving us or fighting for us. There is nothing He won't give to save us."

The words touched a chord inside of Jack. His brow furrowed as he struggled with the sudden feeling of understanding and trust.

"I can tell that you love your wife and daughter more than anything, and you will fight for them with your own life. Satan wants you to believe you aren't worthy of the kind of love that God has for you. He wants you to give up or to become like the men you hate, but God will never give up on you and has a better plan. I know in my bones that you didn't kill Homer and that your path is in God's hands if you let Him guide you."

Father Diaz left Jack to sit with his words as he headed back to the rectory.

Despite Jack's and Juan's pleas for Siena to remain behind, she was determined to go and was ready and when Sheriff Ramos pulled up next to the rectory. When he got out to talk to Father Diaz, the three stowaways opened the back storage area of the jeep and slid under a black canvas.

Siena carried her Winchester rifle, which she had stored in her truck. "Don't leave home without it," she quipped at Jack's frown.

After several minutes, the driver's side door opened, and Ramos slid into the driver's seat, grunting, "I must be *loco*."

They reached the town limits in about ten minutes and then turned onto a bumpy dirt road leading to the main gate of the ranch. Jack could see the blue sky and an occasional white wispy cloud through the window as the stowaways remained silent.

Ramos stopped at the gate, where a man asked, "Sheriff, *¿qué puedo hacer por usted hoy?*"

"*Buenos dias.* I'm checking every establishment in Van

Horn to see if the murderer of Homer Beeker might be hiding out. It's just a routine check," replied Ramos.

The guard talked on a walkie-talkie and then waved Ramos through the gate as it opened.

Ramos drove down a long dirt drive before stopping at a second gate attended by a friendlier guard. "Sheriff Ramos. *Bienvenido.* You are looking for a fugitive, no?"

"I am. His name is Jack Russo. I need to make sure I check all possibilities. You know the murder happened on the road right behind your ranch," said Ramos.

Jack could make out the man's rough face and a rifle strapped over his shoulder.

After a long pause, the man responded, "Leave your car here, and I can take you around the ranch."

When Ramos and the guard were out of sight, Jack eased the back door of the jeep outward and slipped outside to get a better look. The narrow guard shack blocked their view from the ranch house, and Juan and Siena were able to slide under the partially opened door. The question was how they were going to get from there to the other buildings in broad daylight. Jack felt as if they were sitting ducks, or more like dead ducks, if they stayed in their current position much longer.

Suddenly, he could hear the sound of a vehicle coming down the drive, and he waved to Siena and Juan to stay low. It looked like a horse trailer coming through. The driver stopped at the second gate and then proceeded through the gate slowly. Jack grabbed Siena and Juan and motioned them to grab onto the open slots on the back of the trailer. Siena peered into the trailer and whispered, "That is a beautiful horse."

Jack smiled nervously and motioned them to jump off as the trailer pulled alongside the large stable barn. He peered into a window, hoping that he might see a young woman inside that could be Rosalina. There was no such luck as he only saw

145

a stable hand and two men bringing in the horse from the trailer. Disappointment coursed through Jack's veins. Staying low, they moved around to the back of the barn until they reached the far corner, where they could see Ramos coming out of the ranch house with the guard, heading to the front of the barn. With no one in the yard, the three took the chance of scrambling to the back of the ranch house.

Pausing to calm his breathing and his heightened nerves, Jack whispered, "I'm going into the house alone to see if anyone is there. Stay down. There's got to be men on the lookout."

As Jack crouched forward, Siena grabbed his arm and handed him her Winchester rifle. She gazed into his eyes. "Please be careful, Russo."

Jack nodded and moved along the backside of the ranch house until he reached a door. He slowly turned the knob, only to find it locked. He continued until he turned the corner, where he tried to open a small window to the basement. It didn't budge, so he pushed harder, and the window opened, allowing him to squeeze into the dark basement. Once his eyes became accustomed to the dark, he could see wooden crates, similar to those being transported from Prâxedis to the Van Horn warehouse a few nights earlier.

He approached a set of wooden stairs that he ascended each step with utmost care to minimize the squeak until he reached the door to the first floor. Other than the pulsing beat of his own heart, he could hear nothing. He slowly made a full turn of the knob before opening it wide enough to slip through. When he started to creep forward, his heart stopped, and his blood felt as if it drained from his veins. A short but solid barrel-chested man with a square face, high cheekbones, deep-set eyes, and pitted weather-beaten skin stared down at him with the smile of a hunter who had cornered his prey.

Chapter 26

The man waved his automatic weapon at Jack and motioned for him to hand over the Winchester. One hand in the air, Jack slowly handed him the rifle, then placed both hands behind his head, and glanced around the seemingly empty house as he was marched toward the front door. The place looked more like a family home instead of a bunkhouse for cartel members. He could feel the gun barrel in his spine sharply nudging him forward until he was outside in the dusty yard.

Jack couldn't see Siena or Juan as he scanned the yard on the way to the stable barn. He soon found them on their knees in the center of the barn with Ramos. The man with the high cheekbones grunted, "Join your amigos, Mr. Russo." Jack kept his hands behind his head and knelt down between Siena and Ramos, then he spotted two other men with guns pointed at them. "You seem awfully interested in visiting our facilities. Why the curiosity?"

Jack replied, "I was looking to buy a horse for my daughter."

The man slammed the butt of his rifle into Jack's gut, driving him to the ground with the pain. Ramos moved to help but was pulled back by one of the other men.

The high cheek-boned man's half-smile disappeared as his eyes narrowed, and he asked in a more serious tone, "Why are you so interested in our ranches?"

Looking worried and scared, Siena helped pull Jack back to his knees. Out of the corner of his eye, Jack caught sight of a tall, thin man in black emerging from the shadows, puffing on a cigarillo—Maldito, wearing his black hat and dark sunglasses. As he reached the center of the barn, he took the Winchester rifle from the man with the high cheekbones, aimed it at Jack, and peered through the gunsight. Siena moved toward Jack, and Maldito lowered the gun. "Bring her

---

to the house," he ordered, nodding in Siena's direction.

One of the men grabbed her arm, and Jack said, "Why are you taking her?"

The man escorted her toward the large opening of the barn without responding.

Maldito laughed. "You don't even know who she is, do you?" He paused before adding, "Haven't you been looking for her your whole life?"

Jack's eyes darted toward Siena as she looked over her shoulder and peered into his eyes with a yearning expression.

He could barely get the words out as she disappeared around the corner. "Rosalina?"

"It's a shame you won't be available for the family reunion," hissed Maldito as he turned his attention to Juan. "Stand up, *hermano pequeño cerdo*," he ordered with a mocking tone.

Climbing to his feet, Juan narrowed his eyes at Maldito.

Maldito sneered at him. "I thought you looked familiar. Your brother had the same look of fear before he squealed like the pig cop he was."

Jack could see fury rising up in Juan, who edged closer with fire in his eyes. From his belt, Maldito pulled the long hunting knife he had taken from Siena and hissed, "Let's see if you sound like he did." Just as Maldito raised the knife to Juan's throat, Jack sprung to his feet and then recoiled as a loud gun blast went off.

Maldito's dark glasses fell as he dropped to the ground, shot in the back. Jack turned to see Sam standing with a gun in his hand. Another cartel man fired twice, hitting Sam, who returned fire and shot the man dead before dropping to the ground.

Jack rushed to Sam's side. Blood flowed from a wound in his friend's thigh. Ramos jumped up, and Siena came running into the barn screaming as gunfire exploded right behind her. Sam yelled to the sheriff, "Get them out of here!"

Jack snapped, "We're not leaving you here. Ramos, can you get to your jeep?"

Ramos grabbed the Winchester lying next to Maldito's body and headed to the jeep amidst the gunfire. Jack and Juan picked Sam up from the floor and dragged him closer to the barn door opening, while Siena waved Ramos on. Bullets were flying, some hitting the jeep, as Ramos reached the barn, where they loaded Sam in the back and jumped in before he sped through the gate. Gunshots spat at them from behind as they approached the next guard shack, where the guard shot directly at them. Ramos sped up, crashing through the gate and down the long bumpy dirt road until he reached the main road. Jack put pressure on Sam's wound, and Juan tied a cord around his leg.

"We're getting you to the hospital, Sam. What are you crazy? Risking your life like that?"

Sam smiled, wincing at the same time. "Tell me you wouldn't have done the same?"

Jack continued to put pressure on the wound while Siena wiped Sam's brow. Jack replied, "How on earth did you find us?"

"I searched all night for you in Juarez after the incident with those guys in the bar. When I couldn't find you, I figured you'd come back here to finish what you came to do. I asked around town and heard that Sheriff Ramos was heading to the ranch, so I came in through the fence off the back road. I'm just glad I was in time."

"So am I."

Sam winced again and closed his eyes, drifting off into unconsciousness.

Jack felt a bump on the back of Sam's head where he must have banged it against the ground during his fall. He pushed down on the wound and then turned to Siena. She was already gazing at him and smiled broadly as Jack's eyes met hers.

He asked, "Is it really you?"

"Well, I've always been me, Russo," she laughed, putting her arm around his shoulder and drawing her head into his shoulder, breathing in.

Luckily, the small Culberson Hospital was in Van Horn, and Ramos had called ahead for the surgical team to be ready when they arrived.

While the doctors were taking care of Sam's wound, Ramos went back to the courthouse to report the incident. Jack sat on a bench with Siena and Juan in awkward silence. Finally, Juan stood up and said, "I don't know."

Siena's brow tightened. "What don't you know?"

"I don't know how I feel. All this time, I wanted justice. I wanted vengeance. Now Jesus's killer is dead, and rightly so, but I feel no sense of peace, no satisfaction. I still feel as if nothing has been fixed or made right." Juan paced back and forth. "I need some time to think," he added as he traipsed to the hospital entrance and then out the door.

Siena turned to Jack. "I don't know what to do for him. He's been in such pain for so long. If he killed that man with his own hands, I don't know if he'd have felt any better or not."

Jack sighed. "I feel the same way. I wanted Maldito stopped from doing any more harm, but there is no sense of peace for—" Jack paused as he searched for how to refer to Maria.

"For my mother? Is that what you wanted to say?" Siena clasped Jack's hand.

Jack nodded. "I feel dazed by what Maldito said. I didn't feel I could trust anything he said. Part of me feels it would be like trusting the devil himself, but here you are. I've sensed something about you since we met. It seems like too much of a coincidence that you remembered that ranch, attended that school, and lost your parents so young. This would be my biggest dream come true." Jack smiled as he wiped away the tear that rolled from Siena's eye.

Siena laughed awkwardly. "You know I've enjoyed being

with you, and I missed you when you were gone. I've never really let myself feel very attached to anyone in my life, and I wasn't expecting you to be my father—just someone who cared for me because he liked me and not because he had to."

Jack cupped her chin in his hand and gazed into her eyes. "I care for you because I like you—a lot. A lot, a lot. I think you're a very special young lady and very worth caring about." She leaned in and rested her head against his chest. Jack put his arm around her and held her close. "I'm glad it's you."

Chapter 27

Four hours later, they were allowed to visit Sam in his hospital room. The doctor informed them that all had gone well with the surgery, and he'd be on his feet in a few days.

Sam was sitting up when Jack entered the room and greeted him with a grin. "So, how is the hero of Texas?"

"Oh, a little woozy right now, but feeling pretty good."

Jack added, "The doc said there was no serious damage done to your leg, and you were lucky that the bullet to your chest didn't penetrate. Well, I guess coming to a gunfight with a bullet-proof vest was more than luck."

Sam raised his eyebrows. "I've been working in these parts for a while now. Taking precautions in the right situations is something you learn fast. For good or bad—I guess I've learned not to trust anyone these days."

Siena entered the room, and Jack took her hand. "Sam, I don't think you two have formally met, but this is Siena. She is Rosalina."

"What?" Sam gasped. "How did this happen?"

"Maldito told me in the barn."

Sam winced as he straightened himself in the bed. "Maldito? No offense, but can you trust him?"

"I thought the same thing, but I'm pretty certain that he was one of the men in the apartment that day and was responsible for Maria and then taking Rosalina. He must have been keeping tabs on her or something—and he seemed to react to her when she came to the ranch in Prâxedis," replied Jack.

"Huh. Well, that's unbelievably great news, then!" Sam turned his attention to Siena. "How do you feel about this, Rosa—I'm mean, Siena? It must be a bit of a shock to you too?"

Siena grinned as she turned to Jack. "I guess I could get used to it. I really want to thank you, too, for coming to our rescue."

Sam stared more intently at her. "It's the least I could do for my goddaughter, don't you think?" Then he said to Jack, "So, Jimmy, what will you do? Does this mean you're heading back to Boston?"

Jack shrugged.

"He's a Boston boy, through and through. He's not telling you the truth if he says anything else," Sam said to Siena.

They left Sam to rest and returned to the lobby, where Juan was talking to Sheriff Ramos. As they approached, they could hear Juan saying, "How is that possible?"

Jack tilted his head. "How's what possible? What's going on?"

Ramos replied, "I went back to the ranch with a group of state marshals and just got back."

"And?"

"And there was nothing there. Not a soul, no horses, no bodies, no guards at the gates, no evidence that anything happened. It was like a ghost town," insisted Ramos. "It was spooky."

Jack narrowed his eyes at him. "That's crazy. Maybe we scared them off?"

"Maybe. Something's not right," muttered Ramos, walking off before turning to Jack and pointing at him, "And you're still under arrest, Mr. Russo."

Jack sighed and turned his attention to Juan. "How're you feeling?"

Juan shook his head. "Uneasy. Something's weird about this town."

Siena patted his shoulder. "I imagine it brings up a lot of feelings. Oh, we just saw Sam, and he's gonna be okay."

Juan gave half a smile. "That's good. I should thank him for saving my life. Hey, what was Maldito saying to you about Siena, anyway?"

"That we've got a lot of catching up to do," said Jack with a smile, leaving Juan appearing even more confused. "Why don't I take you two for lunch at Lizy's?"

As they entered Lizy's Café, Maggie glanced over with a smile and pointed to the booth by the window.

She laughed as she approached them. "You wouldn't be the first fugitive to eat here." Jack ducked his head, and she added, "Oh, I'm not worried. I heard the sheriff doesn't think you did it. It's still sad about old Homer, though."

They all nodded and put in their orders. After the waitress left, Siena broke the short silence. "Juan, Maldito told Russo that the daughter he's been looking for all these years is me."

Juan's jaw dropped. "What? Really? That's great. That's really great. So, we all got what we came for today."

Siena reached across the table to clutch Juan's arm. "You certainly don't look like it."

Juan sighed deeply. "I don't feel like it, either."

Siena frowned. "Russo said that guy admitted to it. Your brother's death has been vindicated. I know that's not what you really want, but at least he's been stopped for good."

"It just doesn't feel like it, and Maldito took orders from someone. I feel like there's someone responsible who hasn't paid his debt."

Jack chided. "You mean *El Patron?*"

Maggie came back with drinks, and Jack asked, "Maggie, have you heard anything about the owner of that large ranch in town or the warehouse on the main route?"

"You're talking about *El Patron?*" Maggie slid the drinks in place.

Jack nodded.

"I don't know. If the owner of the ranch is him, he did come in here and was nice to everyone. I haven't heard anything bad about him, but I don't know that I can say the same about some of the men that work for him. Just fishy, you know?"

As Maggie bustled off, Jack sipped his drink and turned to Juan, dropping his voice to a whisper. "He seems like an enigma. What are you thinking of doing? Nothing stupid, I hope. Nothing can replace the loss of your brother. He'd want you to live—" He glanced at Siena. "And you have family members to protect and think of." It hit Jack that he lived the past twenty years as if he'd had nothing to lose, but now he did. The risk now wouldn't only be to him.

After lunch, Juan agreed that he couldn't miss another final exam and needed to get back. Siena drove them on Route 10 toward El Paso. Halfway between Van Horn and El Paso, Siena called out, "Isn't that Ramos's jeep over there?"

Juan blurted, "I think you're right, but what's that black vehicle racing up behind him? I think I recognize it from the ranch."

In a cloud of dust, Siena spun her truck around on the dirt strip between the east and westbound sides of the highway. "Hold onto your hats, boys!" she yelled as the back wheels slid sideways before she straightened out, and she took off after the vehicles heading back toward Van Horn.

Up ahead, they could tell that Ramos had picked up speed, and gun blasts that shot across the valley.

"This doesn't look good," said Jack.

Siena reached back and opened up her compartment where the Winchester rifle lay. "I hope y'all know how to pull the trigger on this baby."

The black vehicle had gained ground on Ramos's jeep, and they continued to hear the loud blasts as Siena pressed the accelerator.

Suddenly, Ramos's jeep swerved on the road and then spun off into the desert sand as the black vehicle sped away. Siena let her foot off the pedal until she pulled off the side of the road next to Ramos.

Jack yanked open the jeep door. Ramos was hunched over his steering wheel, the horn was blaring, and blood was visible on the back of his shirt. He put his hand to Ramos's neck and could feel a pulse. "He's alive! We need to get him to the hospital—fast!" Siena backed up the truck to the jeep as

Jack and Juan carefully lifted him out and laid him out onto the flatbed of the truck.

"Siena, we'll stay back here to keep the pressure on the wound. See if you can keep the ride as smooth as you can."

"Sure thing, Pops," she replied with a shaky smile.

It took almost an hour to reach the emergency entrance of the Culberson Hospital. While the staff rushed Ramos into surgery, the three of them returned to the lobby to wait for an update.

Father Diaz arrived shortly afterward. "Any word on how he's doing?"

"Not yet." Jack stood and shook the priest's hand.

"What happened out there at that ranch today?' asked Father Diaz.

Jack wrung his hands. "We've been trying to piece that together ourselves. Someone's trying to silence any inquiries into that ranch, but this has gotten way out of control. I think we need to double up on those prayers."

It was several hours later before the doctor came out to report on Ramos' surgery. "I don't know if you guys are lucky or just dangerous to hang around with."

Jack asked, "What do you mean, Doc?"

The doctor chuckled. "Well, everyone around you is getting shot. That's not great, but both your friend Sam and the sheriff were very lucky—neither of their wounds hit anything vital or did too much damage. They should be able to go home in a few days."

After the doctor left them, Siena asked, "Russo, that was good news. What's the concerned look about?"

Jack responded, "With no police in town and two intended targets alive, I'm afraid they might come to finish the job."

Jack remained on guard in front of the hospital, holding the Winchester rifle visible, while Juan and Siena drove into town to get a few things from the sheriff's office. As night began to fall, Jack stood guard with Juan, who was wearing the sheriff's hat and jacket. They hoped their silhouettes would look convincingly like police officers in the dimly lit doorway. At one point, a set of headlights on a dark vehicle approached the entrance. Jack whispered, "Stand straight and hold the rifle so that it shows in the light."

Juan shook as he breathed deeply and watched the vehicle slow down, circling the curved drive in front before taking off.

Juan wiped his brow. "Do you think that was them?"

Jack replied, "I don't know of any joy riders that check out local hospitals this time of night."

They took turns trying to nap on the couch in the lobby as someone stood guard, but there was little sleep to be had even without the return of any unwelcome visitors.

In the morning, Sheriff Ramos was able to receive visitors. There were bandages on his shoulder and a broad smile on his face. "I hear that I owe you guys a big thank you!"

Jack approached. "You've been sticking your neck out for us. I think it was the least we could do."

Juan added, "It looks like they may have tried to come back last night to finish the job."

"What?" Ramos' eyes widened.

Siena responded, "A large SUV approached, and I think it was the same one chasing you on the highway yesterday. Luckily, these two imposters do a good job of acting like armed police guards. They might be vying for your job. "

Ramos said, "I don't believe it!"

Siena blurted, "Why don't you believe me?"

Ramos lifted his healthy shoulder and pointed toward the doorway. "I believe you, but not that." Sam was standing in the doorway with only crutches to support him.

"What did I miss?" Sam laughed.

Jack, Siena, and Juan stepped to the door to greet him.

"Oh, nothing much," replied Jack. "Just another deadly cartel assassination attempt. Luckily for you two, they can't shoot straight enough to get rid of you," replied Jack as he put his arm around Sam. "How are you doing?"

Tentatively, Sam bobbed his head. "I guess better than the alternative. The leg is sore, but I can put weight on it, so I should be getting around pretty good sooner than later."

Juan approached Sam and shook his hand. "*Señor* Engres. I wanted to thank you for saving my life and serving justice by stopping the evil of that animal."

Sam firmly shook Juan's hand. "I'm glad I was there in time. I don't believe in luck, so I think we know who to really thank."

Juan nodded, and Siena's smile clearly agreed.

Sam made his way over to Ramos's bedside. "Are you planning on staying in that bed all day?"

Ramos laughed. "Not if I can help it. It's good to see you vertical so soon. All four of you are heroes in my book." Turning to Jack, he said, "Even though some of you are technically on work release."

Father Diaz appeared at the doorway. "I heard there was a party going on here, and you know how much I like a party." He grinned as he saw his friend Ramos was sitting up. "What are we going to do about the evil that has invaded our small community?"

Ramos raised the head of the bed. "When I went back to the ranch and saw no signs that we had ever been there—no dead bodies, no blood, no sign of anyone there, no horses, *nada*—" Ramos paused. "I had a contact of mine do some digging to find out who the real owner of the ranch was. And it was the same as the owner of the warehouse."

"Huh. That *El Patron* guy?" asked Jack.

Ramos nodded. "He's The Boss."

"Did you say, 'The Boss'?" inquired Jack as his eyes narrowed.

"*Sí*. That's what *El Patron* means—The Boss. Why do you ask?" queried Ramos.

Jack shook his head in disbelief. "Nothing. Did you find him?"

Ramos winced and put his hand to his chest. "I did and went to see him in Juarez. Hector Engando."

Sam shifted his weight on his crutches and appeared dismayed. "Hector? Did you say Hector Engando?"

Ramos nodded again. "The same. Why?"

"I've been doing work for him. I can't believe he'd be involved in anything like this," countered Sam.

Jack put his hands on Sam's shoulders. "All those years, you must have seen or suspected something—didn't you?"

Sam dropped his gaze. "Nothing like this. He's not like that. I knew his business wasn't always legal, but I think he seriously wanted to change that. The things he did focused on minor stuff—not the hard drugs, murder, extortion, and kidnappings the cartels were trying to push on him. That's why he was so keen to move into new types of the transportation business, where I spent my time. I can't believe he would be involved in what we saw."

Jack exhaled. "I want to believe you, but this took place on his property—and I'd assume with his men. Why were we attacked by those men in the bar just after he told you his men would help you?"

"I don't know," said Sam.

"Why would he have a man like Maldito working for him— a man we know brutally killed Juan's brother and how many others? Why was a man who worked for him in my family's apartment when I was shot, Maria burned to death, and my daughter kidnapped if he wasn't that kind of man? Why did they attack the sheriff just after seeing Hector?"

Sam dropped down on an available chair, rubbed the sides of his face as his eyes squeezed tight. "I don't know!"

Jack glanced at Ramos to see his reaction.

Then Jack walked out of the room, down the corridor, and out the front door of the small hospital. He was flooded with emotions that had consumed his life for so long, plagued with questions he couldn't believe were possible. Was his father-in-law so angry, feeling so disrespected, that he would kill his son-in-law? Yes. His own daughter? No. He couldn't believe it. Would he take away his only grandchild's parents just because they got married without his consent? Jack didn't know what to think. He only knew that the adrenaline running through his veins was overwhelming him. All he wanted to do was drive to Juarez and confront Hector, once and for all.

Chapter 28

Thoughts of Hector consumed Jack to the point that he no longer cared about the danger or the consequences. He went back into the hospital and asked Sam if they could talk alone.

Sam led him down the hall to a visitor's room.

"You're getting around pretty good on that leg," said Jack.

Sam smirked. "Guess I was lucky. What did you want to talk about?"

"I want to see Hector. I need to have this out with him."

Sam sat down on the metal chair. "Jack, I know how you feel. I'm pissed off, myself, about all the possibilities running through my head. I still can't believe any of them, though."

Jack rubbed the back of his head. "I need to know where he lives now. Is it the same place as twenty years ago?"

Sam shook his head. "No. He said that it got too dangerous for the family. I don't know what to do here. I don't want to see you hurt. What about Rosalina; I mean Siena—which name is she going by?"

Jack turned. "I don't want her involved."

"I know, but you being dead isn't what she wants either. Let me heal and think about it. I'd want to go with you and plead your case—and also to find out what happened in Juarez the other day. I think I can reason with him."

"Sam, I don't want to wait, and I don't want you risking your life again for me."

Sam stood up and grabbed Jack's arm. "You're angry right now."

"You're damn right I'm angry!" snapped Jack.

"That's not going to help you. We need to have a game plan, or nothing is going to get resolved. If you trust my friendship and love for you, you should take your daughter back to Boston and forget all of this. Leave the past and have the life with her you've both missed. What else could be more important?"

Jack patted Sam's back. "I should trust you. Perhaps you're right. Maybe I'm just out for revenge; that won't be any good for Siena. Look, you stay here and heal, and I'll try to take some time to think about this."

Relief flowed over Sam's face as Jack walked him back to his room.

In the lobby, Jack met Juan and Siena. Siena stared at him. "What's the plan? I can tell ya have one."

Jack pursed his lips. "You're not going to like it, but I can't risk taking you along."

"Since when did you become my—well, look, I'm not goin' to sit on my thumbs while you get yourself hurt or worse!"

Jack tilted his head to make eye contact. "I need you to protect these two here while Juan and I go back to Prâxedis. He knows the area better, and we can't leave Ramos and Sam unprotected here. I'm not trying to treat you like a child. I really need you to do this."

Siena nodded. "I hate it when you make sense."

Jack turned to Juan. "Are you willing to go back to that ranch in Prâxedis ?"

Juan nodded as Siena reluctantly handed over the keys to her truck. Siena turned to Jack, blinking back tears. "I don't want to lose you."

Pulled into the moment, Jack gazed back into her piercing eyes and felt his heart torn in two. Isn't she why he was searching for all these years? Was revenge more important than being with her? He tightened his brow. "I know. I promise it will be okay."

She hugged him and then turned away as they left.

On the ride down, Juan asked, "*Señor* Russo, how did you realize who *El Patron* was when the sheriff was telling about his visit?"

"Good question. When I was in Juarez, before you were born, people used to always refer to Hector Engando as 'The Boss.' All this time that we've been talking about *El Patron*, it never dawned on me that it meant the same thing. It seems so obvious now. He must have bought that ranch to have a safer place to get away with the family. I need to find out where he lives in Juarez and talk to him face to face. I need to bring some closure to this thing."

Juan stared out the window at the barren desert lining both sides of the highway. "I know how you feel. It's as if nothing was resolved when Maldito died—like there's still no justice for my brother and family."

"I know. Can you show me how to get to Calle's house?" asked Jack.

Juan shifted uncomfortably in this seat. "Yeah, but I don't think we should ask her to risk going back out there."

Jack was quiet for most of the drive as Juan directed him to the town and then to Calle's home, where her truck and horse trailer could be seen in the back of her house. He knocked on the back door, and Calle opened it, appearing relieved.

"I'm so glad to see both of you alive." She peered around and let them in. They told her what happened at the ranch, about the tunnel, the warehouse escape, and the incident at the ranch in Van Horn. Calle seemed to hang on to their every word. "So, why are you back in Prâxedis ?"

Juan replied, "We need to go back to the ranch. We don't want you coming, but we want to ask you if we could use your trailer to get us to the gate."

Calle anxiously rubbed her hands together and sighed. "I haven't gone out to take care of the stables yet today. I don't know. From what you're telling me, I think you're both going to get yourselves killed."

Jack made eye contact. "We need to do this."

Calle thought for several moments before going into the kitchen and coming out with a large rolling pin. Before Jack could ask what it was for, Calle gave herself a hard whack across her cheekbone with the pin. "That should leave a nice bruise—one that you two left me with when you ambushed me and stole my truck and trailer. Please be careful."

Since Juan was smaller and his skin darker, he drove the small truck, wearing Calle's hat. Jack rode in the back trailer. As they approached the guard on the road to the ranch, Juan kept his head down. When he lifted it, the guard stepped back, holding his weapon. "*¿Dónde está Calle?*"

Before Juan could answer, Jack came down hard on the guard's neck with a chop and then knocked him cold with a solid punch to his head. They dragged him into the guard shack, tied his hands and feet, and took his weapon. Juan pressed the guard's walkie-talkie and did his best imitation of the guard's voice as he said that Calle was coming to take care of the stables. They proceeded slowly down the long dirt road to the busy ranch compound. The next guard waved them to the stable. Juan pulled alongside the building, and they slid out into the stable to determine how best to make their next move.

Juan began working the stalls, and Jack studied the compound, looking for an opportunity. Before long, he spotted Emilio heading toward the stable barn. Jack grabbed a bale of hay to shield his face as Juan brushed down one of the horses.

Emilio entered the barn. "*¿Tienes todo lo que necesitas, Calle?*"

Jack turned with the bale of hay and grabbed Emilio. He held Siena's hunting knife to the man's throat. "We left in such a hurry last time that we didn't get to say goodbye or thank you for your hospitality."

Emilio didn't express any sign of panic as he glanced at something. "*Señor* Russo, I could just yell out, and you'd be both dead in a matter of minutes."

Jack pulled the knife a little closer to Emilio's throat. "You could, but you wouldn't be around to see it, would you?"

Emilio's eyes shifted to see Jack's face. "What is it you want?"

"Only one thing. I need to know where *El Patron* lives in Juarez," replied Jack.

Juan watched out the barn door.

Emilio chuckled lightly. "I would be a dead man if I told you that."

"Maybe, but you'll definitely be a dead man if you don't tell me," snapped Jack, tightening his hold on Emilio.

"Señor Russo, there is death and there is death. I believe yours would be much more pleasant than if I was a *sapo*," muttered Emilio. "It is possible that we will all be dead before the end of the day. The boy is young."

Juan turned to Emilio with a serious stare. "Not too young to deliver justice for my family."

Emilio muttered, "So you both seek justice while others play."

Jack tightened his grip and pressed the knife harder. "What does that mean?"

Emilio laughed. "You'll find out."

Suddenly, one of the horses shook and neighed. As Jack and Juan looked up, there were two dark silhouettes at the doorway with the bright sun behind them. Jack shook his head to make sure he wasn't seeing things, but there stood a tall, thin man in black, with dark sunglasses, a black cowboy hat, and the puff of smoke from the cigarillo in his mouth. Maldito was supposed to be dead or severely wounded, but here he stood without any sign of injury. The husky man next to him had a nasty look behind his long mustache as he held an automatic rifle, waving it as a command for Jack to drop the knife.

Jack's mind raced as he debated whether or not to drop the only leverage he had. If he dropped the knife, they would surely be taken out to be killed and buried. If he held the knife to Emilio's throat, he might be able to buy some time or even their escape. Maldito gave his cigarillo a long puff, letting the smoke drift from his face. "I can see you're struggling to know your best play. What if I made the decision easier for you?" Without hesitation and with one motion, he drew a black handgun from behind his back and cocked it. The sound as he fired it was deafening.

Chapter 29

It took a second for both Jack and Juan to open their eyes to see that Maldito had shot Emilio in the chest, who dropped to the ground while Jack stood horrified at the coldness of this killer. As Jack raised his arms overhead, he let the knife slip from his grip and fall to the ground. Juan, instead, approached Maldito, fury blazing in his eyes, and Maldito struck him hard with his backhand, sending Juan to the dusty floor with a thud. The second man grabbed Jack and pressed a gun to his back.

Maldito snapped, "Take this nuisance and the dead pig's brother into the barn, and don't let them escape this time. Let them imagine their last moments before we finish them for good."

The short, husky bandit pulled Juan to his feet and marched them to the large barn where they had been held a handful of days before. This time their pockets were checked, and the man took Jack's pen knife from him. Then he pushed them into the stable cell and slammed the heavy door shut, locking it tight.

"Are you okay, Juan?" Jack gestured to the dark bruise beginning to show itself on the side of Juan's face where he had been struck by Maldito.

Juan snapped, "I don't think this bruise is what's going to do me in. How are we going to get out of this?"

Jack scanned the dim stable cell and slammed his hand against the cell wall. "Why did I ever get you involved with this? You're only a kid."

Juan stared, serious. "Well, I'm a kid whose brother was brutally murdered by that sadist. I knew there was a reason I felt like something was wrong or unfinished the other day.

Justice felt empty, and now I know why. Don't ever apologize for me being here."

Jack paced the enclosed area, kicking the dirty straw beneath his feet. "What do you mean you 'knew there was a reason'?"

Juan shook his head. "I don't know. There was something fishy about that day, and here we see a dead man walking around as if nothing happened. Think of what Emilio said: 'You seek justice while others play.' What did he mean by that? All I know is that this guy is evil."

Jack patted Juan on the back. "We may have some time to figure something out. Either he wants us to sweat it out for a while, or he has to wait for someone's okay. Maybe that's Hector?"

Juan muttered, "I don't know. He didn't hesitate to shoot one of his own men."

Later that evening, they heard the door being unlocked, and then a rifle appeared through the opening. The lighting was poor, and a short, barrel-chested man entered the room, waving them back with his rifle. He held a bucket in the other hand that he lowered to the ground as he kept his eyes on Jack and Juan. It was the high cheekbones, deep-set eyes, and weather-beaten skin that caught Jack's attention as the man grunted and then left, slamming the door shut and turning the lock.

Juan checked out the food and water bottles in the bucket as Jack remained deep in thought. "What is it?" asked Juan.

"I've seen that man before."

"Probably here. We've seen lots of nasty-looking men here," whispered Juan. "What's so interesting about him?"

"I don't know. He has a pretty distinctive look. That's it!"

"What's it?" asked Juan.

"He's the man who was with Maldito in the Van Horn barn. He's the other guy that Sam shot—dead, I thought."

"*Señor* Russo, what's going on here?" asked Juan, rubbing his face with one hand.

"I wish I knew. We know Sam was shot, but it's not likely this guy and Maldito took bullets. They are walking around as if nothing happened. I also know Maldito is out of patience with us. You are much too young to—well, you know." Jack's voice trailed off.

Juan stared down at the ground. "You are not so old, yourself. I've wanted so badly to bring Jesus's killer to justice that I was willing to die to make that happen, but now—" He paused. "But it looks like I'll die without any justice. Do you ever think about dying? I mean, really dying?"

Jack thought about Juan's question. "Yeah. Part of me almost looked forward to it, to end the agony memories, but another part of me wouldn't let death rob me of making things right. I'm coming to believe that killing Maria's killer won't make things right. It would only satisfy my desire for revenge, which may not solve anything. Maria would still be gone, and I'd still be alone. Still, the thought of him not paying for what he did makes me sick. I want him to pay. I still *need* him to pay, so I don't want to die."

"But have you ever thought about death, you know, what happens after?" pressed Juan.

Jack replied, "Oh, I see. Well, I've thought a lot about seeing my wife again someday, so I guess I have. I had a tough time for a while believing God would allow that to happen, but I think I was just angry with God. I still believed. A lot of priests keep reminding me that we can't change the way God loves us; it's really about us seeing and trusting God's will. I'm working on it."

Juan said, "So you believe in heaven?"

Jack nodded.

"I know my mother and grandmother believe it without any question. No matter how hard life has been, they never seem to doubt. It's like their source of strength. I guess that's always made an impression on me, but I've kind of stopped going to church since college. And I feel like something's missing."

"Juan, you are as impressive a kid as I've ever run into. You have a good heart, and you want to do the right thing for your family. I'm not giving up hope here, either."

"But you can't go to heaven if you have grave sin on your soul— if you've turned your back on his commandments. I've had anger and hate in my heart for so long now. I haven't worked on my relationship with God, and I've wanted my brother's killer dead. I've wanted to be the one who does it. Might be a roadblock to heaven, huh?"

Jack put his arm around Juan's shoulder. "I guess we're in the same boat. It's never too late to be sorry for those things. I've been told that God will always forgive us if we are truly sorry. Plus, I have a feeling that you have a few people at home praying for you every day."

Nodding, Juan said, "And you have Siena now. I think it would mean a lot to her if you stay alive. Before she found out you were her father, she told me she admired you, felt a connection. She's not a shy girl, by any means, but she doesn't get close to anyone. I think she's been afraid to, but you've been different for her. I can tell."

Jack said, "That's nice of you to say. I know you've been a good friend to her, and I appreciate it. Now, let's see if we can figure out how to get ourselves out of this."

Since there was no exit to the stable cell, they talked about rushing the guard as he entered and seeing if they could make a break for it. What else could they do but take advantage of the first opportunity they had before Maldito's plans for their execution?

The evening was quiet as they tried to sleep. Jack thought about the likelihood that neither he nor Juan would survive the next day. What would his fate in the afterlife be? He had drifted from his faith in many ways but never lost touch with its place in his life. This was mostly due to his relationship with Father Tom in Boston. Did that count as attending to his faith and preparing his soul? He'd been so obsessed with his hunt for justice that he neglected making his life a meaningful one, a giving one. Father Diaz said that Jesus didn't ask us to be vengeful; He asked us to be loving, forgiving, and selfless. Father Tom never gave him a specific answer to what criteria God used to send people to heaven or hell. Did we have to be exceptionally good saints or just not evil? How could people that dedicated their lives to others get the same treatment as those who never bothered to be truly Christian at heart or in their actions?

Turbulent thoughts raced through his head most of the night, along with images about the actual confrontation to come with Maldito. As much as he worked to maintain a calm and rational exterior, interiorly, anxiety was beginning to overwhelm him as the early light of day filled the narrow opening under the door. It was several hours before they heard the loud click of the door. Jack's heart raced when he realized they had missed their chance to jump the guard on the way in when the door opened. Like a dark specter, Maldito stood before them and aimed a gun at them.

Maldito gestured for Jack to get onto his feet. "I'd like to wish you a good morning, but I don't think you are going to have one today. Come with me, Mr. Russo."

Juan jumped up. "Where are you taking him?"

Jack could picture his squinty eyes behind the dark sunglasses that rested on his hawk-like nose. He offered a sadistic half-smile. "*Entonces, ¿quieres mirar, hermano del cerdo?*"

Jack could see the fire in Juan's eyes as he spat back, "Don't ever call my brother a pig again!"

Maldito snorted. "I like your spunk, *pequeño cerdo*. Would you like to watch your friend's last morning of being a nuisance to me?"

171

Juan surprised Jack by rushing Maldito, who, without hesitation, pulled the trigger of his gun. The loud blast sent Juan to the ground, blood running down the wound in his shoulder. "I didn't want to make things too quick, but don't test me," he warned as he motioned both of them out into the larger center of the barn.

They sat down on two short stools in the dark shadows. Juan alternately winced and glared as he clutched his shoulder to stop the bleeding.

Maldito held the gun by his side, eyeing his two condemned prisoners. "You two have been a thorn in my side, and I don't much like thorns. Your brother was a thorn for too long."

Clearly, Juan seethed as he tried to watch for an opportunity to rush his executioner.

Maldito turned to Jack. "So, Mr. Russo, you should know what you're being convicted of to deserve such a harsh sentence."

"I appreciate that," replied Jack trying to buy some time.

Maldito smiled. "So calm and calculating. First, you came and showed no respect to an important man. You, an arrogant American *gringo*, defied him, stole his daughter, and showed no regard for Mexican family honor. That alone deserves the death penalty, for sure. You have violated our businesses and have seen too much to let you go. I can tell you'd like to kill me out of revenge, and any reasonable man could claim self-defense."

"Let the boy go," demanded Jack.

Maldito laughed. "You are in no position to make any demands—and I don't think he's any less dangerous to me than you. Now, tell me why you think I have a choice in this matter."

Jack sat up. "I treated Maria with love and respect. I didn't want to disrespect her family, but I couldn't live without her. It is you who disrespected the family by brutally killing Maria. You were there that day, weren't you? You left

Hector's granddaughter without her parents. *You're* the guilty one."

Maldito tilted his head, exposing the sinister eyes behind his sunglasses. "There is much you don't know, and it's a shame you'll never know the whole story nor spend time with your daughter now."

Jack thought about Siena and fought off the nightmarish images of Maria burning in the fire. "You won't get away with this. Others will come until you pay the price. If it isn't the sheriff, it will be Sam. Their sense of loyalty is based on something you'll never know anything about in your selfish and empty world."

Maldito stepped toward Jack. "I wish I had more time to shed some light on your fantasy, but it's time—or should I say the end of your time."

Before Jack could react, Maldito held the gun to his head. Jack shook inside as he felt the hard metal against his skull. He heard the blast and the deafening ringing in his left ear. There was no feeling of pain as his eyes opened, and Maldito fell forward on top of him. Behind him stood Juan holding a large knife covered in the blood of the devil himself.

Jack pushed the dead weight of Maldito's body off him, and it slumped to the dirt floor of the large empty barn. He rolled him over, his glasses mangled and dirt on his face as his sinister eyes barely opened. Still alive, he smiled at Jack to utter his last words with a pained laugh. "You really think Sam is a loyal friend, don't you? I guess I get the last laugh," he mumbled as his last breath drifted from his lungs.

Frozen, the stunned expression remained on Juan's face. "Is he dead?"

"You saved my life—and your own. I have no doubt that you were next. You had no choice." Jack pressed his hand against Maldito's chest and could feel no signs of a bullet hole from Sam's gun.

Juan stared down at Maldito's lifeless body contorted on the ground and muttered, "I know. I don't feel anything except relief."

Jack cautioned, "That won't last long. They're going to be expecting him to come out of this barn soon. He pointed to Juan's hand that held the knife. "Where did you get that?" asked Jack.

Juan shook his head to break his trance-like state. "What? This is Siena's knife. When you dropped it in the stable, I let him strike me so that I could fall on top of it. I didn't want you to know I had it, in case you wanted to take it from me."

"Let's see if you can be as clever and get us out of here."

Chapter 30

Jack and Juan cautiously approached the barn door opening, staying in the shadows. Jack ran back to Maldito's body. He tugged off his black shirt, slipped off his sunglasses, and grabbed his black hat, and put them on. "If we make our way across the compound, we may be able to make it back to the truck."

Juan said, "It's risky, but we don't have time for any alternative plans."

They waited until several men headed into the ranch house and a truck drove off. The compound yard remained quiet, and Jack held Maldito's gun to Juan's head as he marched him across the open area to the truck and horse trailer still parked alongside the stable barn. They quietly opened the doors and climbed in. Jack started up the engine, but before he could put the truck in gear. "*¿Jefe, a dónde lo llevas?*" His heart dropped as he heard a voice approach the driver's-side window.

As Jack turned his head toward the voice, he could tell it was the man with the high-cheekbones he had encountered earlier. Jack leaped from the truck, and the man immediately recognized that he wasn't Maldito. Jack gave him a hard chop behind the neck and pulled him into the back cab before jumping back in and taking off, waving at the guard at the gate as he sped off. A mile down the road, he pulled over and dragged the man with the high-cheekbones from the back cab and dropped him on the side of the road. In minutes, he returned in Calle's truck and then headed out of Prâxedis and across the border toward Van Horn.

"Keep pressing on that wound," Jack pleaded with Juan. "We'll get that taken care of. How're you doing?"

Juan looked at the blood on his hand and pressed down harder. "I'll be okay."

"I mean, how are you doing inside?"

Juan stared out the passenger-side window. "I'm okay. How are you?"

"I wish I knew. I feel like there's still some unfinished business," replied Jack.

"What do you think he meant—about never knowing the whole story and about Sam's loyalty?"

Jack sighed. "I'm trying to sort that out. I haven't wanted to believe it, but I have a feeling that Hector is behind this, and maybe Sam knows something about it. I don't know, but *I'm fixin' to find out*," replied Jack with a twang to his voice.

Juan chuckled. "You've been spending way too much time in Texas."

"Y'all think so?" Jack sped down the highway, trying to piece together what he was missing. *Why did Maldito say, "You really think Sam is a loyal friend, don't you? I guess I get the last laugh." Why would he have the last laugh? When they were in the barn in Van Horn, three men were shot, Maldito, the man with the high cheekbones, and Sam. All shot in the upper body and now all showing no signs that they were hit. Sam was the only one with a wound to his leg. Why would Maldito shoot Emilio when I had Siena's knife to his throat? He could have just let me do the dirty work. I can't trust a guy like Maldito to do anything but try to poison the well. He killed Maria, and now he's dead.*

Jack reached the hospital in a little more than an hour. The registration administrator glanced up at Juan and then at Jack. Raising her eyebrows, she said, "I know one thing. I don't think I'd be hanging around with you these days. It seems like everyone gets shot!"

Jack agreed as he wished Juan good luck before heading down the hall to see how Sam and Ramos were doing.

Siena spotted him in the hallway. Relief flooded her face as she ran to him. "You had me so worried," she exclaimed as she wrapped Jack in a hug.

"We're okay," said Jack as he embraced her.

"Where's Juan?" she asked, staring down the hallway.

"He's going to be okay. He took a bullet to his shoulder area, but it doesn't look too serious."

Her brow tightened with concern. "Easy for you to say when he's the one who's shot. What happened?"

Jack relayed the events of the two days and how Maldito met his final demise, first to her and then to Ramos and Sam.

"What the heck is happening?" pleaded Sam as he stood, appearing much stronger on his feet.

Jack shook his head. "I'm not sure, Sam. I think the only course I have is to see Hector face-to-face and find out the whole story. I need you to tell me where he lives in Juarez."

Sam shook his head. "That's just not a good idea, especially after what happened to us the last time. Let me see if I can reason with him and find out what's going on. Can you hang on to let me do that? My guess is that you're better off dropping this and taking your girl home to Boston. Start living your life. I would think that's what Maria would want, instead of risking something seriously dangerous happening."

Jack walked over and patted Sam's shoulder. "You're my best and oldest friend, Sam. I trust you more than anyone, but I need to do this before I can move on."

Sam glanced at Siena. "Please, talk some sense into this guy." He grabbed Jack's arm. "This isn't a game down here. I don't know what the deal is, but I can't see it making anything better. I need you to trust me on this."

The intensity in Sam's eyes spoke volumes. As he walked out of the room, visibly upset, Jack started after him, stopped only by the sound of Ramos's hushed voice. "Russo!"

Curious, Jack reversed his direction and stepped over to Ramos's hospital bed. "What is it?" Ramos rolled his eyes toward Siena and then back to Jack, who apologetically motioned Siena out of the room. She reluctantly left, and Jack repeated his question. "What is it?"

"I don't know anything for sure on this, but I wanted to let you know that I had the county police check on a few things while I've been in here."

Jack furrowed his brow in confused curiosity. "What kind of things?"

"They got a call from Detective Sergeant Brooks in Boston. It appears that they uncovered an officer in his squad being paid to provide information to someone down here—on you."

"Me?" exclaimed Jack. "What kind of things?"

Ramos replied, "He got him to confess to having told someone that you've been alive all these years and have been looking for Maria's killer and Rosalina's kidnapper. If you were getting close, they were to be informed. When Father Fitzpatrick told you about the girl's photo in that school in El Paso, they were told."

Open-mouthed, Jack dropped into the leather cushioned visitor's chair. "That might explain the sudden fire to destroy all the records at the school? I wonder if that explains the attack on the highway to El Paso where I was left to be run over? Did he say who this cop has been talking to?"

Ramos shook his head. "He only had a number and a code name, *Doses*, but there's more."

Suddenly, the door to Ramos' room slammed shut. Jack darted over to try to open the door, but it was jammed shut. He could only bang on the heavy frame as he heard several screams from the other side, screams that became fainter each time. Jack turned and faced the police officer. "What's going on?"

Ramos blurted, "Sam was wearing a bullet-proof vest when he was brought into the hospital. That explains why the first shot to his body didn't penetrate, and he only received a wound to his leg."

Jack banged again on the door. "What does that have to do with anything? He said he came prepared."

Ramos said, "He showed up at just the right time to save the day. The same way he showed up just in time to find you in Van Horn."

Jack shook his head as he approached Ramos and chided, "What are you saying? Sam was trying to help me!" Jack turned to the window and spotted Sam shoving Siena into the back seat of a yellow car as another woman stood with her hands over her head, screaming at Sam. He couldn't believe what he was seeing. Where was Sam taking Siena, and why was he being so rough with her? He squeezed his eyes shut as the room started to spin. "Are you trying to say that Sam is somehow involved with Maldito and his gang?"

Ramos replied, "His vest and the gun he used were both purchased at the same time as a shipment for similar armor, and guns were shipped to that warehouse."

Jack darted to the door as it opened, and a nurse came in.

Ramos yelled out, "Russo, where are you going?"

With fresh fury, Jack glared at Ramos. "I just saw Sam forcing Siena into a stolen car. I'm going after him!"

Chapter 31

Jack sprinted down the hall and out the hospital door, fishing keys out of his pocket before jumping into Siena's pickup truck. He drove out of town in the direction he saw Sam drive but was too far behind to see the yellow car. They were heading in the direction of *El Patron's* ranch. Jack reached back to the storage case in Siena's car and pulled out the Winchester rifle. Before he reached the road to the ranch, he saw the yellow car off to the side of the road. Panicked, he jumped out of the car and checked. The car was abandoned. In the distance, the dust of a large black vehicle continued down the highway, back toward Van Horn.

He quickly jumped back into the truck and sped after them, going close to 120 miles per hour. As he closed the gap, the black vehicle accelerated and tore down the road taking a right, heading north onto Route 54. Siena's old truck couldn't keep up with the black car, but Jack kept an eye on the vehicle far ahead as drivers veered to the shoulder to avoid being hit in the high-speed chase.

Ten miles had passed with no turns off of Route 54, and the black vehicle continued to pull further ahead toward the rocky mountain range. As he raced after him, Jack wondered if he was chasing the right car. *There's got to be an explanation for Sam's behavior. What is he afraid of? How mixed up was he in this? And where the hell is he going?*

After another twenty miles of highway, he could only catch a glimmer of the black vehicle up ahead, along with signs for Guadalupe National Park and Guadalupe Peak. Looking down and noticing the gas gauge reading close to empty, anxiety welled up in him. He wouldn't be able to stay with him if this chase went on for too long and he couldn't find the phone Juan had left with him. For the next thirty miles,

180

thoughts raced through his head while he continued to check the gauge, getting closer and closer to the empty mark.

The low fuel warning light finally came on, and rage tore through him at the thought of losing his daughter because of an empty gas tank. He banged his fist on the steering wheel. *Where is he going?!*

He felt as if the mountains were now on top of him, seeing signs for *El Capitan,* Guadalupe Peak, and several hiking trails. The raw beauty of the land was not something he could appreciate at the moment. He pressed down harder on the gas pedal, hoping the high speed would keep him going, even if the tank ran dry. He squinted as he thought he could just make out the black car turning off the road up ahead. By the time he reached the turn-off, he noticed the sign for Pine Spring Canyon and made a quick turn, running out of gas about a half-mile down the road. Grabbing the rifle and slamming the door shut, he sprinted down the road, which turned out to be less than a quarter-mile to the parking area where an abandoned black SUV was parked on the edge of the road. Sam must have left the car outside the ranch when he surprised them in the barn.

The day was hot, and there was only one other car in the parking area as he spotted two hikers—a young man and a woman—heading toward him, appearing shaken. The man wore a bandana around his long frizzy hair that matched his uneven beard. He was pulling the girl behind him when he noticed the rifle in Jack's hand.

Jack called out, "Don't worry. You don't have to worry about me. Did you see a man with a young woman?"

The young man pointed toward the trail they had just returned on. "Something's not right. The girl's hands were tied, and a man with a gun was pulling her along. They're probably half to three-quarters of a mile down the trail to Devil's Hall."

Jack pleaded, "Was the girl okay?"

"She was struggling and angry, but she didn't appear to be injured. We tried to say something, but the man held out his gun and warned us to take off. We hauled back here to get to the park ranger and report it," stammered the worried young man.

Racing along the rocky path, Jack yelled over his shoulder, "Call the police as quick as you can!"

Jack thought the wound in Sam's leg would slow him down. How could he have gotten this far on that leg? Then he remembered how the pain had never stopped Sam in the past when he had a job to do or a game to compete in. Underneath his playful exterior, he was a driven man in many aspects of his life. He wasn't one to be beaten at anything.

Jack reached a fifty-foot tiered rock staircase made out of thin layers of eroding limestone. The stone steps were so narrow and slippery that he had a hard time scaling the rock ledges. At one point, he slipped and noticed fresh blood on the limestone and a small piece of colorful blue-and-white worn fabric. The material appeared familiar to him, but he couldn't quite place where he'd seen it before. At the top of a set of steps, there was a pool of water and the second set of stairs, followed by a winding canyon with fallen boulders. He concentrated on the rocky trail.

Suddenly, he came upon a narrow slot canyon with hundred-foot tall vertical limestone walls that were no more than fifteen feet apart and much narrower in some sections. With the sun being blocked by the sides of the cliffs on each side, there was an eerie feeling about entering the dark corridor, and he wondered if he had entered the infamous Devil's Hall. At the base, Jack spotted another small piece of blue-and-white cloth material. He now remembered seeing the material before; it was the threadbare, blue-and-white kerchief that Siena had let him use to wipe his scraped cheek when she saved him on the highway to El Paso.

As he entered the narrow canyon corridor, his heart

pounded. Holding the small piece of material, he yelled out, "Siena!" Her name echoed off the canyon walls.

What echoed louder was a bullet shot from above into the canyon, which ricocheted off of the limestone rock just behind him. He ducked down and peered up to see where the shot had come from. "Sam? Sam, let's talk this out! There's got to be a reasonable explanation."

Another shot ricocheted closer to his head and off one side of the canyon wall, creating a cloud of limestone dust. "There's nothing to talk about, Jimmy! Just go back to Boston, where you belong!"

Jack kept moving ahead, shifting from side to side to see if he could tell where Sam was. "Tell me that Siena is all right!"

Sam yelled down, "Just go back, and she will be well taken care of." Sam shot again, down into the canyon, missing him by a wider margin, making Jack think that he had lost sight of him on this side of the canyon.

Jack squatted down and tossed a stone across to the other side. There was a shot that hit the spot where the stone had landed, leaving Jack to think that Sam was seriously trying to hit him. What was he so afraid of? They had once been the best of friends. "Sam, Maldito is dead. You have nothing to fear now. I can help you!"

Sam's laugh echoed through the walls of the narrow canyon. "You're going to help me? Help me do what? Help me have the life I wanted? You had a family growing up. You had your own family with Maria and Rosalina. Why does everything I desperately wanted come so easily to you? If you really want to help me get what I want, what I deserved—then leave and never come back!"

Jack made a quick move to another boulder and pulled back as he heard the blast and the dust spray from another bullet striking the limestone wall. "You've always been my best and most loyal friend. Why are you trying to kill me? What did I do?"

Silence.

Jack stretched his neck and could see nothing. He darted further down the corridor to total silence. Finally, he reached the end of Devil's Hall and noticed another small piece of cloth on the rocks above. He had to scale the rocky slope until he reached the top, but there was no sight of Sam or Siena. The last thing he wanted to do was to go in the wrong direction. Frantic, he ran one way and then up another trail to search for a clue or a fragment of the blue-and-white cloth. His chest tightened painfully until he finally noticed a piece of cloth at the base of a jagged stone.

Despite the rugged path of the trail ascending the mountain, Jack managed to jump from stone to stone and running where the trail allowed, then climbing the rock face where it became more vertical. At one juncture, he stopped to squeeze through the narrow part of a carved-out stone, trying to determine if they could have come this way—when there was an echo of a gunshot from a distance that hit the rock face and grazed the back of his neck. Reflexively, he quickly grabbed his neck, feeling the wetness of a trickle of blood as he ducked down. He could barely hear Sam's voice in the distance. "Go back!"

"Why are you doing this?" Jack screamed.

"Just go back! Why try to live in the past?! I'll give you the girl if you promise to never come back!" yelled Sam.

Jack thought about Sam's offer. Could he make this promise to save his daughter and let go of finding Maria's killer? He was pretty sure it was Maldito, and maybe justice had already been served, but, like Juan, he knew perfectly well there was more to this story. He didn't know if Siena would come to Boston, and he didn't want to leave her. Why was Sam giving him this ultimatum? "Put down your gun, and let's talk about it!" yelled Jack. "I'm sure there's some mistake!"

The next words he heard had been the same ones that had haunted him for two decades. "The mistake was yours!" yelled Sam.

Jack felt dizzy as he heard the words in Sam's voice. The same words he heard from the men in black that invaded his home that day. Jack dropped to the ground behind a boulder, a flood of thoughts racing through his mind. He squeezed his eyes tight until there was nothing but darkness—picturing the door burst open. Four men in black with black masks and guns. He could clearly see the man to the left puffing on the cigarillo as he pleaded with them, "There must be some mistake!"

The response didn't come from Maldito but from the man in the middle. He could hear the words being slowly spoken: "The mistake was yours." And then there was a flash of light, no sound, only the feeling of being hit by a cannonball in the abdomen. Maldito didn't shoot him! It had to have come from one of the other men, possibly the one standing in the middle, the man who had uttered those words in that same voice. Jack squeezed his eyes tighter as an avalanche of emotions and thoughts flooded him. He couldn't process what he was thinking, but the pieces of the puzzle seemed to only confirm it. If Sam was one of the men in black and the one who pulled the trigger, how did he know Jack had lived? He would have to be the one to whom the informant in the Boston Police Department was feeding information. *What was the code name—'Doses'? Doses. Sam Engres, Doses. What does that mean? Dos means 'two'. And the letters 'e' and 's' were the initials for Sam Engres, backward. Sam was a junior. Sam Engres II. Sam always played with code names you had to decipher in college.* "Oh my God."

After a long moment of silence, Sam yelled down, "Are you still alive down there?"

"Yes, but no thanks to you! Why? Why did you do it?" cried Jack. "Why did you try to kill me?"

Silence.

Jack lifted the Winchester to see if Sam would fire, but there was no shot. He must be on the move again. Jack carefully got

185

up, still crouching to make sure he was not being set up. He started back up the side of the mountain, periodically finding small pieces of Siena's kerchief to keep him on the trail and to let him know she was still okay. Jack figured her mouth had been gagged, or she would have been screaming out for him, regardless of the danger. The ascent became steeper and more challenging as he got closer to the summit, where he, finally, caught a glimpse of two figures.

Jack reached another spot where he had to squeeze through and pull himself up while trying to find places to secure his footing. Two rapid shots hit the rock that his hand was clutching.

"I'm not going to make the same offer a third time!" yelled Sam.

"Before I accept, tell me why you tried to kill me! In the apartment, and then outside of El Paso? You are *Doses*, right?"

Sam's laugh carried down the mountain. "Very clever. Yes, I found out that you lived and kept tabs on you, but you were never close enough to worry about. When your priest friend told you about the photo, I had to get rid of the evidence. And when you came down, I couldn't let you keep poking your nose in places it didn't belong!"

"Why did you have to kill Maria?"

There was a long pause with no response. "That was an accident!"

"You killed Homer to set me up, didn't you?!"

"It was a way of getting you out of the way and letting you live. You should have been grateful!" yelled Sam as he pulled the trigger, narrowly missing Jack.

"What happened? Why did you do this?" cried Jack as he maneuvered out of the creviced area of the rock and made his way closer, shielded by thick brush.

"You don't know what it's like to have no family to give you a home and love. I deserved better. I needed better than that.

I liked you, but I wanted what you had, what I needed, and what you didn't appreciate," screamed Sam hysterically. "When you met Maria, you took the girl I loved. That's right; I loved Maria! It was painful to watch you two being so happy together, and then when you had Rosalina, you had the family that should have been mine. I envied you and your family. I felt contempt and anger. I couldn't take it anymore, but you wanted me to be Rosalina's godfather—to watch you, up close and personal, have the life *I* wanted. Do you know how that made me feel?!" screamed Sam.

Jack crept up behind Sam. "Put the gun down, Sam. Let's talk."

Sam didn't turn. Instead, he raised his gun toward Siena. "Drop your gun," Sam said, "and I promise she will live."

Something hit the ground.

Jack had kicked a rock, and Sam turned and aimed his gun at Jack, most likely assuming the noise had been the Winchester being dropped. Jack dropped to the ground and rolled to avoid the round of fire.

"I told you I wouldn't make the offer a third time!"

As Sam aimed at Jack, Siena, with tied hands and tape over her mouth, kicked Sam in the side, making his shot go astray. Sam pushed her off with his free hand, sending her over the side of the mountain. Sam peered down to where she fell as Jack turned and fired the Winchester for the first time, narrowly missing Sam, who ducked, glaring at Jack. He fired back several rounds at Jack, but Jack's only thought was getting to Siena to see if she was alive. He wedged himself behind a boulder and pulled the trigger, coming closer to Sam. "Sam, let's cut this out. She may need help!"

Sam took cover behind the stone at the peak and fired back at Jack, hitting the boulder in front of him. "You had plenty of chances to avoid this. Just go back home!" He fired his rifle again, just missing Jack's head as he tried to steal a look from the rock.

Jack, looking for a spot with a better vantage point, yelled, "Just answer me one thing. Did Hector order his men to come to Boston?"

Sam let go of three more rounds. "Yes, but what's the difference?"

"All the difference in the world," replied Jack as he shot and darted to another spot, dodging a return shot. "I can understand him coming after me, but not Maria. If you loved Maria so much, why would you be part of it?"

"I told you, that was an accident. Not part of the plan. It was your fault, and now you're letting another person you love die!" shouted Sam as he aimed for another round.

Without further hesitation, Jack aimed his gun. "Not if I can help it!" He stood and fired the Winchester. The bullet slammed into Sam, lifting him off his feet and onto his back. Jack sprinted toward him with his rifle ready, grabbed Sam's rifle, and hurled it from the peak and down the side of the mountain. His heart raced as he scanned the mountainside to spot Siena. No sight. He scaled down the vertical cliff and found her lying on a rock landing.

Jack saw blood beneath her head, and her arm contorted from the fall. He frantically felt for a pulse, almost in too much of a panic to feel the faint throb in the vein of her neck. He quickly lifted her unconscious body, hoisted her over his shoulder, and started down the steep decline. "You're too strong to let this lick you. Don't die on me now," he said aloud as he maneuvered each step of the trail, zig-zagging down until he reached the crossroad with the Devil's Hall Trail, where he met two park rangers, who had been alerted by the two hikers.

"We've got to get her to the hospital, now!" shouted Jack.

One of the rangers replied, "Don't worry. With all the shots, we ordered a Medivac helicopter, and it should be here in a matter of minutes. Are you okay? There's blood on the back of your shirt."

"I'm fine. There's a man shot at the peak of the mountain, so your Medivac is going to need to take another trip." Within minutes, the chopper was hovering above, and the medics carefully placed Siena into the stretcher and lifted it to the open door. Once she was in and they got the thumbs up from the EMT, Jack started to climb back up the mountain trail.

"Sir, where are you going with that rifle?" questioned the ranger.

Jack turned and handed it to him. "Hold this. I need to go back up." One ranger took the rifle while the other followed Jack up the trail.

Chapter 32

By the time Jack and the ranger had reached the peak, there was no sign of Sam. Jack scanned the area for a clue but could only find blood from his wound where he had collapsed. "See if you can see any blood heading out from this spot," said Jack.

The ranger inquired, "How was he wounded?"

"He injured the girl and tried to kill me, so I shot him in self-defense."

The ranger scratched his head. "He tried to kill you, and now you're trying to save him?"

Jack shrugged. "To tell you the truth, I don't know if I came up here to save him or finish him off." They made wider circles around the area until they found blood spots leading down a back trail, where they found Sam on the ground, blood covering the front of this shirt. Sam opened his eyes and jerked back as Jack came at him, but Jack only tore a piece of his own shirt and pressed firmly on the wound to stop the bleeding. "Hang on. There's a helicopter coming."

"Why are you helping me?" murmured Sam as he winced with pain. "Just let me die here."

Jack smirked. "That might be too good for you. Plus, I don't think I hit your heart—not that it would've made a difference. Siena told me to aim an inch above what I wanted to hit with that old Winchester, so I aimed two inches. Stupid loyalty thing I have."

It was around twenty minutes before the Medivac returned to take Sam to the hospital. After the helicopter left, Jack and the ranger hiked back down the mountainside.

Ramos stood at the bottom of the trail, appearing relieved that Jack was still alive. Jack smiled and shook his head, seeing Ramos with his arm in a sling. "I'm looking for a new

190

deputy, Mr. Russo." Before he could pat Jack on the back, he saw the blood on the back of his shirt and turned his body to see the wound on the back of Jack's neck. "Let's have that taken care of, Cowboy Jack."

"I'm sure the ranger here can clean this up himself. I have someone to see," replied Jack.

"And who might that be? We've got Sam."

Jack replied, "Sam just gave me Hector Encando's address in Juarez, and I have some unfinished business to discuss."

Ramos shook his head. "If this is *El Patron*, I'd better go with you."

Shaking his head, Jack said, "I need to do this myself. You make sure Sam doesn't escape and Siena and Juan are doing okay." As he started for the truck, he turned and added, "Please make sure they take care of Siena."

Jack took off for the border to the Juarez Valley. On the way, he found himself praying for Siena, hoping her injuries weren't too serious. The hour-and-a-half ride seemed to take forever as he continued to have flashbacks of courting Maria, then being rejected by Hector, and finally, the attack on his family in Boston. He started anticipating what to expect when he got to Hector's residence. Would he be stopped or even killed at the gate? And, if he did get in, how would Hector react to him after all these years?

He finally found his way through the maze of streets to the gate in front of Hector's home. It was not the same home in which he had spent time with Maria. He passed the entrance before pulling over, then glanced down at the Winchester laying in the back but decided not to take it. He opened the truck door and approached the gate where two men stood. He stepped toward the gate entrance, waiting for the guards to stop him, but surprisingly, one of them merely looked him over, then opened the large iron entrance gate. Behind it was a long driveway of pea stones and finely landscaped gardens on each side. He couldn't turn back, but tension mounted in his chest as he got closer to the large home built of finely cut stone. Another two guards stood by the large carved wooden doors to the front entrance. Again, they said nothing and made no move to stop him, checking only to see if he was armed before opening the doors to the home.

The odds were that this was a setup and possibly the last moments of his life, so he made a quick Sign of the Cross, and his eardrums pulsed with the rapid beating of his heart. He took a deep breath as he stepped carefully, crossing through the foyer, and then peered into a large open room, full of antiques and artifacts of Mexican history, obvious signs that Hector's business had made him an even richer man than he had been twenty years earlier when Jack had first met him.

In the next room, where lights hung over a long shiny wooden table, he could see a gray-haired figure sitting with his hands folded on the table and smoking a large cigar. The room was dimly lit, so it took him several seconds to recognize the man—Hector *"El Patron"* Engando.

"Come in. I've been expecting you," said the gravelly, almost hoarse-sounding man.

Except for Hector's jet-black hair now being gray, Jack recognized him immediately. He could never forget the deep-set coffee brown eyes under his thick eyebrows, the coarse bronze skin, and his broad facial structure. He was an imposing figure, physically and with the strong aura he projected. Neither one of them said a word for several minutes, determining how this was best going to play out. Jack expected some of Hector's men to make an entrance from behind, but here they were, alone in this large dining room.

Hector spoke. "You look good for someone who's been dead for twenty years."

Jack's eyes narrowed. "On your orders?"

Hector shook his head. "I told my men to bring back the daughter who had been taken from me, nothing more."

Jack snorted, then snapped his words, "You told them to kill your own daughter?"

Hector held his cigar in his right hand as the smoke drifted upward. "You of all people know I could never do that—*would* never do that!"

Jack glared at him. "Don't your men follow your orders?"

"Yes, they do. The only orders were to bring back Maria and Rosalina. At the time, I felt that you had no right to them. You did not respect the family, which showed me that you did not deserve Maria, that you wouldn't know how to love her for life," replied Hector in a stern tone.

Jack paused. "I was young, and you were right to demand more from the man that would deserve Maria's hand in marriage. I loved her, even if it was infatuation at first. I loved your daughter—and I still do."

"I know you do," responded Hector.

"What?" Surprised, Jack wanted answers.

"I know you loved her and were willing to unselfishly give her your love for life, but I did not believe that then, and I was angry. I should not have made my rejection of your proposal so definite. I put you in an impossible situation. I'm sorry for that, and I'm sorry for the agony of the last twenty years." Hector met Jack's gaze across the long table.

Jack shook his head. He was still angry, but conflicting emotions battled inside him as tears rolled down his face. "What are you saying? How can you say what you are saying?"

"Diego, I couldn't have been angrier than I was when you took Maria from us after I told you that she could not marry you. Your actions were the ultimate insult to our family, but what was even more important was knowing she was with a man who was not a man of integrity, not a man that deserved a girl such as Maria. When I found out where you were, I told my men to bring them back, not to harm you. Your friend, Sam Engres, was not part of the plan. He had worked for me when you were here in college and made a proposition to help develop more legitimate businesses for me if I would hire him permanently. What I did not know was that he, too, was in love with my daughter and would do anything to get her away from you. He only wanted to work for me to be near her, to have her and Rosalina to himself."

Jack pleaded, "He told you that?"

Hector stood up and approached Jack. "I only found out much of this very recently. Sam Engres has two very distinct sides to his nature—a friendly guy, a great businessman, and very thoughtful when it came to my family. He built up the legal part of our business, or so I thought."

"So you thought?"

Hector shook his head at Sam's deception. "He formed an alliance with some of my men."

"Maldito?"

"Yes, and some of his soldiers. They used our operations to expand the business into more profitable areas: drugs, kidnapping, and extortion. They allied with the Sinaloa cartel in the Valley, destroying towns like Guadalupe and Prâxedis. They used killing and fear to take over these areas and used my ranch for smuggling things I never wanted to be part of. Emilio found out about these traitors and also about you still being alive," explained Hector.

Jack nodded. "So that is why Maldito shot Emilio without hesitation?"

Hector's eyes dropped. "I think so. I had built the ranch and transportation warehouse in Van Horn to get my family away from the dangers of the war here in the valley, but they only used them for their own purposes. I've been trying to distance us from all of this, but it's not so easy in this business to do so without losing your family." Hector stared at the smoke rising from his cigar.

"Why are you telling me all of this? Why aren't you trying to kill me?" demanded Jack.

"Because you are my—" He cleared his throat before he

finished, "You are my son."

Jack dropped into an open chair at these words. His eyes narrowed in disbelief at what he was hearing.

Hector pulled up a chair and sat next to him. "I know this is confusing. I am just processing this myself. There is a Mexican proverb that goes, '*La verdadera amistad es un alma campartida por dos cuerpos.*'"

Jack shook his head, indicating that he didn't understand.

"'True friendship is one soul shared by two bodies.' Even after all these years, I think you love my daughter and would sacrifice your own life for her or even for her memory. You never gave up on her or your own daughter. Am I not right?"

Jack nodded. He wiped his tears with the back of his hand. "How can you know this? How can you know how much I loved her and how much I mourn that she is gone?"

Hector put the palm of his hands on both of Jack's shoulders. "Diego, Maria is not dead. She was not killed in that fire."

Jack's mouth dropped open as he stared in disbelief at Hector through his teared-filled eyes. "What?" His heart began to ache at this cruel attempt at a joke, but he knew Hector wouldn't joke about his only daughter this way.

Chapter 33

Jack pleaded with Hector, "Don't do this to me if you're not serious."

Hector walked over to a table against the wall and picked up a photograph in a glass frame, carried it back, and handed it to Jack. Despite the years, he knew in an instant it was Maria. Not Maria at twenty, but now at forty, and more beautiful than the image he had held only in his mind over all these years. "She is very much alive."

Jack's face tightened, squeezing his eyes shut. "How? They found her remains in that fire. What happened? Where is she?"

"From what Emilio found out, Sam never went there to kill you, only to take Maria and Rosalina. His shot was meant to wound you. He wasn't ready for the rifle Maldito gave him to use. He planned to knock you out and drag you outside while the fire was set in your apartment."

"But the charred remains? Her necklace?"

Hector nodded, "Sam made connections with a man that worked a night shift in the police morgue. They would take in homeless and unidentified men and women who had died and needed to be buried. He paid for the body of a younger woman who had died and planted her body in the fire, putting Maria's necklace around her. You had been blown out the window and were presumed dead already. Sam was a man possessed by my daughter. The only story I was told was that my daughter and granddaughter were back home, and you had been accidentally killed in the process. I will admit that I shed no tears for you at the time."

Jack paced the room, trying to work off all the energy running through his body. "What did Maria think when she arrived home? She must have believed you ordered a hit on me."

Hector stared at the grain of the fine wooden table. "Ahh, she was told by my men that they acted alone to bring her and respect back to our home—that I had nothing to do with it, and you were shot in self-defense when you attacked one of the men. She's too smart to know something didn't seem right with the story, and she believed I wasn't telling her the whole truth. She had to deal with the reality that her husband and the father of her daughter was gone, but she refused to live here with us."

"Where did she go?"

Hector ran his hand across his cheek and sighed. "She lives in an apartment in El Paso."

Jack thought that made sense since Siena went to school in El Paso and lived there.

"Sam insisted on paying for it and eventually Rosalina's college. He is devoted to them in every way."

Hector brought another picture over with Maria and Rosalina together. Jack took the photo from him, staring in disbelief. "This isn't Siena. Who is this?"

"Your daughter. The most beautiful gift of a granddaughter I could've ever wished for."

Jack continued to shake his head. "This isn't Rosa—" But he stopped short as he looked into her eyes and saw the same thing that Father Tom had. This was his baby girl, the daughter he had searched for all these years. "I don't understand. Maldito told me that Siena was my daughter, and Sam confirmed it."

Hector took Jack's arm. "They wanted you to believe it, hoping you might return to Boston with her and never come back—never finding out the truth. I believe that girl went to school with Rosalina and came to the ranch to ride a few times, but she is not Rosalina."

Jack peered into Hector's eyes. They seemed different than he remembered, not physically but in empathy. "Why are you telling me all of this? You never liked me and certainly don't

197

want me staying in the picture, do you?"

Something Jack hadn't thought possible was happening before his eyes. Hector's eyes welled up. "Sam offered Maria everything she could have asked for, a home, protection, friendship, loyalty, and even love, but she could never give him that last thing. She loved you and only you. She told me how much she loved you and how much you loved her. How you treated her and how dedicated you were to her and then to Rosalina. As much as I fought believing it, she convinced me that you were created for her and her for you, that you were the only person that would ever be for her—you made her happy. I have watched her grieve for you, even to this very day. And I have seen that love she has for you, even to this day."

Biting his lip, Jack tried to hold back the tears, but to no avail. "I'm so sorry for taking her from you. I would probably do it again, but I was wrong in how I did it. Where is Maria now? Where's Rosalina?"

Hector smiled. "They are coming back today. Rosalina goes to school at St. Mary's in San Antonio, and she was taking a summer course. Maria drove down yesterday, and they spent the day together. I do think they will need a little warning before they see you, though."

One of Hector's men came into the room and leaned over to whisper something in his ear. Before Hector was able to say anything to Jack, a striking young woman entered the dining room. "*Abu!*" she exclaimed as she put her arms around Hector and nestled her head into his chest. "*¡Es tan bueno verte!* I feel like I haven't seen you in so long." She glanced up to catch a glimpse of Jack and then stepped back, squinting her eyes. "Do I know you?"

Jack gazed into her eyes, unable to say a word in response. She was the girl in the photo. This was his baby, Rosalina, now a young woman, looking like just the kind of woman he would have prayed his daughter would grow up to be. Hector took her hand in his. "Rosalina, this man has been searching for his daughter her entire life, never giving up hope of finding her and giving her all the love she deserves."

Rosalina smiled. "She sounds very special."

Jack stepped forward. "She is more than that." He took another step. "She was loved from the moment she came to be and deserves to know how loved and cherished she is." His eyes welled up as he took another step closer and gazed deeply into her eyes. "She should know that she is the most precious daughter this father could ever have wished for and that he is so sorry she didn't have him with her every day to know it, to believe it in her heart and soul."

As she watched the tears roll down his cheeks, her eyes welled up with a look of confusion and hope. "Why don't you tell her this in person?"

"I am finally doing that right now."

She glanced at her grandfather, and he nodded with a smile.

Jack took another step and slowly put his arms around her. "I've missed you so much," he said as he held her tight while she sobbed.

In a muffled voice that shook, she asked, "How can this be?"

Before he could explain, Maria entered the room to see her daughter in the arms of a man. Jack lifted his head and smiled as he gazed upon the love of his life. He was shaking inside at the sight of someone he thought he had lost forever. Maria closed her eyes and then shook her head as she collapsed to the tiled floor.

Jack let go of Rosalina and raced to Maria. He dropped to his knees and lifted her head into his lap. He stroked her hair as he glanced up at Rosalina and said, "I'm sorry to surprise you like this, but it's really me."

Rosalina turned to Hector who nodded, again. "He's been looking for you all these years."

Maria sat up, her mouth open and speechless. She looked even more beautiful than he remembered. He didn't wait for words, and he kissed her, his body still shaking. Then he stood and lifted her to her feet, gazing deeply into her eyes. "Maria, it's a very long story, and I'm in as much shock as you must be right now. I thought you were dead all these years as I searched the country for Rosalina. I can't give you back the time we lost, but I can give you the rest of my life, if you'll have me again."

Hector nodded to Maria with a smile.

Maria wrapped her arms around Jack and held him tight, breathing in the scent from his shirt as her tears drenched his shoulder. "Every day, I've prayed for Our Lady to take care of you, but I never imagined this." She held out her hand as it trembled, and Jack took it.

They spent the rest of the afternoon and evening crying, laughing, and catching up on all the years they had missed as a family. They also told Maria and Rosalina about Sam and his involvement in the destruction of their family. Maria couldn't accept it and shuddered at the thought of all the times she had trusted Rosalina with him over the years.

Chapter 34

While Jack felt as if he was in a daze processing all the revelations of the day, the sincerity of Hector's feelings toward him seemed even more genuine when Hector set aside a suite for them in the southern wing of the house. They were almost as awkward and nervous as they were on their honeymoon night, but just holding Maria in his arms felt like heaven. He had to keep telling himself that she was really alive and they were together again as a family. How did he deserve this with all the hate he had carried in his heart for so long?

In the morning, Hector had a breakfast feast prepared on the veranda. Rosalina's eyes danced as she watched her mother smile more than ever.

Hector took a seat. "I hope everyone slept well. Let me know if there's anything different you'd like for breakfast."

Jack laughed as he took in the table at the fruits, omelets, meats, pastries, and assorted juices to go with their coffee. "I can't imagine there's anything you don't have here. I want to thank you for your hospitality, Hector. It means more to me than you know."

Hector lifted his cup of coffee. "To family. May we always be close."

Rosalina said, "I like that, but it still feels like a dream to me. Mamma talked to me about you all the time, but it's not the same as you being right here—alive." She blushed and added, "I have a father!"

Reaching over to kiss her on the cheek, Jack replied, "And I have a daughter—and a lovely one at that." Jack glanced at Maria and said, "But I'm not surprised."

Maria gazed at Rosalina. "I think she has a lot of her father in her, and that's not a bad thing." Then she turned to Hector with a smirk. "Of course, her stubborn side could have come from you, too."

Rosalina quipped, "Hey, we like to call that determination. So, what happens now?"

Jack replied, "That's a very good question. I feel as if I need to come to some closure with Sam to move forward. I've been angry and vengeful for so many years now that I need to be able to process knowing who the man is that I've hated for so long. I'm trying to reconcile the Sam I thought I knew with the man he's become and what he's done to our family."

Maria sighed. "I'm having a hard time myself with this. I knew how he felt about Rosalina and me and why he may have been so good to us over the years, but I can't see him as a killer or into all the horrible things you both say he was doing."

Jack stood up, trying to keep calm. "Maria, he tried to kill me twice, now. Even if he intended to only wound me in Boston, he must have shot at me fifty times on Guadalupe Mountain. That's not the sign of a good man nor a trusted friend."

Maria took Jack's hand. "I know." She paused. "Did you say he shot at you fifty times and missed?"

"Well, he did get me with a ricochet, but yeah, he missed me. I wasn't trying to get hit," said Jack.

Maria shook her head.

"What is it?"

Maria replied, "I'm certainly glad you didn't get hit, but Sam's too good a shot to miss his target. If he wanted to hit you, he would have. I've never seen anyone practice his marksmanship as much as Sam did. He got really good at it—extremely accurate at long distances too."

Jack glanced up at Hector, who nodded. "It must have spooked him when he shot you in Boston and being around the dangers in this area. He might be the best shot I've seen in these parts."

Jack sat back and murmured, "Are you trying to say he was only trying to scare me off? He did keep pleading for me to go back to Boston and never come back and to take Siena with me." Jack turned to Rosalina. "Do you remember a girl at Our Lady of Mount Carmel School named Rose? She was probably more stubborn, or let's say determined, than your grandfather and I."

Rosalina paused to think back.

Jack added, "She would have come to the ranch in Prâxedis when you were maybe five or six years old."

Rosalina replied, "Huh, Rose? I think I remember a girl like that. We used to kid about almost having the same names, and she loved horses. I don't know that she had a good family situation. Why do you ask?"

Jack chuckled. "I met her in El Paso, and Sam tried to convince me that she was you and that I should take her back to Boston. I think you'd like her. I guess I'm getting off-topic. So, you think Sam wasn't trying to kill me—*and* you don't believe he would be involved in some of the nasty business of hard drugs, kidnapping, and extortion?"

Maria shook her head. "I can't see it."

Jack retorted, "Do you know he shot a sweet ninety-five-year-old man in the head in Van Horn and tried to frame me for it? Does that sound like sweet Sam?"

Maria stared wide-eyed at him. "Oh my gosh. Are you serious? I can't believe it. I can't believe it!" She began crying and rushed back into the house. Rosalina lifted her hand. "I'll check on her." She darted into the house after her mother.

Hector's demeanor darkened.

Jack asked, "What are you thinking?"

Hector breathed out what could have been fire from his nostrils. "I'm thinking that Sam has been playing us. He destroyed our family and has been completely disloyal to me, working with my enemies and putting our family in danger. If everything we think we know is true, the man's nothing but a liar and the devil himself!"

Jack knew Hector's point was valid, and it raised some of

the same toxic hate that he had wallowed in over the years. Now he had someone real to aim it at and seek justice against with a passion. Didn't Father Diaz say that God had a passion for setting things right? He also remembered a Mexican saying that he never quite understood before. *No hay mal que por bien no venga*—there's no evil that doesn't come with some good in it. Was there some good that came with the evil in Sam? If there was, Jack couldn't see it. He'd never felt this level of conflict before. Part of him wanted to trust that Sam could be redeemed, and part of him wanted to put his hands around the man's neck and administer the justice he deserved. As Hector said, he not only destroyed their family, his greed and selfishness put Maria and Rosalina's very lives at risk with this cartel war. The adrenaline and anger swelling inside of him made him too restless to sit thinking about what was true or not. He needed to end this cancer and protect his family.

Chapter 35

Jack found Maria in their room crying while Rosalina tried to comfort her. He sat down on the bed next to Maria and reached out to stroke her back.

"I hate this greed, dishonesty, and violence, but I can't believe Sam is involved. I just can't," insisted Maria.

Jack replied, "I don't know what to think. We never really know what's inside another person's mind and heart."

"I don't believe that. I've known him for over twenty years now," insisted Maria as she faced Jack, her cheeks wet from tears.

Jack felt a twinge of jealousy with that reality. He and Maria were married, intimate, but had only that one year before they were separated for decades. After twenty years, was Sam now closer to Maria than he was? In her heart, did she know and trust Sam more than him? The thought of this stolen and disingenuous intimacy with Maria infuriated him. It reminded him of the injustice and pain caused by Sam's deceptive disloyalty then and now.

What about poor Homer Beeker and his widow, a murder Sam tried to frame him for? How could she be so trusting of a man that would put a gun to an old man's head and pull the trigger? What was Sam capable of doing to his family?

Jack tried his best to hide the fury welling up inside of him. He quietly took several breaths and stroked her hair as he spoke softly. "I need to go back to Van Horn today. I want to visit a young man named Juan, who saved my life and to talk to the sheriff. Are you okay here if I leave shortly?"

Maria pulled him close. "Diego, I don't want to lose you again. Please don't risk your life again. We've hardly had a chance to believe you are actually here with us—here to stay." Maria put her other arm around their daughter and held them close—a closeness that he had dreamed impossible only a day before.

Jack left in Siena's truck without telling Hector he was heading back to Van Horn. On the drive, any denial about Sam being capable or responsible for acts of evil being driven by envy and greed had given way to a strong belief that he was guilty and never the man or friend he had pretended to be. Jack wondered how he had ever believed Sam was like a brother that could be trusted beyond question, someone he enjoyed, even loved. All a sham. This realization allowed Jack's anger and resentment for all the years lost to well inside of him and be aimed at the rightful owner of the unforgivable injustice to his family and him.

Jack had planned on seeing Sheriff Ramos first, but, instead, his growing rage created a sense of impatience and immediacy. He drove directly to the hospital. As he sat outside the entrance in the truck, his chest tightened, his breaths shortened, and his stomach rolled. All those years of being cheated, the damage was compressed into this single moment, like carbon into a diamond. He opened the compartment on the floor of the truck and gripped the handle of Siena's knife, the one with which Juan had killed Maldito. It was still coated with blood. He tucked it under his shirt and entered the hospital, asking first for Siena's room. He couldn't let his family be harmed again.

Jack entered her room quietly and stared at her. In her unconscious state, she looked peaceful behind the bruising and wounds on her face. The sight of her beaten up and the fear of what could have happened only added to his anger. He reached over and gently stroked the hair, pushing it off her forehead and gazing at her. He may have incorrectly believed she was his daughter for a short while, but he found himself caring a great deal about her. He wanted to stay with her until she woke up, to protect her. If Sam was able to finagle his way out of jail time, would she ever be safe from him? Would any of them be safe? He knew that he had unfinished business to take care of.

The door to the room next to Siena was open, so Jack could see Juan sitting up, trying to pour himself some water from one of those plastic hospital pitchers. Jack stepped in and took the pitcher to fill Juan's cup. "How is my savior doing today? That was a nasty wound."

Juan tried to smile. "A little lightheaded. What happened? Is Siena okay?"

Jack nodded. "She's next door, still unconscious, but she should be okay. Sam took her up into the Guadalupe Mountains and pushed her off the peak after she risked her own life to save mine. I guess I owe you both a huge debt of gratitude."

Juan's brow tightened, looking as if he was trying to put the pieces of the puzzle together. "But you're okay. What happened to your friend?"

"Well, I don't know how much of a friend he ever really was. He's responsible for almost everything we've been trying to figure out and for everything that has happened to my family." Jack tugged his shirt down as he was sure Juan had spotted the bloody knife tucked into his pants. Jack was doing a bad job hiding his anger, a feeling that Juan most likely knew all too well.

Juan asked, "*Señor* Russo, what are you going to do?"

"I don't know, but what I do know is that you need to get healthy." Jack patted Juan's good shoulder.

Out in the hall, an armed guard was stationed outside the last room several doors down. He slipped into a supply closet with shelves of light blue hospital scrubs. He put them on, grabbed a cart, and made his way to the guarded room. Head down, staring at the clipboard on this cart, he mumbled, "Need to take the patient's vitals." The guard nodded and stepped aside, allowing Jack to proceed, pushing the wheeled cart toward Sam's bed.

Jack lifted Sam's arm in the pretense of putting on a blood pressure cuff when Sam's eyes opened. Sam's face remained blank, no panic or fear, even though he must have known that Jack wouldn't be at his bedside disguised as a hospital worker if he wasn't there to settle the score. In a hushed tone, Sam said, "You look good cleaned up."

Jack wrapped the blood-pressure band around Sam's bicep and whispered in response, "I always try to look my best for the funeral of an old friend of mine."

Sam nodded, appearing resigned to his fate. "You'll be doing me a favor. Relieve me of this loneliness, the emptiness of this black hole that only gets bigger."

As the guard peered in, Jack picked up the clipboard to feign jotting down some numbers. "Don't talk to me about those years. What happened to you? Were you ever the friend I thought you were?"

Sam didn't respond.

"You nearly destroyed my family and tried to kill me. You lied to Hector, trafficking in the worst kind of crimes and putting Maria and Rosalina in the middle of the most dangerous cartel war in the world. How could you become a man like Maldito, a man who killed and tortured for pleasure? How could you murder a sweet old man like Homer Beeker in cold blood and frame me for it? You lied to me about Siena. You tried to kill her." Jack had slipped the knife into his hand and held it to Sam's side. Sam stared motionless, a faraway look in his eyes.

Slowly, Sam shifted his gaze to peer into Jack's eyes. "End it, Jimmy. End it."

All the years of grief, sadness, anger, and relentless desire for revenge crystallized into that single moment as he visualized pushing the tip of the hunting knife into Sam's side. It felt as if it were the only way to relieve all the pain and to stop the threat to the family. The fact that Sam didn't offer any apology only heightened his belief that Sam's death would be justified, that it would end his anger, would put the past to right. Yet, as he closed his eyes to do just that, tears filled his eyes and wouldn't stop, no matter how much tight he squeezed them.

Jack turned and rolled the cart out of the room without looking back, without saying a word to the guard. Walking out of the hospital, still wearing the scrubs, he jumped into the truck and drove without consciously thinking of where he was headed. On the edge of town, he pulled to the curb to calm his breathing and to think. As his mind settled and he released his grip from the steering wheel, he could hear the church bells of Our Lady's Church nearby. Jack got out of the truck and walked into the welcoming shade of the garden grotto.

The door to the small church was open, and the sunlight streamed in behind him as he entered. He was alone, or so he felt, kneeling in one of the back pews, weeping. He had no idea why, but he felt as if a dam had burst. Sobbing, he repeated to himself, "I'm sorry. I'm sorry," until he felt a hand on his shoulder.

Father Diaz gazed at him with concern and friendship. "Are you okay?"

Jack wiped his face. "I don't know. I don't know what I am."

He slid over in the pew, and Father Diaz sat with him, peering at the crucifix over the altar. "You've been through a lot."

Jack lifted his head. "I just found out that my wife, Maria, has been alive this whole time, and my daughter has been with her. It's a little unsettling to meet your daughter for the first time as a grown woman."

A broad smile came to Father Diaz's face. "That sounds like better news than you could have dreamed of, but you seem more troubled than happy. What is keeping you from restarting your life with your family again?"

Jack shook his head, telling Father Diaz about all the things

Sam had been responsible for and how angry it made him, angry enough that he considered killing him to bring justice and safety to his family.

Father Diaz glanced down at Siena's hunting knife with Maldito's dried blood on it, visible at Jack's waist, but remained silent.

"I wanted to kill him. I really did. I don't know what stopped me."

Father Diaz smiled. "I'm glad to hear that the blood on your knife is not his. You know, resisting temptation is a sign of something good. It means that we didn't let the devil win. You do have a right to be angry, very angry. And you have a right to protect your family from any further risk."

Jack ran his hand through his hair. "Don't I have the responsibility to protect them and to make things right? He never asked for forgiveness. He asked me to end it for him, his loneliness—he called it a black hole growing inside of him. I don't know why, but I felt pity for him, at that moment, instead of hate."

"Ahh, a spark of the love we talked about," said Father Diaz.

"Love? Forgiveness? Is that all you have?" snapped Jack. He stood up.

Father Diaz glanced at him and then at the crucifix hanging in front of the church and then back at Jack. "Tell me this: If Sam asked for forgiveness and truly repented, was truly sorry for all that he did, how would you feel?"

The question threw Jack off, and he dropped back down into the pew. He wanted Sam to see how bad his actions were and to plead for forgiveness. He shook his head. "I don't know. He's not sorry, so what's the point of the question?"

"We never know what's truly in another man's heart, what fears, pain, and motivations come into play. We also don't always even know everything that happened, even when we feel completely certain. If the cartel found him, tortured, and killed him, would you feel better?" asked Father Diaz.

To his surprise, Jack's first thought was not one of justice or relief. He imagined himself trying to stop it from happening. He felt as if he would want to save Sam from that fate. He shook his head. "No."

Father Diaz gazed at the crucifix again. "You know, God wants the best for you, no matter how many times you turn your back on him, reject him, spit in his face, beat him to a pulp, and take his life in the most violent way possible. We owe him everything, yet we treat him pretty lousy most of the time. He gives us our very lives, love, friendship, mercy, forgiveness, beauty, children, and purpose, and what do we give him back? Yet he keeps wishing the best for us, always ready to welcome us back with open arms. We are all prodigal sons with a loving father waiting to welcome us home."

Jack felt frustrated. "I know, God is great, and we are lousy good-for-nothings."

"He doesn't think so. He thinks we can be pretty wonderful and worth loving."

Jack squirmed in his seat. "Look, we can't be expected to be like God. If he is asking me to just forget everything, act as if nothing happened, and hand out forgiveness like lollipops at a parade, he's asking too much. People could never do it. I could never do it."

"I agree," replied Father Diaz with a smile.

Jack was confused by his response. "What?"

Father Diaz stood up and stepped out from the pew, genuflecting toward the tabernacle, then he waved Jack to follow him as he walked around the back of the church and down the side aisle next to the stained glass windows with the scenes of the Stations of the Cross in between each set of windows. He walked by several of the stations where Jesus was carrying the cross and one where he stumbled and fell. Jack's chest tightened, feeling as if he wanted to help Jesus up. Father Diaz stopped at a light fixture on the wall and pointed to it.

"It's a light," said Jack sarcastically.

"Very good," said Father Diaz with a chuckle. "Anything about it that's different?"

Jack peered around the church and noticed that it was the only light along the wall that was not lit. "It's not on. Do I win something?"

"You're definitely in the running. This light has been trying to shine for quite some time, but it can't."

Jack smiled. "It's just a bad bulb. Throw it out and put in a new one."

Father Diaz touched the bulb. "That's what I thought, but it's a perfectly fine bulb. What I finally figured out was that it wasn't plugged in. See, there's a short cord and plug in the back of the light, and it wasn't connected, so it didn't have the power on its own to do what it was made to do."

"Okay, so you passed Electrician 101," Jack said, feeling more confused than before.

Father Diaz smiled. "You said that what God is asking us to do is too much to ask, too hard for a human being to do. I agreed with you—if we try to do it alone if we are not plugged into Christ and his grace. Paul said, *'For I can do all things in Christ, who gives me strength.'* Think about that for a bit. We can't do it without his strength, his example, and his grace, but he does ask us to do it. Plug yourself in, and you can be a light. You can find the strength to do what he asks."

Father Diaz left Jack standing at the light. He reached up and pressed the plug behind the fixture in, and it illuminated the space. It could do what it was designed to do, but not on its own. Jack dropped down into a pew, perplexed at what Father Diaz was asking him to do. He struggled as he glanced up at the crucifix and then down at the wooden bench he was sitting in, a bench many had sat in when they struggled in their life.

As Jack sat in silence, his heartrate slowed, and the tightness eased from his chest. He tried to listen for a voice or

212

some sort of sign for what to do next. He had spent every day of the past two decades on a single mission, and it was, for all intents and purposes, over, yet he felt as if it wasn't over. Would he have solved anything if he had followed through with his plan at the hospital? Sam would be dead and justice served. Jack would be a murderer and would've spent years in prison and not with his beloved wife and daughter.

There was a missal on the pew beside him. He remembered his mother following along with the Mass and the Scripture readings for the day in the missal. He used to play with the colored ribbon markers between pages. He pulled on the end of the red one and opened the missal to that page. *Ephesians 4:31-32. Get rid of all bitterness, rage, and anger, brawling and slander, along with every form of malice. Be kind to one another, tenderhearted, forgiving one another as God in Christ forgave you.* Jack glanced over at the Station, the figure of Christ on the ground with the cross on top of him. *I shouldn't ask for a sign if I don't want to hear the answer.*

Jack stood up and walked through the doorway at the back of the church, squinting in the bright sunlight. He was still angry at Sam and probably always would be, but he didn't want to kill him any longer. He wanted Sam to see what he had done and be sorry for it, to change who he had become. Jack wasn't going to become the enemy he had been fighting against his entire life.

He wanted to thank Father Diaz for taking the time to listen to him without judgment and to let him know that he wouldn't be trying to pursue justice through vengeance. If he knew one thing now, it was that serving final justice wasn't his place. That job belonged to God.

Chapter 36

Jack headed to the rectory and wasn't surprised to see Sheriff Ramos talking to Father Diaz in the kitchen, but he wasn't prepared to see Hector Engando sitting there chatting with either a sheriff or a priest. No one spoke as they all turned to Jack, who said, "Is this a party or an intervention?"

Father Diaz replied, "It could be both. Come in."

Sheriff Ramos said, "Been to the hospital today?"

Jack said, "Why do you ask that?"

"Unless you've enrolled in medical school recently, it was just a wild guess," said Ramos with a smile, looking Jack up and down before taking a step forward and lifting Jack's shirt to remove the bloody hunting knife from his belt. "I'm glad your visit was a peaceful one."

Hector put his hand around Jack's shoulder. "Diego, sit down. We've found out a few things more that you should know."

"Look, I just want to make sure that Sam gets what's coming to him and that Maria and Rosalina are safe," chided Jack as he sat at the kitchen table with the others.

Father Diaz said, "Jack, remember what we talked about in the church—about not knowing everything in another man's heart, well—"

Ramos interrupted, "We may have had some things wrong."

Jack scratched his head, glancing around the table for a clue. "Wrong? He murdered Homer, put my family at risk, lied about—"

Ramos said, "Russo, I know what you believe, and you want to protect your family, but we found out some things that change the picture a bit. The coroner's report came back. It appears that Homer died of a heart attack and not a gunshot wound. I questioned Mr. Engres, and he admitted that he and

Maldito found Homer already dead in his car sometime after he dropped you off at Daisy's. He said that Maldito had decided to kill you and Juan, but Sam pleaded with him to find another way to get you out of the picture. He was hoping you would go back to Boston with Siena if you thought she was your daughter, a daughter you wanted to protect. When he found out how intent Maldito was, Sam convinced him to frame you for the murder to keep him from killing you, then later he would figure out a way of getting you off and keeping you alive."

Jack stood up. "What? Are you saying Sam was trying to save me? Why was he trying to kill me on the mountain?"

Hector countered, "Sam was definitely envious of you and wanted Maria and Rosalina to be his family, so it was easy for Maldito to convince him to be part of the attack in Boston. The thing was, Maldito hated you for taking Maria and disrespecting the family—I can't say that I didn't feel the same way at the time. Sam was only supposed to wound you, but Maldito gave him a much more powerful gun than he expected."

Jack shook his head in confusion. "What does that have to do with him trying to kill me in the mountains?"

Hector continued, "What happened in Boston shook Sam, and he also knew that now his life was always going to be in danger, so he practiced and became quite a marksman handling a gun. Maria told you that if he wanted to hit you, he would have, but he was just trying to scare you off—to go back to Boston with Siena and never look back."

Jack rubbed his cheek. "I don't understand. What about him getting your business more involved with trafficking hard drugs, kidnapping, and extortion? They destroyed those small border towns. All those families live in fear through intimidation and the threat of murder of their family and friends. You, yourself, said he lied to you and used your organization to do just the opposite of what he had told you."

Anger rekindled in Jack as he thought about all the pain and suffering created for nothing but greed and the desire for power.

Hector nodded. "Up until this morning, I believed the same thing. I brought one of Maldito's men in and questioned him." Hector glanced over at Ramos with caution. "Let's say it wasn't a friendly conversation, but he confessed that Maldito started working his own agenda many years ago, even before you met Maria, and he had also been in alliance with the Sinaloa cartel that was trying to take over smuggling routes in the Jaurez Valley. Sam had come down to do some more work for me shortly after you and Maria were married. He overheard Maldito's plans to kill you, and me for that matter, so Sam approached him with the idea that would save your life. It may have served his own purposes to have Maria to himself, but his friendship loyalties to you were more important. He convinced Maldito that he would leverage my business to help Maldito get what he wanted. It intrigued him enough to keep us both alive as they carried out their plans."

Jack paced the floor, trying to wrap his mind around Hector's information. "Surely, he could have come to you about this, and Maldito could have been stopped?"

Hector pursed his lips as his eyes flashed in suppressed fury. "Maldito excelled at manipulating people's fears with his lies and extortion techniques. It appears that he told Sam he would kill me, Maria, and Rosalina if Sam didn't help him achieve his plans to move in directions I would not go along with. That eventually led Maldito to form an alliance with the Sinaloa cartel, who wanted access to the tunnel Sam had convinced me to invest in."

"Why did you do it?" inquired Ramos.

Hector shook his head. "He said it would be safer for the people we helped to cross the border and would be good for business. In my gut, I knew it was the wrong thing to do. Not because it wasn't a great business idea, but because I built that ranch as an escape from the city for Maria and Rosalina. Once it became the main distribution point for the business, the ranch wasn't the same. It didn't feel safe, so we went there less—which gave Maldito more room to operate in those towns through brutality and intimidation. He started using the tunnel to move drugs across to the US and guns back into Mexico for the Sinaloas. Destroying the towns and killing off the police gave them free rein to operate. That was when I began looking for a safer place to build another ranch. Rosalina loved to ride her horses. You should have seen the look on her face when she visited the ranch to be with her horses."

Dropping back into his chair, Jack buried his face into the palms of his hands as he tried to sort everything out that he was hearing. Father Diaz put his hand on Jack's shoulder, which brought some comfort that he wasn't alone, but it didn't solve his state of confusion. "Are you trying to tell me that everything Sam did was to protect our family, that it was all good?"

Hector replied, "I don't know everything he was thinking or that his motivations were all unselfish. I know he has tried in vain to win over Maria's love and be a father to Rosalina. He may have been torn between two desires, as we all are, at times." Hector eyed Ramos again. "I, myself, started out trying to survive and then got greedy for money and power. When Maria and Rosalina came back, my priorities started to change. I wanted to become a better person and to protect my family. People change, but I'm wondering if Sam has always wanted the best for you."

Jack sat, stunned. "I don't know what to think anymore."

In a quiet voice, Father Diaz offered, "Jack, you've just been thrown a complete change to what you have believed to be true. Give yourself some time to let it sink in. Don't beat yourself up for something you didn't know until now."

Jack raised his hands. "You don't understand. I went to the

hospital to take my revenge out on Sam. I went there with the full intent of sticking that knife in him and ending his life. I was so close to pushing that blade into this side, and he pleaded with me to 'end it' for him, to end his loneliness, his pain, the black hole of emptiness he's lived with his entire life. I didn't go there with any desire to help him, to show him loyalty, love, or forgiveness. I went there to kill him to fulfill my own need for vengeance."

Ramos spoke out. "But you didn't. Good thing, because you would have had two murders on your wanted poster. Maybe you need to find out the truth from Mr. Engres, himself?"

Chapter 37

Jack sat in the front of Siena's truck for a half-hour outside of the hospital. Finally, he decided it was time to go in.

Nervous tension rose in his chest as he stood outside the door to Sam's room for the second time that day. This time the objective was different than the first. Ramos had also driven over and relieved the guard on duty since charges were no longer going to be made against Sam. Jack walked in alone. Sam was sleeping. He gazed upon his old friend in a different light this time, now wondering if Sam would forgive him.

He sat next to the bed and apologized to God for his wasted years of hate and desire for revenge, not being of any positive value to anyone. He realized with regret that his hate had kept him from living. He had been a prisoner. He asked for guidance to navigate the time ahead of him in a way that could make up for those lost years, thanking God for a second chance with Maria, Rosalina, and even Sam.

When he glanced over, he realized Sam was awake and staring at him. "Sam! How are you?"

Sam's eyes narrowed, looking suspiciously at Jack. "Unfortunately for both of us, I'm still alive."

"Don't say that."

Sam shook his head, wincing at the pain in his shoulder. "What's going on, Jimmy?"

Jack moved closer to the bed. "I've, um—I've come to apologize to you."

Sam's brow tightened. "What? You've come to me to apologize? For what? For taking away your family? For putting them in danger? For hurting Siena? For not being the friend you needed? You wanted to kill me earlier, and now you're apologizing? What's going on?"

Jack cracked half a smile. "Sam, you were the best friend I

ever had. I just found out that you still are."

Sam's head moved slightly forward. "Is this a joke?"

"Look, I know you loved Maria and envied me for having her and a family. But I know why family is so important to you. I also know that you didn't kill Homer. I know you didn't want to kill me in Boston. I know you were forced into this nasty business down here to protect Maria, Rosalina, Hector, and Marta. I know Maldito threatened to kill them to take over the business and form an alliance with the Sinaloa cartel, and you worked, instead, to save them."

Sam's eyes glazed with unspilled tears.

Jack continued, "I know you were only trying to desperately save my life by trying to convince me that Siena was Rosalina and have me go back to Boston where I'd be safe. And I found out you are too good a shot with a rifle these days to miss me that many times on the Guadalupe trail."

Tears rolled down Sam's cheeks. "How do you know all this? How can you come this morning to stick a knife into me and, now suddenly, know all of this?"

Jack smiled. "I know two more things. I know that you cared for Maria and Rosalina with love and respect all these years, and, most of all, I know that you have been a loyal friend whom I should never have doubted." Jack reached out his hand to Sam. "Can you ever forgive me?"

Sam reached out with his left hand and slapped away Jack's hand with a gesture to instead embrace his friend. "Not too hard; this still smarts. You're a pretty good shot yourself, you know. I'm glad Siena's calibrations for the sights on that Winchester were accurate. Is she okay? I really didn't want to hurt her. I was panicking that I couldn't get you to leave with her."

Jack nodded. "I think so. She is a few rooms down the hall here, still out, but stable."

Sam sighed with relief and glanced over Jack's shoulder toward the doorway. Jack turned and could see Ramos,

Father Diaz, and Hector standing there. Sam said, "Jimmy, it looks like you get to witness my arrest, Last Rites, and execution if I know why these three are here."

Sam gave a wary glance as Hector approached the bed, but Hector's calm expression quickly seemed to put him at ease.

"I found out the true story behind Maldito's antics," Hector said, "and how you have been working to protect my family. I wanted to express my gratitude and promise, now, to protect you with my own life. You never have to worry again about the bad seeds in my business. I'm going to work here with the sheriff to get it dismantled." Hector patted Sam on the shoulder as if he were a son of his own.

Ramos said, "I'm not saying that all of me feels completely comfortable with this after what happened to the young lady, but I had a long talk with your friend, Mr. Russo. If Siena agrees, they'll be no arrest or charges to worry about from the Van Horn police."

Father Diaz smiled. "And no Last Rites, yet. I hope there are a good many years before you have to worry about that—although, you may want to start attending Mass again if you know what's good for you."

Jack winked at Father Diaz. "We'll see if we can get him plugged in too, Father."

Hector had left the room while they talked to Sam. After several minutes of conversation, Jack and Sam glanced over to the doorway and saw Hector standing in the doorway. When he stepped aside, there was Maria and Rosalina. It was obvious to Jack that Hector had let them know all the news about Sam, and they entered the room with cautious smiles, cautious until Jack hugged each of them and said, "Maria, Rosalina, let me introduce you to my reclaimed friend, Sam Engres." Maria stroked Sam's shoulder with a smile, and Rosalina kissed him on the cheek.

Turning to Sam, Jack quipped, "Do me a favor and don't ever say that you don't have a family again. This will always be your family, even though I think you are still young enough to find someone."

Sam flashed a genuine smile as a tear made it to the corner of one eye. "I would like that."

Jack asked Sam if he would excuse them for a few minutes and motioned to Rosalina and Maria to come with him. They followed him down the hall to Siena's room. Jack felt relief when he saw that Siena was conscious and sitting up. He motioned for Maria and Rosalina to wait as he entered alone.

Siena looked toward the door and rolled her eyes at Jack. "I've got to get you some lessons with that Winchester, Russo, or I wouldn't be in here—now, would I?"

Jack stepped into the room. "Probably not, but I'm glad you're looking better."

"I've survived worse, and if I keep hanging around with y'all, I'm sure I'll see worse," said Siena, holding her head as she winced a bit with pain.

"I'm sure you will," replied Jack, gazing into her eyes. She may not have turned out to be his daughter but seeing her tugged at his heart. "Uhm."

"Why are ya looking at me that way. I'm not dying, am I?"

Jack half-smiled. "Not on my watch. I just don't like seeing you all bruised up, and—I guess I missed you."

Her eyes softened, and she smiled back. He hesitated to continue.

She squinted. "There's somethin' yer not sayin'. I can tell. Am I right?" she asked as she tilted her head. "I can always read ya."

He continued to gaze at her and moved closer. "Yes, you can." With a deep sigh, she said, "You know how I said you can never trust anything that Maldito said?"

She squinted more and nodded.

"Um." Jack shifted.

"I can take whatever it is."

Jack had to force the words out. "It turns out that he was

lying about you being my daughter."

She brought her hand to her lips, her eyes glistening. "Well, at least I had you for a little while. That's better than—" she stopped herself short.

Jack waved Rosalina and Maria into the room. "I want you to meet someone. Well, actually, you two may have already met at Mount Carmel School in El Paso. Rosalina, this is Siena Connors. You may have known her as—"

"Rose," interrupted Rosalina with a broad smile on her face.

Siena tilted her head and squinted her eyes with curiosity. "How did you know that?"

"Your eyes. I remember those eyes. We were best friends that year when I didn't have one. Now, I remember us playing that we were twins because we looked alike, and both of us loved to ride horses at Abu's ranch," said Rosalina. "I felt bad when I changed schools. How have you been?"

Siena smiled. "I can't believe you remember me." She turned to Jack and said with a half-smile, "So, Russo, ya found what you've been looking for—your family. I'm happy for you."

Jack put his arm around Maria and gave Rosalina a loving glance. "I did, but not without your help."

Siena nodded and pressed her lips together. "So, I guess y'all will be headin' back home to Boston to be together."

Jack half-shrugged. "My home is where my family is, so I may be sticking around here if *y'all* don't mind." He could see a tear making its way to the corner of Siena's eye. "I haven't checked in with the team, but I'd like you to be part of our family. I'd actually like that very much."

Siena glanced at Rosalina, who nodded in agreement.

"There's a strict family rule that you have to save the hide of someone in the family three times to get in, and I think you qualify. Plus, I do need to stick around to defend my mechanical bull championship victory!"

Jack leaned over, wiped her tears with one of the small pieces of blue-and-white kerchief pieces he retrieved from his pocket. Siena wrapped both arms around him and gave him a long hug, whispering in his ear, "On one condition, I still get to call ya Russo."

Maria and Rosalina gave Siena a hug and kisses. Hector had entered the room and nodded with welcoming eyes. Genuine peace and happiness filled Jack as he watched his family in the first time in forever.

When Sheriff Ramos and Father Diaz joined them, he thanked them for believing in him enough to give him a chance for this moment.

He glanced back at Siena, who winked at him. She was happy for him too.

The End

Acknowledgments

Writing an intriguing and meaningful novel is truly a team effort.

I want to thank the Holy Spirit for guiding this story, my wife, Joanne, for her encouragement and always critical first-pass editing expertise, Michelle Buckman for her mentorship and professional editing expertise, and Ellen and James Hrkach for their incredible support in publishing this story and cover.

One of the things I enjoy is researching to ensure these stories are as authentic as possible. Writing a story about the land and, more importantly, the people on the Mexico/Texas border, I want to thank readers Irene, Jess, and Erika for offering their unique perspective and expertise to ensure the story and characters respect and realistically capture the Mexican culture and dignity of its people.

About the Author

Jim Sano grew up in an Irish/Italian family in Massachusetts. Jim is a husband, father, lifelong Catholic and has worked as a teacher, consultant, and businessman. He has degrees from Boston College and Bentley University and is currently attending Franciscan University for a master's degree in Catechetics and Evangelization. He has also attended certificate programs at The Theological Institute for the New Evangelization at St. John's Seminary and the Apologetics Academy. Jim is a member of the Catholic Writers Guild and has enjoyed growing in his faith and now sharing it through writing novels. *Van Horn* is Sano's fourth novel.

Jim resides in Medfield, Massachusetts, with his wife, Joanne, and has two daughters, Emily and Megan.

Published by
Full Quiver Publishing
PO Box 244
Pakenham, ON K0A2X0
Canada
www.fullquiverpublishing.com

Made in United States
North Haven, CT
29 March 2024